HEIST

PENGUIN BOOKS

PENGUIN BOOKS

UK | USA | Canada | Ireland | Australia
India | New Zealand | South Africa | China

Penguin Random House Australia

Penguin Random House Australia is part of the Penguin Random House group of companies whose addresses can be found at global.penguinrandomhouse.com.

First published by Penguin, an imprint of Penguin Random House Australia Pty Ltd, in 2025

Cover design by Kristy Lund-White © Penguin Random House Australia Pty Ltd
Illustrations by Aaron Blecha
Internal design and typesetting by Midland Typesetters, Australia

Printed and bound in Australia by Griffin Press, an accredited
ISO AS/NZS 14001 Environmental Management Systems printer

Penguin Random House Australia uses papers that are natural and recyclable products, made from wood grown in sustainable forests. The logging and manufacture processes are expected to conform to the environmental regulations of the country of origin.

NATIONAL LIBRARY OF AUSTRALIA
A catalogue record for this book is available from the National Library of Australia

FSC www.fsc.org MIX Paper | Supporting responsible forestry FSC® C018684

ISBN 978 1 76135 027 6

penguin.com.au

We at Penguin Random House Australia acknowledge that Aboriginal and Torres Strait Islander peoples are the Traditional Custodians and the first storytellers of the lands on which we live and work. We honour Aboriginal and Torres Strait Islander peoples' continuous connection to Country, waters, skies and communities. We celebrate Aboriginal and Torres Strait Islander stories, traditions and living cultures; and we pay our respects to Elders past and present.

To the ones who don't feel like they belong.
Those who haven't found their squad . . . yet.
Geez, that can be so difficult.

My hope is that the raucous,
unexpected friendship
of this squad
might even lead you,
in some way,
toward finding your own.

The serendipitous friendships
that are born, most often,
out of a choice . . .
to open yourself,
just a little.

MEET THE TEAM

Andy McGee

Marlie Balooby

Jasmine Quinn

Fleassy Davies

Nick Delancey

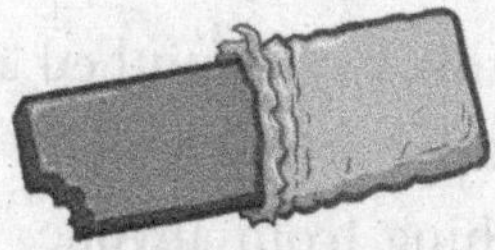

PROLOGUE

Let's start from the beginning. After all, these things have to begin somewhere. You can't have a caper without something to caper about. And if you are going to engage in such caperous activity (pretty sure I just made up a word there), it had better be a worthwhile caper, indeed.

Marlie, who you'll meet soon, tells me that 'caper' is actually the name of a little edible something or other from the Mediterranean. But, I assure you, this caper is not a salty treat from the Mediterranean. It is, rather, the thievery kind of caper. A heist story. A theft. A symphony of cunning minds and nimble fingers. Or, perhaps, more a cacophony of immature minds, sticky fingers and hot-headed know-it-alls. Either way, it is a caper of magnificence.

Ah, you may say, but who are you to decide whether this particular caper truly is so magnificent?

Well, I must confess, I am the one who steals the chocolate. Me. Andy McGee.

Actually, it isn't just me. It's Marlie and the rest of my team, too. We all do the deed but, somehow, I end up as the ringleader of this sweet-toothed affair.

Please don't judge me, though. I promise I don't usually steal anything from anyone. My intentions are admirable. This is not a stealing of chocolate for stealing's sake. No way. This particular crime NEEDS to be committed.

For, I tell you, if we were to NOT steal the chocolate, then this world would be in utter peril. And by *world* I am not speaking metaphorically. I do mean the actual entire population of Earth. And by *peril*, I mean gone. Caput! Vamoosh! Annihilated! Literally, the entire human race stamped out like a tiny squished bug on the windshield of existence.

Lucky this world has me and my team to steal the chocolate and save the day.

Don't believe me? Yeah, I probably wouldn't, either. So, let me tell you the story.

This is the tale of how I, Andy McGee, save the entire planet.

Well, Marlie and I. Oh! And Fleassy, Nick and Jasmine, too.

The best heist squad this world has ever seen.

SEVEN DAYS BEFORE THE HEIST

WHERE ALL THINGS BEGIN

MONDAY AFTERNOON

This particular tale begins right at that moment when all things begin, which is when you don't actually realise that something is about to begin. It was an insignificant Monday lunchtime, just like every other insignificant Monday lunchtime.

Or so I thought.

There I was, living my best ordinary teenage life, walking to the school canteen to get something to eat. Which, if you have been in a school like mine, you would know is more like traversing a battlefield than a relaxing stroll.

One hop right to avoid a spitball. A quick dodge left to narrowly save my eyeball from a paper plane. A leap and a jump over the wad of gooey pink chewing gum. A skid around the corner to flatten myself against the wall and avoid five burly Year Ten footballers who were charging along, squishing everything in their path.

I breathed a sigh of relief.

'What are you looking at?' growled a voice.

Ah, you see what I mean? I didn't focus for two seconds and some senior-high kid was about to eat me for lunch just because I didn't realise I was staring at him. I walked straight past, head down, trying to look anywhere but his beady eyes. Thankfully, I noticed just in time his outstretched leg, stuck out for the tripping. Gripping my bag strap, I jumped over the foot and continued the perilous journey to lunch.

Your feet have gotta be nimble in high school – head on a swivel, eyes peeled for any great big SOMETHING that might be hurtling through the air toward you. For instance, the avocado that was about to turn my face into a smashed-avo breakfast. I ducked, swerved, pivoted and twirled down the corridor, narrowly avoiding a green splattering.

Such wariness in the school corridors is especially necessary when you've only just graduated to high school a few months earlier. From king of the primary school playground to scum of Year Seven. On the social ladder I wasn't much higher than the sticky gum I had just leapt over.

Whoever decided that the transition to high school should happen right at the time of awkward stumbling limbs, a body that feels too big, weird hair growing in strange places and a voice that might hiccup into a badly played violin at any moment . . . they should be court-martialled.

So, there I was, attempting to get lunch, avoiding school bullies and just generally trying to stay alive in a body that felt like it would betray me at any moment.

Welcome to Year Seven.

'Andy! Andy! Have you heard? Andy!'

I knew the voice behind me, but I chose to ignore it. Still, she persisted.

'Andy, wait up. Wait up!'

Marlie Balooby. That is her actual name. Can you even believe that? I've known her since we started primary school together. Yep, seven years of primary, and then she was the only other kid from our primary school who came to Bellington High. She thought that meant we'd be friends here. I did not. Hence, why she was now chasing me down the corridor.

Reluctantly, I turned around to greet her. Bouncing curly brown hair, a big toothy smile, olive skin and glasses so thick her green eyes looked magnified. She was the kinda person who answered EVERY question in class and did ALL the homework and so, all the teachers LOVED her! Marlie was the epitome of everything I did not want to be known as in high school . . . A nerd girl.

As in, she's the nerd girl. I'm a nerd boy. No! I mean, I am not a nerd boy. Just a *boy*. Just your average, brown-haired, slightly skinny, freckly faced ROCKSTAR! Okay, all of that is true except for the rockstar bit. In primary school, I admit, I was the kinda kid you'd find practising a magic-show routine, or looking up into space with a telescope, or reading through an encyclopedia. Yep, if you can believe it, my parents still owned a set of encyclopedias. But now I was in high school, I had put all that behind me. I was determined to be one of the cool kids. Or, at least, cooler than I had been.

On that particular Monday, Marlie had somehow collected at least a metre of toilet paper on the bottom of her shoe. It trailed along behind her, licking up into the air like a kite that had forgotten it was actually a thin piece of paper used to wipe people's . . . Anyway, you get what I mean.

I could see others around, all sniggering in their disdain, about to call out some humiliating taunt. That is, until they saw who they were sniggering at. Every single one of them quickly stifled their laughter and nervously looked around to make sure they hadn't been seen.

The whole school knew that Marlie Balooby was under the protection of her brother, the infamous Henry Balooby. Or, as he was more commonly known, The Cleaner.

Now, *he* is someone you don't want to get caught staring at. His nickname was not, as you might assume, because he had a side job as a cleaner. No, The Cleaner was named as such because of a toilet. Yep. That's right. He had his own cubicle in the boys' toilets. Cubicle Three.

Not a cubicle used for what you might usually use a toilet for – the launching of submarines. No, this cubicle was known for something much more flush-worthy. Namely, the wailing head of a little junior-high kid like me, or for anyone else who would be silly enough to tease his beloved sister. He could clean the insolence right out of them with one flush of that loo.

The Cleaner. I shuddered at the thought.

'Gosh, you walk fast for someone with such small legs,' said Marlie as she reached me, out of breath. The limp she's had all the time I've known her might have slowed her down, but it certainly didn't seem like it.

'Sorry . . . I, ah . . . have to get to the canteen before the last . . . um, roll-in-a-roll goes.' A roll-in-a-roll being a sausage roll, all toasty and crusty and meaty and warm, put inside a big, buttery hot-dog roll and covered in a bucket of tomato sauce. It was basically a clogged artery in a meal and it was *delicious*.

'Oh, don't worry. My brother has a standing order of three of those each lunchtime, and most of the time he only eats two. I'll just get you one of his.'

'No. No. Don't! I mean, thanks for the offer, but . . . I'll be okay.'

I could just picture the laughter on The Cleaner's face as his sister begged a roll-in-a-roll while I stood awkwardly at her side. That was NOT something I was willing to let happen.

'Have you heard?' Marlie asked again.

'Heard what?' I replied nonchalantly, turning to keep walking.

'That school is cancelled next Monday?'

That got my interest. 'What? No it's not. I haven't heard anything about it.'

'It is. I just found out. The teachers have something on. I don't know, a development day somewhere offsite or something, and they're doing building works here, too.'

'Oh geez, really? Wow, cool. Ah . . . thanks. Now . . . I gotta . . .' I was edging away, trying to escape the conversation before anyone started connecting me with her.

'So, what are you gonna do?'

'When?'

'What are you gonna do next Monday?'

'Oh, um . . . stay home, I guess. 'Cause it's a school-free day, like you said.'

'Right. But maybe, like, I wonder if, maybe, we could hang out or something?'

'Oh. Right, ah . . . look . . . ah, I ah, I . . .' I really couldn't think of anything to say. 'I, sure . . . maybe . . . let's play it by ear, okay?'

'Yes. That'll be amazing. I'll tell my brother you're coming.'

'Cough. Choke. Gurgle. Cough.' (That was me, expressing my horror by having a completely justifiable coughing fit.) 'What?' I asked, recovering.

'My brother, Henry – I'll tell him you're going to come over to our house on Monday, just so he knows.'

'Ah . . . Um . . .'

I don't know if you have ever heard the phrase 'catch 22' before. It basically means that with any choice you make, you are doomed to fail. Like choosing between jumping into a plummeting elevator or staying trapped in a room full of grinning clowns. Either way, you're pretty much dead meat.

I was now going to have to either rock up to the Balooby household, or have a one-on-one conversation with the toilet bowl in Cubicle Three. Talk about being stuck between porcelain and a punch-in-the-face. Sheesh.

'You don't have to do that. I'll just come. It'll be great. Yeah, that's fine,' I responded, with as much enthusiasm as I could muster.

However, as is the way, by the next class it had spread around the entire year that McGee was going on a date with Balooby. By home time, everybody in the school knew. Including, gulp, The Cleaner. The bus trip home was nothing short of humiliation. Every kid I walked past spluttered a, '*Cough*, Balooby sucks. *Cough, cough*.' All followed by a surprisingly well synchronised 'Oooooooooh Baloooooooooby!' from the whole bus as I left. I guess they figured that if they *all* joined in the taunt, then The Cleaner wouldn't flush all their heads. In my rage, I hoped they were wrong.

By the time I got home, I was a frazzled stick of dynamite, a short fuse ready to blow. My mum's cheerful greeting sounded like fingers scratching down a blackboard.

'Welcome home!' she chirped from the kitchen. A surprise. Not the chirpiness, but Mum being in the kitchen. In our house, that room is solely under the occupancy of my father, a super-passionate chef. Like, wildly passionate. A Chef Consultant, they call him. Designing menus for the latest hoity-toity restaurant about to open in our town.

Our kitchen looked more like an evil scientist's laboratory than a place to make a sandwich. Pots and pans of boiling multicoloured sauces. Test tubes with who-knows-what in them. Strange odours. Smoke from liquid nitrogen as my dad, with his big red gloves, froze some kind of dessert. I really cannot complain, though. We ate like royalty in this house. Or perhaps we were just lab rats forced to take part in Dad's culinary experiments. Either way, I was happy with that arrangement.

That's my dad. My mum, however, she couldn't cook if her life depended on it. I guess monkeys don't need exotic foods. She's a zoologist. Works at the local zoo looking after all the animals. And she loves her job. So much so that she often brings it home. The animals, that is. She takes care of the sick native ones in our backyard when they need more care than in just her working hours.

She doesn't just love her job, she actually loves everything, my mum. Absolutely everything. An eternal optimist. It is SO annoying.

'Ughhh,' I mumbled as she made her way from the kitchen to the front door.

'How was your day, dear?' she asked with way too much cheer.

'Fine.'

'Of course it was. But tell me something interesting that happened.'

'Nothing. Nothing happened, all right?' I said with an overly bitter conviction, thus giving the game away entirely.

'Honey, are you okay?'

'I'm fine,' I lied, and stormed to my room. Thankfully, she didn't follow. An hour passed of me angrily throwing a red rubber ball at the wall before my dad appeared with a soft knock on the door.

'Mate, you in there?'

'Maybe,' I said with no enthusiasm. The door cracked open.

'Just got some quail legs with tamarind glaze and fig chutney for your pre-dinner snack here, buddy.'

Dad walked in carrying what would be better served in a five-star restaurant than wasted on a grumpy teenager. Thankfully, I really liked the fancy food Dad made.

'Ughhh. Thanks.'

'You all right, mate? Mum said you were in a slight bit of a mood when you got home.'

'I'm fine,' I said, picking at the quail like it was a pile of cold French fries.

'Right . . . But, just say you weren't, would there be something that would cause you to . . .' he pointed up to the wall, 'redecorate?'

It was only then I realised that the white wall now looked like it was blushing from the many circles of rubber red smudged all over it, stained by the bounce of my ball.

'Oh. Sorry. I didn't realise.'

'Nothing a lick of paint won't fix.'

My dad was not the type to get angry. I know some parents would go full-on-Godzilla mode if their child had redecorated the wall with a red rubber ball. Not my folks.

That wall had once been filled with pictures of galaxies and nebulas and planets and star charts. I'd taken all of them down when I started high school. Now, it looked like the remains of a strawberry battlefield.

'I just . . . I hate high school. It sucks.'

'Oh, mate. Sorry, I thought you loved learning new stuff. You always have. Things a bit harder in high school, though, hey?'

'You can say that again.'

'Oh, mate. Sorry, I thought you loved learning new stuff. You always have. Things a bit harder in high school, though, hey?'

'Shut up, Dad.'

'Sorry. It was some low-hanging fruit for a dad joke. I was just picking some papa-joke berries. Would you like some papa-joke ber–?'

'Oh my gosh, Dad, I can't even . . .'

'Right. Right. Sorry, mate. Tell me what's making high school hard?'

'It just . . . it sucks. I do everything to not stand out and be so . . . I don't know . . . nerdy . . . and . . . then Marlie –'

'Oh, I like Marlie, she's the one from your old school. The one with the –'

'Big head and even bigger mouth . . . yes.'

'No, I was going to say, the one with the big brains, just like my son.'

'Ah, she is so annoying.'

'Andy, sometimes the people who seem really annoying in our lives are, well, more than that.'

'Good talk, Dad. Yep. More than annoying. You're absolutely right she is.'

'You know what I mean, don't you? I know it sounds clichéd, but don't judge Marlie 'cause she's different to you. She might actually be more similar to you than you realise. You never know, she might just be the very friend you need.'

'Pffft! Doubt it, Dad. She was always so frustrating at primary school, and now she's the only one who came to Bellington High and so she's –'

'Lonely?'

'I was going to say clingy.'

'Hmm . . .'

'I don't know. I'm not really hungry, Dad. I'll just eat the quail and go to bed.'

'All right, mate. Remember, though, Mum and I are just down the hall if you need us. Well, your mum will probably be elbow-deep in wombat poo, but she's around.'

'Gross, Dad.'

That's it. That's where it all began, this whole caper (not the Mediterranean edibles). Did you notice? Probably not. I didn't, either. But, as I said, that's the way with the beginnings of things. You don't even realise that they're happening until you're swept off the ground like a wayward balloon heading straight into a hurricane. For now, Monday had come and gone and, by the end of it, I had agreed to a play date with Marlie, been teased on the bus by a chorus of gigantic prats and painted my bedroom wall in angry circles of red.

What I didn't know was that, one week later, instead of being on a date, that Monday would actually be the day Balooby and I would be saving the entire human race. But, I must not get ahead of myself. To understand the Monday, you have to understand the Sunday and the Saturday and the Friday and the . . . well, you get the picture. So, let's talk about the Tuesday, six days before the heist.

SIX DAYS BEFORE THE HEIST

ENTERING THE PRISON

TUESDAY MORNING

Tuesday morning began with one of those particularly painful parental car rides. You know the type, when your parent wants to *be there for you,* but they just come across as sappy and sentimental. Yep, it was one of *those* car rides. My mother was intentionally dialling down her normal enthusiasm for life because she knew I was not in the mood. But when someone who cannot help being a perky rooster chooses to not be, it's like sticky tape on a dam wall. Sooner or later, it's gonna explode in a flood of wild optimism.

'Did you get your homework done last night?' she asked in way too serious a tone for my mum.

'No,' I replied curtly.

'Right. Right. You were, ah, painting the walls, hey?'

'I already said sorry to Dad about that.'

'Yep. You did. Thanks, Andy. You're a good kid, you know, son.'

'Mum, stop!'

'No, it's true. You always have been. I remember when the next-door neighbour lost their cat and you spent hours looking for it.'

The truth was that I had spent hours reading on my bed while everyone else was out looking when suddenly the cat jumped in through my window like a furry thief. I got to claim the victory on that one.

'Or that time that your cousin Freddy fell over and almost broke his ankle, and you were the one who helped him all the way back home.'

The truth of this one was that Freddy had nicked a bike off one of the kids at the park and was riding off with it and stacked badly. Then he forced me, under duress, to help him home, threatening what he would do to me if I said a word.

'Mum, you don't have to try to cheer me up.'

'I know, son. I just hate to see you like this. So, come on, the rollercoaster that is high school will get better. Right now, it just feels like you're zooming through a loop-the-loop after eating a gigantic hot dog. But it'll even out. You'll make some friends, I know you will. You're a lovable fellow. You are a butterfly emerging, Andy. You are the lead role in the sitcom of your life. *Andy McGee, human extraordinaire*. You are the –'

(I told you the dam would break.)

'Enough, enough!'

'Okay. Sorry. Just getting a little carried away there.'

'Yeah, I realised.'

Thankfully, the car then pulled up at the school. I pecked Mum on the cheek and hopped out, making sure to walk as fast as I could into the school. Hoping . . . Hoping . . . But no, true to form, Mum opened up the window and yelled, 'Love you, my little star fruit!'

I lowered my head in shame and shuffled quickly into school. Luckily, no one heard.

The big and black iron gates of Bellington High School loomed above me. At least three storeys high, they were ludicrously large, and each bar was as thick as my arm. Gates built to keep non-students out. Or perhaps, more truthfully, built to keep us students in.

Prisoners. Literally.

I kid you not, Bellington High was NOT designed by the winner of Best Architecture Australia. No! My high school was designed by the best prison architect in Australia. It's true. I am reminded of it every time I walk through those iron gates, which were installed just to break up the concrete brutalism. They were the only way into Bellington Penitentiary. I mean, Bellington High School.

Concrete walls surrounded concrete buildings. Concrete floors. Concrete passageways. Concrete trees . . . Nah, just kidding, there were no trees. Oh, except for the big stump of an old fig tree that was right in the centre of the main quadrangle. Otherwise, it was concrete, concrete and more concrete. A concrete school of four concrete blocks.

A-block for Administration. Though, we called it the PW block. Prison-Warden block. It was where the warden, Principal Jenkins, and his cronies had their offices.

B-block was where English and Maths offenders served their sentences.

C-block was for Creativity, so said the teachers. True, all things science and artistry happened in this block. But we called it the Correctional Centre, where inquisitive souls were confined by cursed prison guards.

And finally there was **D-block**. The school gym. Better known as Dante's Dungeon, so-named after the Physical Education teacher, Mr Dante. All things hellish happened in that block.

These buildings were double-storey monstrosities that surrounded central courtyards (made of concrete), all of which was encircled by a massive concrete perimeter wall. The only opening in the wall being a cut-in walkway a few metres wide, with concrete walls just as high as the perimeter wall itself. This was the entryway that led to the big black gates.

What is important to know is that the school, when it was shut up at night, was impenetrable. Impossible to break into and, during school hours, impossible to break out of. A very effective prison indeed.

I quickly walked into the school away from my mum – head down, shoulders hunched – when . . .

Whack!

Yep, I'd run headfirst into someone. Principal Jenkins, the prison warden himself. I looked up just as spittle and spray rained down on my forehead. Jenkins was what you'd call a LOUD TALKER. Everything he said was at a volume WAY TOO LOUD and was often then accompanied by a subsequent spit shower. It was not fun to be caught in his spray.

'SLOW DOWN, YOUNG MAN! SLOW DOWN!' Principal Jenkins spoke in his usual decibel-breaking voice. He was looking at me through his dark sunglasses. I wasn't sure why he was wearing sunglasses on this cloudy day, but he was. He had a wrinkled forehead, an unshaven chin and eyebrows as bushy as . . . well . . . a bush.

'AND WHO IS IT WE HAVE HERE NOT LOOKING WHERE THEY ARE GOING SO EARLY IN THE MORNING?'

'Ah, sorry, sir. Sorry. It's me . . . Andy McGee,' I said, tempted to put my fingers in my ears to block out some of his booming voice.

'IS IT, YOUNG MAN? IS IT, INDEED? ANDY MCGEE, YOU SAY, ONE OF OUR NEW YEAR SEVEN STUDENTS, ARE YOU?'

'Ah . . . Yes, sir,' I said. This was not my first time meeting Principal Jenkins. But I supposed he must meet a lot of students, being that there are eight-hundred inmates in this school. He continued to scowl at me but, thankfully, at that moment, the bell rang.

Ding. Dong. Ding. Dong.

'WELL, INTO CLASS WITH YOU, YOUNG MAN. AND NEXT TIME . . .' He waited as though I should know what he was going to say and should fill in the blank. But I had no idea.

'Um?'

'. . . WATCH WHERE YOU ARE GOING!'

'Oh! Yes, sir. Yep, I will.'

I walked off toward English class, glancing back to see Principal Jenkins shouting to some late students, 'COME ON, YOU LATECOMERS!'

Weirdly, at the same time, he was scratching his neck with one hand, his lower back with his other and his right shoe was scratching at his left calf. He must have really itchy skin, I thought, or he's practising for a contemporary contortionist routine. I watched him flail his way over to the gates and heft the giant iron bars closed on their squealing hinges.

BOOM!

The great iron gates slammed shut upon the prisoners stuck inside. Jenkins was having the time of his life as he hummed a little tune. It was a song I had heard him hum before, but I didn't know what it was. He took a great big black key that was hanging around his neck and, with one click, locked the gate. A shiver ran down my spine as a strange look of glee swept across his face. Though, it was gone in a moment. I had only ever seen the scowl of Jenkins, but the glee was somehow more disturbing. A menacing prison warden with too much power, or maybe just a principal who *really* loved his job. Who could tell?

Suddenly, he turned and saw me watching him out of the corner of his eye. I ducked around the corner as fast as I could, walked quickly through the corridor and straight into English class.

Thankfully, Marlie wasn't in English with me. But a few sniggers and laughs from surrounding tables proved

I wasn't going to live down the humiliation of the very public 'date' I was to have with Marlie.

Maths was next. Easy. We were doing sentence problems. You know, like, 'If a farmer has twelve apple trees and cuts down half of them, how sweet is the orange juice he has for lunch?' That kind of thing. I wasn't as much of a brainiac as Marlie was with maths. Marlie was in the other top maths class, so I didn't have to see her then, either.

Recess break was spent, you guessed it, trying to avoid Marlie. I didn't want to give any more credence to any talk of a date with her. I was grateful that the school gossip mill was as fickle as social media and, by recess, everyone was talking about a Year Twelve kid who had crashed his car on the way to school. Such news easily outweighed the silly rumours of a supposed Year Seven romance, even if it was The Cleaner's little sister.

Science class was after recess. This is where things really began to heat up. And not just because of the Bunsen burners. (Yep, bad dad joke, I know.) Science class was what changed things.

It was what changed *everything*.

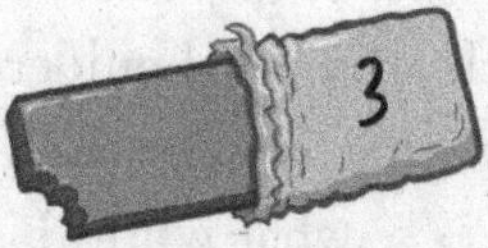

A SPLATTERING OF FROG GUTS

TUESDAY MORNING (SCIENCE CLASS)

I walked in and there was Marlie, front and centre, sitting at the science table, looking straight at me. I couldn't avoid her. And, to make matters worse, she patted the stool next to her and called out, 'Hey! Andy! I saved you a seat!'

This was followed by an 'Ooooooooooooohhh!!!' from other kids already in the classroom.

That was it. I couldn't sit there. I couldn't do it. Instead, I did what any self-respecting person might do in my circumstance. I pretended I didn't see her. Even as she stared directly at my face. Yep. Great move, Andy McGee, really honourable.

Look, it wasn't my finest hour. I walked straight past her and flung my bag down next to Nick Delancey.

Did I feel bad about it? Yes. Yes, I did.

Marlie turned as I sat, and there was a look in her magnified eyes that reminded me of the look parents give that says, 'I'm so disappointed in you I do not even need to show you how angry I am.' You know the one.

She turned back around, shoulders slumped.

Lonely. That's what my dad had suggested. Marlie was lonely, and I . . . what could I . . . I couldn't . . . I just . . .

All right, I was a jerk. A total jerk. But that's not why I was telling you about science class. So forget about that and just let me get on with the story, would you? Stop rubbing my face in my jerkiness. I get it. Stop judging me. You're the jerk. You . . . judging . . . jerky jerk.

Okay. So, Nick Delancey. I sat next to Nick. It was a bold move on my part. A move not well thought out in the rush of potential humiliation. Nick Delancey was one of the cool kids of Year Seven. The kind of kid who could talk his way out of anything. Literally, anything. Any trouble that he had ever gotten himself into, he just as quickly talked himself out of. He prided himself on this fact. On his *charm*.

Nick's name was spoken by teachers in a loud voice, with an edge. Until, moments later, he'd have them laughing and convinced it wasn't his fault in the first place. Nothing was ever his fault. He was buttery smooth, always making people laugh and feel good. Even in his first month at Bellington High, he'd used his *charm* to get a number of kids, as well as entire classes, off detention.

So, Nick was already a Year Seven hero, and I was . . . very much not. Choosing to sit next to him then was, ironically, a heroic kind of move. Well, if it hadn't been out of sheer cowardice toward Marlie, then it would have been heroic. But don't you start judging me again about that.

Nick looked me up and down when I sat next to him, as if deciding whether to let me into his good graces or do something to humiliate me.

He nodded. 'You're McGee, ain't you? I don't think we've ever sat together.'

'Ah . . . no. No, I don't think we have. And, yep, I'm McGee. Andy McGee.' I held out my hand.

He looked at it and raised an eyebrow. I instantly felt foolish.

'All right, all right,' he laughed. 'Being a little formal for science class, aren't we? I'm Delancey, anyways. Nick Delancey. You might have heard of me from the narrowly missed week-long detention of Seven-F a fortnight ago, or the bamboozling of Principal Jenkins in music class last week, or the smoothie incident in the staff car park. Anyways, good to meet you, McGee. Aren't you the one dating Marlie? Why aren't you sitting with her?'

'I am NOT dating Marlie,' I whispered, a little too frantically.

'All right, all right. Chill, brother. It's all good if you like –'

'Hey, do you need this?' Thankfully, our next-table neighbour, Jasmine Quinn, cut off whatever Nick was about to say. She appeared out of nowhere, taking hold of a pen on the desk and, before either of us had a chance to answer, was already back at her table.

Jasmine Quinn was a flitter, a flutter, an impression of a movement you thought you saw, but then forgot.

A whisper, barely spoken. It's what she prided herself on – not being noticed. She was as quiet as a mouse. An extremely discreet one, at that. She didn't want to be seen, so she wasn't. I envied her that right now. Hiding away in the shadows, she would let the world pass her by without making the barest imprint upon it. It was like she had designed everything about herself so you'd just forget. To prove the point, both Nick and I instantly forgot she'd even borrowed a pen.

'Ah . . . where were we?' Nick asked.

'We were talking about the smoothies you put on the teachers' windscreens.'

'Oh, were we? Yes, well, you should have seen –'

I stopped listening at that point. Images of Marlie going straight to her brother in tears after our science lesson and the inevitability of a visit to Cubicle Three loomed heavy in my anxious thoughts. Nick kept talking and I kept nodding until the teacher showed up minutes later.

Mrs Grouse was a science teacher whose love of the periodic table bordered on obsessive. Every time she talked about an element, it was like she was talking about someone she'd fallen in love with. It was gross. Today's lesson was all about the shining beauty of Magnificent Magnesium, as she called him. I mean *it*, as she called *it*.

It was not a bad lesson. Bunsen burners, tongs and eyewear, and we all got to burn little pieces of magnesium. Within minutes, the magnesium was blazing, Mrs Grouse was gushing and students were trying to *not* look too intently at the burning bright-white flame while also trying to get their neighbour *to* look intently at the bright-white flame.

Nick had at least ten suggestions for how we might better use such an element, like sticking it down the butt crack of Peter Damsen, who was sitting in front of us. Thankfully, he didn't attempt it. But he did quickly pocket a few pieces of magnesium. I guessed, to burn somewhere later with his mates.

'What are you doing, Nick Delancey?!' Mrs Grouse spoke. I thought he was busted, his hands deep in his pockets.

'Ah, nothing, miss, just admiring magnificent magnesium.'

'Well, stop doing nothing and take your hands out of your pockets and help your partner.'

'Yes, miss. And I must say, I am really loving this lesson.'

'Oh, I am glad, Nick. That's great.'

'What's your favourite element, do you think, Mrs Grouse?'

The lesson continued with more burning of magnesium and teaching from Mrs Grouse, and Marlie's disappointed glances backwards. I wasn't sure how much more of the shame I could take. Finally, the bell rang, only for me to realise it was a double period.

In this second period, our attention turned from the elements to biology, from magnesium to frogs. You guessed it – dissection. Half the class cheered as Mrs Grouse returned from the science lab's storeroom pushing a cart with stacked trays of dead frogs. The other half cried out in disgust. To the sound of more squeals and fake vomiting, Mrs Grouse demonstrated for us on one frog. We were then given our own frogs, and the dissecting began – to a chorus of hollering and dry-retching.

But this was when it happened.

This was when everything changed.

Fleassy Davies came into the classroom. Fleassy Davies was a joker. *The* joker. Not the Batman *the* Joker, but *the* joker of Year Seven at Bellington High. The kind of person whose idea of a good time was picking her nose and wiping it down some fancy person's expensive suit as she stood behind them in a line. Unlike Nick Delancey, though, she had no ability to turn on a sweet voice. In fact, she'd rather a detention than suck up to any teacher. If Nick was buttery smooth, Fleassy was sandpaper – gritty and grating.

'Nice of you to show up, Ms Davies,' commented Mrs Grouse.

'It is, isn't it, miss?! I . . . got stuck doing something.'

'That is not good enough, Fleassy.'

'But it's true, miss. For one of the other teachers. I was doing something.'

'And which teacher was that, Fleassy?'

'Ah, it was . . . um . . . ya mum!'

The whole class burst into laughter. I told you she was no Nick Delancey.

'Right, that's lunchtime detention for you, Fleassy. Both today and tomorrow. One for missing first period with no valid excuse, and one for giving me cheek.'

'Awww, but –'

'And don't you give me one more word or I'll put you on afternoon detention as well.'

I was expecting Fleassy to lose it. But, for once, she didn't say anything. She didn't even seem angry. She just made her way over from the door and sat on our table.

'What's he sitting here for?' was all she said. She and Nick had been at primary school together.

'I don't know. I think he's trying to escape Marlie . . . but he's all right.'

'I am not escaping Marlie! I am –'

'Look, I really don't care.' Fleassy cut me off.

Suddenly, though, her face softened and she held out her hand. 'Good to meet ya . . . My name's Fleassy.'

'I know . . . ah . . . who you are.' I shook her hand, warily. 'Good to meet you, too. I'm Andy. Andy McGee. I'm actually in a few of your, um, other classes.' I stumbled over my words, but they eventually came out. I tried to let go of her hand but she kept hold of mine, continuing to shake it.

'What is it with all the hand-shaking today?' laughed Nick.

'Well, it's good ya here, McGee.' Fleassy continued squeezing my hand. ''Cause I need ya for something.'

'What?'

'I . . . need . . . you . . . for . . . some . . . thing.'

'No, right, I heard you. I just –'

'Great. You're in then.'

'What? No! I . . .'

But before I could say anything, Fleassy had picked up the half-dissected frog from our table and was wobbling it toward me. Mrs Grouse had turned to the whiteboard and didn't see.

'Wanna kiss the frog, Andy?' Fleassy whispered.

'Yeah, Andy, kiss the frog,' Nick joined in.

I wasn't sure how this moment had very suddenly turned into a barrage against me, but I lashed out at that frog and then watched, in slow motion, as it went flying out of Fleassy's hand and up in the air. An amphibious discus in the science Olympics. Due to the centrifugal force (See? Science has taught me something!), its insides were spurting out as it flew . . . up and up . . . then down and down . . . straight toward Mrs Grouse.

SPLAT!

Squashed frog. It had struck the whiteboard next to Mrs Grouse. Ironically, she had been drawing the anatomy of said frog on the board. Now, the frog's anatomy was . . . on the board. Only, it was dripping down it.

But it wasn't just on the board. The impact exploded that frog like a piñata. The rain of inner-froggy bits was now dripping down the face of Mrs Grouse. She turned. Her expression was contorted into a creature of rage and disgust. It was like a horror show.

'Who did this?' She shook as she whispered the words.

'Who DID THIS?!' Her whisper became a barely-held-back scream of rage. And that is when I saw it . . .

Fleassy Davies, that snitchinator, pointing her finger right at me. Followed by my new best buddy, Nick

Delancey, also pointing his double-crossinator finger right at me. The class caught on and, before I knew it, at least ten others were pointing at me. A whole class of snitchinators.

'I . . . ah . . . I . . .'

Everyone was staring, fingers raised. I was done for. I looked at Marlie. She had turned toward me from the front and was staring, too. I waited for her finger to raise, as payback for my snub at the start of class.

'It wasn't Andy, miss, it was me,' is all she said. Marlie Balooby, she was offering to take the fall. I couldn't believe it.

'Well, which of you was it? Andy McGee? Or you, Marlie?' the teacher barked.

Without even realising I was speaking, I heard my own voice betray me. 'Miss, it was me, miss.'

'No, Andy, it was me,' Marlie spoke again.

'It was not, it was –'

'It was –'

'All right! Stop it! Both of you. I don't care which of you did it. You are both on lunchtime detention.'

A snigger sounded from beside me.

'You think this is funny, Nick Delancey?'

'No, miss. Just a croak in the throat, miss, you understand.'

The class erupted in laughter.

'That's detention for you, too, Nick.'

'Wait, that's not fair.'

'Do you think I care what is FAIR OR NOT right now, Nick?'

Even his charm was not going to counter this moment.

'Does anyone else want to test me? I assure you, I've got more lunchtime detention spots to fill today.'

The class was silent. Mrs Grouse washed her face. For the rest of the period, no one spoke. I cleaned up the murder scene of sprayed frog. Fleassy sat there smirking. Nick was fuming. Marlie was expressionless. Finally, the bell rang and everyone filed outside. Except those on detention. We sat and were lectured at for at least five minutes before she told us not to move a muscle and plonked herself down behind the table in front. We sank into our seats for a looooong lunchtime detention. Until a few minutes later, when . . .

'Wait for it!' Fleassy whispered, looking at her watch.

'Wait for what?' I whispered back.

She ignored me. 'Wait for it,' she whispered again.

RING. RING. RING.

Fleassy smiled. The phone on the science-room wall rang out. Mrs Grouse got up to take the call. Something strange was going on.

'Hello, Mrs Grouse here,' she answered with a frown. A frown that twisted into a grimace as she listened. A grimace that turned into a scowl. A scowl that turned into what can only be described as a furious bald-headed uakari. If you don't know what a uakari is, then you must look it up. Now! Go and do it!

Enough to say, she was beyond angry. It seemed her day was getting worse and worse. Without even a look at us, she slammed down the phone, picked up her keys from the desk and flew out of the room.

'Don't you move!' she yelled as she slammed the door shut.

'What the heck just happened?' asked Nick Delancey.

We all looked at Fleassy.

'What just happened,' she said with a wicked grin, 'is that youse just became my accomplices.'

'What?!' we all said in shock.

'Accomplices in what?' Marlie asked.

'You'll just have to come and see, won't you, Balooby? Come on, we only have a few minutes.'

And with that, Fleassy picked up her bag, walked to the front of the room and straight into the science storeroom beyond. Marlie looked at me. I looked at Nick. Nick looked at Marlie.

'I'm not going,' I said flatly.

'What else are we going to do?' Nick said as he got up from the stool. Marlie looked at me, just for a moment.

'Yeah, what else are we going to do?' she asked, narrowing her big eyes at me. I seriously wondered if a laser was about to strike out of them and cut me down. Thankfully, she walked after Nick.

'Marlie, I . . .'

She kept walking.

'Marlie . . .' I pleaded.

She did not turn back.

With a heavy sigh, I forced myself to stand up and follow, knowing the whole time that I was certain to regret it.

'Yeah, what else are we going to do?' I asked the nobody that was left in the now-empty science room as I walked to the storeroom door.

‘Good point,’ the empty room answered. Like, literally, it answered.

I nearly jumped out of my skin. I turned back and there was Jasmine Quinn walking out of the shadows at the back of the class, grinning as though she had always been there.

‘Jasmine? How the . . .? What the . . .?’

‘Sorry about the fright, Andy. I knew Fleassy was up to something, so I stayed back to find out.’

‘But how did you just . . . appear?’

‘It’s just something I do. I was sitting quietly in the shadows at the back of the room the whole time. Don’t worry, I’m a bit of a sneaky sneak like that.’

‘Right?!?’

The two of us walked through the door. The others were just as shocked to see Jasmine as I was. We had no idea what we had just walked into. Or, to be more precise, what Fleassy had lured us into. Or, to be even more precise, what fate had brought together. For this was it. This was us – the heist squad. Five heroes of this story, destined to save the world. At that moment, though, we were just five random kids standing awkwardly in a science storeroom.

A FAILURE AND A WARNING

TUESDAY AFTERNOON
(SCIENCE DETENTION)

'Why are we here, Fleassy?'

'Why? What a silly question, McGee. 'Cause I needed you for this, of course.'

'Right,' Marlie spoke up. 'And what is *this*?' She gestured around to the shelves of Bunsen burners and test tubes and science books. It was a large room filled with all the science equipment the school needed.

'Oh, just a little bit of mischief and thievery in the form of a heist,' Fleassy answered with a smirk.

'*Cough. Cough*. A what?' I asked.

'She said it's a heist,' Jasmine whispered from behind.

'What kind of heist?' asked Marlie. 'Do you want to steal Bunsen burners or something?'

'No. No. I have something else to show you. And it's just through there.'

Fleassy pointed at a big metal door at the back of the science storeroom. A temperature gauge on the door read four degrees in red digital numbers.

'The coolroom? What's in the coolroom? More frogs?' I asked.

'You'll soon see.'

'Fleassy, would you just tell us already?!' Marlie demanded.

'I will not. I –'

'There's a window in the door,' Jasmine interrupted.

We pushed past Fleassy to take a look. Through the small fogged-up window, shelves of frog specimens, soon to be hacked into pieces, lined the walls. BUT, there in the centre, sitting on a pallet, were boxes and boxes of chocolates. M&M's. Maltesers. Dairy Milk. You name it, it was all there, stacked atop that pallet like sugary gold bullion in a vault. I could certainly see how such sweet treasures, gathered like a tower of temptation, could seduce someone into a thieving criminal euphoria. But still, I wanted no part of it. This heist was just . . . wrong.

'Ah, whose chocolates are they?' I asked.

'The Year Twelves'. To raise funds for their formal. And I have done everything I can to ensure we are able to pinch as many as will fit in our bags right now.'

'What?!' Marlie and I exclaimed at the same time before awkwardly looking at each other. Jasmine didn't say a word, she just shook her head. Even Nick looked hesitant.

'You want us to go and steal a whole lot of chocolates from the Year Twelves? That is ridiculous!' I told her bluntly.

'Goodie two-shoes,' she said obstinately. 'Come on,

we're already here and you are already involved, so either you help or we all get busted.'

'Busted for what? We haven't done anything.'

'Really? Haven't you?' Fleassy teased, grabbing the handle and opening the door to the coolroom. With a loud screech it shuddered across the floor. Quite appropriately, cold mist escaped and swirled all around the supervillain Fleassy, who was standing defiant before us.

She winked and, in a flash, she was into the coolroom and back out with a box of M&M's in each hand. The coolroom door half-closed as Fleassy tossed the packets straight at Marlie and me. I grabbed the one aimed at me, but Marlie copped it right in the forehead.

'Hey!' she yelled at Fleassy as the packet dropped from her head into her hand.

'Fleassy, this is not cool.'

'Well, your fingerprints are all over it now, McGee. You, too, Balooby. So, whether you like it or not, you are in. Now, here's what is happening. You two, you need to stand watch at the door. Look out and make sure no teachers are coming. If you see one, yell out. Nick and I will be going in with our schoolbags and filling them up with chocolate. And you, Jasmine, I didn't mean for you to be here. You can, ah . . . oh, I don't know, just be your normal weirdo self.'

'There is no way that I –' I started.

'Shhhhh!' Marlie suddenly put her finger to her lips.

'What?' we all whispered back to her.

But that was when we all heard it. A sound. Not from back out in the classroom. This came from inside the coolroom, or not so much inside the coolroom as, what seemed to be, behind it. Like a latch being clicked.

'Quick, let's go,' Jasmine whispered. Fleassy and Nick bolted past us, knocking the M&M's box in my hand to the floor. I turned and kicked it off to the side of the room. Then I, too, ran for the door, trying to make it back into the science classroom. Jasmine flittered into a shadow and I lost sight of her. Marlie was beside me as I turned to look back into the coolroom. Its back wall seemed to be slowly sliding open. Neither Marlie nor I were going to make it to the classroom in time. A rolling, scraping sound met my ears, and Marlie suddenly grabbed my hand and dragged me down behind the only desk in the room. A large teacher's writing desk. The sound of the sliding wall stopped, just as we landed heavily on the ground. We stayed as still as we could. Breathing. Breathing. Then someone spoke from inside the coolroom. I could hear only snippets.

'WEIRD . . . DOOR . . . OPEN . . . SECURITY . . . DEAD MEAT.'

Marlie and I looked at each other and then down to our hands. One of hers held the box of M&M's Fleassy had thrown at her. We were so busted. Red-handed. Or multi-M&M-colour handed.

Her other hand was still holding mine. We both seemed to realise this in the same moment. I quickly withdrew mine. She did the same.

As quietly as I could, I took the box of M&M's from her hand. I couldn't put it on the floor for fear of it making a rattling sound. So I slid it so very carefully into my school jacket pocket, out of sight.

Quiet footsteps sounded on the cold floor at the entrance to the coolroom. Then silence. I thought maybe I could hear the sound of breathing. A sort of wheezing. Then nothing but a sigh. The footsteps retreated into the coolroom. The door swung shut with a loud creak and scrape. We waited a few moments until a muffled sliding sound brought us relief. It was the wall at the back of the coolroom sliding back into place. Still, we dared not move.

'You two lovebirds all right down there?' It was Nick. He and Fleassy were peeking in through the classroom door into the storeroom.

'Whoever that was, they're gone,' said Fleassy. 'I didn't know there was a door in the back of the coolroom, though.'

'I'm not sure there's meant to be,' said Marlie.

It was very strange indeed.

'Who was it?' asked Nick.

'I know who it was,' a voice spoke out of the darkness. We all turned around as Jasmine stepped out of the shadows in the corner of the storeroom.

'You must stop doing that,' said Nick.

'Did you see who it was?' I asked.

'Yep. It was Principal Jenkins.'

'WHAT?!' the four of us exclaimed together.

'I swear it. He walked to the door, looked around, scratched his neck and his arm and picked up a bunch of the chocolates from the pallet. Then he disappeared through the back of the coolroom again.'

'I don't get it,' I spoke up. 'Why would the –'

'Well, who cares?' Fleassy interrupted. 'Let's just get some of those chocolates and get out of here.'

'We are not going back in,' Marlie protested.

Fleassy ignored her and walked up to the coolroom door. She grabbed the handle. 'It's locked now, damn it. How did he lock it from the inside?'

'I'm outta here,' I said. That was it. It had all been way too intense having to hide like outlaws about to be caught in this gang of Fleassy's. And all because she entrapped us in the situation. This was not how I saw my day going.

'Yeah. Me, too,' Marlie said. Then she cleared her throat and, with a pointing finger at Fleassy, said with a fierceness I was shocked at, 'And Fleassy. Don't you ever do that to me again!'

Marlie and I picked up our bags and left the science classroom. I wasn't even worrying about Mrs Grouse coming back and finding us not in detention. The bell was about to ring, anyway.

It turns out Mrs Grouse didn't come back to school that day because her car had been towed. I have no idea how Fleassy had pulled that off, but I was actually rather impressed that she had.

In fact, aside from the whole unethical and completely wrong nature of the heist, and looking past the entrapment and manipulation and thievery, all of it had been pretty well thought through. To get us all on detention inside the normally locked science labs. To manipulate the two smallest kids in the school to be lookouts. To get the teacher out of there by somehow getting her car towed. It left the coast as clear as possible for Fleassy to stuff as much chocolate in her bag as she could. Not a bad heist plan at all if Jenkins hadn't shown up. Oh, and if it wasn't outright wrong to steal, that is.

Marlie and I walked silently together down the corridor and through the school quad.

I broke the silence. 'You gonna tell your brother about it?' I asked. I wondered what The Cleaner would do to someone who had threatened his little sister like Fleassy had.

'Nah. Not today. I'll let her get away with this one. But geez, what a –'

'Prat?' I offered.

'Um . . . I was thinking more snot-rag.'

'Ha-ha. Good call. Yeah, I can't believe she did that. I'm certainly never sitting next to her again in any class.'

'Yeah.'

I knew what I needed to say as the silence settled between us.

'Marlie . . . I'm . . . I'm sorry,' I said to her.

'Ah, you don't need to be sorry.'

'But I am. I'm sorry. About the start of class.'

'Thanks.'

The bell rang. Lunch was over. But, weirdly, I didn't want to leave Marlie. I suppose it was that feeling of just having gone through an ordeal together.

'Well, I'm in here,' she said as we came to the next door. 'History class.'

'Oh, yeah. Okay. Yep. Ah, have a good afternoon,' I stammered as she moved off into the room. I turned around the next corner, heading to my own history class when . . .

SLAM!

I was thrown to the ground. Looking around I could see two pairs of feet standing either side of me. I looked up, directly into the eyes of Frankie Dwight and Lloyd Botherton. Henry's henchmen.

Gulp.

'The Cleaner wants to see you, McGee.'

I knew what that meant. It was time for my conversation with the porcelain. This was not going to be pleasant.

'Andy McGee, isn't it?' spoke a deep, guttural voice as we turned the corner.

There are moments that break a man and there are moments that make a man. I knew which this was going to be. This day could not get any worse.

'And are you *the* Andy McGee, who has an interest in my little sister?'

'Um . . . I don't know . . . I don't –'

'Well, here is what you need to know.' He spoke, cutting me off and grabbing the scruff of my shirt. 'Marlie means more to me than anything. So, if *someone* should treat her badly, that *someone* is going to get a little gift from me. Do we have an understanding here, McGee?'

'Yes. Yes, sir. I understand,' I managed to squeak out.

'Are you sure?' he said, shaking me and setting off a rattling sound in the bathroom.

'Yes. I'm sure.'

'What you got there?' he asked, shaking me again to hear the rattling sound.

'Oh . . . it's just some . . . ah . . . M and Ms,' I said, reaching into my pocket.

'A gift for me, McGee? You shouldn't have,' The Cleaner said as he grabbed the box of M&M's from my hand, ripped them open and tipped some into his mouth. He then doled out a handful to his two cronies, Frankie and Lloyd, before downing the rest of them and tossing the packet.

'Right, well, McGee, that's a good start. More of those kinds of gifts any time will get you a long way with me. In fact, as I understand it, you and Marlie are having a little date at our place on Monday. Is that right?'

'No, sir. Maybe. I . . .'

'Well, is it, McGee?'

'Ah, yes,' I said, resigned.

'Then I will look forward to a few more packets of these chocolates delivered to my house when you come on Monday.'

I nodded.

'I am glad we've come to an arrangement, McGee.'

'Yeah, me, too, Mr Clean . . . I mean, Henry.'

'All right then. Off you go, back to class, Mc . . . Mc . . . Mc . . . McGee.'

It was strange. Henry Balooby stuttered. He shook his head.

'What are you staring at, Mc . . . McGee?'

Something seemed wrong. His eyes seemed jittery as he stared at me.

'Nothing . . .'

'Right, well you – ARGHHH!!' He grabbed his head.

His two henchmen were not moving. They just stared straight ahead. Against my better judgement, I moved forward to see if Henry was all right. He came up again as my hand reached out to his shoulder.

WHACK!

'What the hell are you doing, trying to hit me?'

'No!' I turned as fast as I could and walked toward the door.

'Andy McGee!' the fierce voice called out after me. I turned around. 'You treat her badly and you know what happens. Got it?' he said, gesturing toward the third cubicle before he started grabbing at his head again. He looked to be in serious pain.

'Got it. Yep. Got it.'

I turned and bolted.

FIVE DAYS BEFORE THE HEIST

AN IMPLOSION

WEDNESDAY MORNING

It was History. First period. I was tired from staying up half the night in anxious fits of worry about the science storeroom incident and about the Balooby problem and, oh, you name it, I lay in bed thinking about it. So I really wasn't listening much as Mrs McGuire droned on and on about the various Greek gods when, all of sudden, she was interrupted by the familiar **ding dong** of the school speaker system. I listened in, then desperately wished I hadn't.

'Sorry for the interruption, classes. Letting you know that Year Twelve exams are happening in the science block from tomorrow lunchtime. No one is allowed in C-block unless they are sitting for an exam. Oh, and Marlie Balooby and Andy McGee, you are to report to the principal's office. Immediately.'

It was like a vacuum had sucked all the air out of my lungs. Oh dear.

'Ooooohhhhhhh,' the class all cooed together.

I wanted to vomit. Marlie wasn't in my history class, so I stood up by myself. Every eye fastened on me. Nick and Fleassy instantly started talking behind cupped hands at the back of the classroom.

'What did you do, McGee?' someone asked.

'Yeah, McGee, what did you do?' called out Nick from the back of the room.

'Hope you didn't skip out of a lunchtime detention or anything,' Fleassy chimed in. But neither of their comments had quite the same level of contempt they normally did. There were slightly worried looks on their faces, too. They knew what this was likely about.

'You better go,' spoke Mrs McGuire as she looked back from writing the names of the Greek gods on the board. She'd just written, *Ares – God of war.* I hoped it wasn't a sign of what I was about to enter into. Without a word, I walked out of the class, down the corridor and straight to Principal Jenkins' office.

The receptionist was sitting at his desk in the hall outside, staring at his computer. He didn't even look up. His fingers were jamming hard on the keyboard. Definitely a computer game.

Bellington High's receptionist was a long-haired yet early-balding, Hawaiian-shirt-wearing, forever-gum-chewing 21-year-old who had hardly left the school before somehow getting a job back here. The shining example of active listening when it came to the parents of the school, the exact opposite when it came to the kids. He had pulled his long hair into a ponytail and was intently staring at the three computer monitors around him. He did not care in the slightest about what students wanted.

'Sit on the seat,' he grumbled, pointing to the four chairs that sat neatly against the wall just outside the principal's office. I sat down and waited. My legs were all jelly and shaking. My heart was pounding, my hands sweaty.

A few moments later, a student I'd never met came round the corner looking decidedly green. Vomit green. Good suggestion for a Colorbond paint colour, I reckon. Vomit green. The kid raced into the sick-bay room a few metres down the corridor, just in time. The sounds of heaving echoed around me. It was not pretty.

'What are you doing?'

I heard Marlie's muffled voice. I took my fingers out of my ears. 'Just trying not to listen to the murder that is happening in sick bay right now.'

'Oh, I hear it now. Gross! Um, should I tell the receptionist I'm here?'

'I wouldn't bother. He doesn't care.'

'Do you know what we're here for?' Marlie asked in a shaky voice.

'Well, I'm guessing it's something to do with the snot-rag herself, Fleassy Davies.'

'*Cough. Cough.*' The receptionist gave a pointed cough toward us with a condescending frown at my language.

'Good guess, I reckon,' whispered Marlie. 'It's not going to be fun, whatever it is.'

'Do we need a story?' I whispered back to her.

'Like, an alibi?'

'Yeah. Some reason we had to leave detention early, or . . . something.'

'Yeah. What about if we –'

But at that moment, the principal's door slammed open. Principal Jenkins stuck his head out, his scowl sending further shivers down my spine as he spoke in his booming voice, 'MARLIE AND ANDY, COME IN RIGHT AWAY!'

We both entered the office. I'd never been in there before. It was like we had walked into a time machine and were suddenly transported from the sticky linoleum floor and flickering fluorescent lights of a high-school hallway into the olden-day study of an aged professor in his country residence. Shaggy mauve carpet in a room complete with plush furniture and wooden panelling.

'TAKE A SEAT!' Principal Jenkins motioned to the two large chairs sitting in front of his grand, wooden desk as he sat down on his leather chair on the other side. He was humming the same tune from the other morning, and he was staring straight at us.

Rising up behind him was a wall of aged books and ornate objects, a silver eagle, a globe with red pins stuck into it (presumably showing where Principal Jenkins had travelled). There was even a wooden crossbow, which I couldn't tear my eyes away from, shuddering to think what it might be used for. That was, until I saw the artwork behind Principal Jenkins. Pride of place, in the centre of the wall, was a large painting of a knight on a horse trampling a dragon, a sword about to pierce its body. What was truly disturbing, though, was that the knight's visor was up and the face scowling out from underneath was the face now scowling at us. It was Principal Jenkins. He was the knight. We were the dragon about to be 'offed'. His tune-humming stopped, and then came the onslaught.

'ANDY MCGEE AND MARLIE BALOOBY!' He spat our names like it was roll call for a firing squad. Neither of us could speak. It would have been the most frightening moment of my life except for one thing . . .

My hand, which was hanging down by the side of the chair, was suddenly taken hold of by Marlie's. It was like an anchor keeping me grounded from the hurricane that was hurtling toward us. Jenkins' eyes were bulging. Marlie's hand, though. His vein pulsing on his forehead. Marlie's hand, though. He kept scratching his neck as he looked down at us. He was huffing and puffing and breathing strangely. But all I could think about was Marlie's hand gripping mine. It's so ridiculous, I know. I don't even . . . she's so annoying! But, in that moment, it was everything. Especially when the hurricane finally hit.

'DON'T YOU TWO THINK FOR A MOMENT I DON'T KNOW WHAT YOU HAVE BEEN UP TO!' Principal Jenkins was fuming. 'DO YOU THINK I AM SOME SOME KIND OF IGNORANT BUFFOON? I TELL YOU, I AM NOT!'

Gulp. He was just warming up. With the hurricane came the tremor of a growing earthquake.

'I WAS THERE, YOU KNOW. YESTERDAY LUNCHTIME, WHEN YOU TWO THIEVES

CAME IN AND STOLE THE CHOCOLATE. I WAS THERE!'

Holy heck. There really was no way out of this. He knew what happened, and we were dead meat. Pulverised dragon meat stuck with the sword of his tongue. He continued his torrent.

'I WAS THERE, I TELL YOU. I COULD SMELL YOU BOTH. I KNOW WHAT YOU SMELL LIKE. AND DO NOT THINK FOR ONE MOMENT THAT YOU SMELL NICE. YOU STINK LIKE THE REST OF THEM!'

I wasn't sure who *the rest of them* were, and by this time I didn't care, for Jenkins' whole body was shaking. My head was spinning. I was seriously about to vomit. Marlie's hand, though. I held on, white-knuckled, riding the worst rollercoaster in the world.

'NOW, WHAT DO YOU TWO HAVE TO SAY ABOUT SUCH THINGS? AND MORE IMPORTANTLY. . .'

And at this point he really let loose.

'WHERE DID YOU TAKE THE CHOCOLATE?'

'We . . . we . . . we . . .' I couldn't speak.

'OUT WITH IT!'

'We didn't mean to,' Marlie whispered.

'YOU DIDN'T MEAN TO? YOU DIDN'T MEAN TO?' Spittle flew out of his mouth. He scratched viciously at his arm. The earthquake hit some new level on the Richter scale. The warrior was about to swing his sword and decapitate us both with one swoop.

'YOU DIDN'T MEAN TOOOOOOOOO?!'

I seriously didn't know if we would make it out of there alive. I had stopped breathing a long time before this point. Who needs breath when you are about to die? His face was so red, his eyes so bulging. I truly thought Jenkins was actually about to explode. I was wrong. Instead, he imploded.

I cannot quite explain it, but in that moment, at the peak of his anger, when all hell was about to break loose, a switch clicked off in the brain of Principal Jenkins. He just, kind of, shut down. His eyes rolled back slightly and he was weirdly staring straight ahead above us both. One of his eyes twitched, and his mouth was contorted. I wondered if his anger had given him a coronary, and we'd be tarnished forever as The Principal Killers.

Whatever it was, he just stood there, slightly swaying and body twitching.

I breathed out slowly for the first time since this had all begun. Marlie and I turned, wide-eyed, to face each other, and quickly let go of one another's hands. I shrugged my shoulders. She did, too.

'Ah, Principal Jenkins?' Marlie whispered, looking back up at the twitching man. 'Is everything okay?'

He kept staring straight ahead.

'Principal Jenkins . . .?' I asked, too. A little louder than Marlie.

The man above us blinked. Once. Twice. Then he shook his head and looked down at us, confusion and fear on his face.

'What . . . what are you two doing in here?' he asked blankly and slowly and much less loudly than usual.

'Um . . . we . . . you asked us to come,' I managed to say.

'Oh right, right. Ah. And what was that about again?'

'It was about the choc–'

I kicked Marlie under the table. 'It was about all the good work we've been doing recently,' I said instead. 'You just wanted to congratulate us.'

'Oh yes. OH YES!' He was back to his normal loud level. 'THAT'S RIGHT, I REMEMBER NOW. YES. YOU TWO. WHAT WERE YOUR NAMES AGAIN?'

'Marlie and Andy,' Marlie offered.

'RIGHT. RIGHT. WELL, CONGRATULATIONS ON ALL THAT HARD WORK. WELL DONE! NOW, I'M AFRAID I'M A LITTLE BUSY HERE. I HAVE . . .' He looked down at the papers on his desk. We looked down, too. A pile of what looked to be blueprints was sitting scattered on it. 'I HAVE THESE TO SORT THROUGH. SO, THANKS FOR COMING, AND KEEP UP THE GOOD WORK!'

Marlie and I left as fast as we could. The receptionist, still engrossed in his computer games, hadn't even heard all the screaming.

'What the heck was that?' I asked as we reached the end of the hall.

'I really don't know. I thought we were both so done for, and then . . .'

'Then his brain imploded.'

'What even was that?' I asked.

'I don't know,' said Marlie, anxious and puzzled. 'And I really don't know what we do now.'

'We never speak of it again. That's what we do. Either what just happened or the science storeroom yesterday.'

'Good idea. I mean, we didn't even have any of the chocolate, anyways.'

'Well, your brother might think differently.'

'What?'

'Your brother, Henry. I, ah, I still had that packet of M and Ms in my pocket yesterday and I, kinda, gave it to him.'

'But, why? You're not friends with him.'

'No. No, definitely not. But he can be rather . . . persuasive.'

'He bullied you, didn't he?'

'No, he, he . . .'

'Oh, I am going to give it to him at home this afternoon. If he thinks he's sick now, he's not going to know what hit him.'

'Marlie, please. No. Don't. Don't mention it to him.'

The thought of the utter humiliation that would occur if Marlie stood up to her brother for me was just beyond what I could handle. I'd be in line for a frequent-flushing rewards card.

'But he . . .'

'Please.'

'Okay. Okay.'

'Wait, what's your brother sick with?' I asked.

'Oh, I don't know. He was acting so strange this morning. Gripping his stomach and rolling around and mumbling to himself. I could hear him from the bathroom. I walked into his room to say hello, and he barely even noticed I was there. Maybe it's a fever or something. I don't know. But my parents are away, so he just stayed home.'

'Weird,' I said.

'I know, right? So strange. I mean, not as strange as old Jenkins, but . . .'

'HEY!' The receptionist was walking toward us down the hall. 'You two should be back in class by now!'

'We better go. Bye.'

'Yeah, see you later.'

A BAG OF MIXED LOLLIES

WEDNESDAY LUNCHTIME

'You two must have have copped it big time!'

Marlie and I exchanged knowing looks. Fleassy and Nick had come over to the wooden table in the quad where Marlie and I were sitting at lunch.

Yes, I was sitting with Marlie at lunchtime. What of it? Don't you start up at me again. I was just trying to be a nice friend, that's all. Yes, I know how hypocritical I am. I may have thrown her under the bus yesterday morning in Science, but, well, things were different now. It's like when people go through war or something together, there comes with it some kind of camaraderie that can never be broken. And what we had faced just that morning with Jenkins was . . . I don't even know what it was. But Marlie felt safe, like an anchor in the storm kinda safe. Or maybe a harbour after the storm that was Jenkins. Or maybe . . . Geez, I don't know. A safe person. That's all I'm saying. I felt safe with her. A fact I was NOT happy about, mind you.

'We didn't cop it,' I said to Fleassy. 'We were actually congratulated by Jenkins on what great work we've been doing.'

'Bull crud you were.'

'It's true,' chimed in Marlie, strawberry jam squishing out of her sandwich as she munched on her lunch.

'No way,' Nick spoke up. 'Surely it was about the science, ah, incident yesterday.'

'What? You mean the incident where Fleassy here forced us into becoming criminals, that incident?' Marlie said.

'The very one,' Fleassy said, smiling.

'It *was* pretty rude, Fleassy,' a soft voice said from next to us.

We all jumped. Jasmine Quinn was suddenly sitting at the same table without any of us noticing her entrance.

'WOULD YOU STOP DOING THAT?!' Nick said, exasperated.

Jasmine gave a double thumbs up with one eyebrow raised and a grin. It was dorky and cute, and we all laughed.

'Why, you guys have a little fright, did you?' she teased. Jasmine was still an utter mystery to me, but I was certainly beginning to like her.

'No, Quinn, you silent stalker! We did not!' Fleassy sneered.

'Nothing I haven't heard before, Fleassy. Get more creative, would you?'

'Anyways,' said Marlie. 'It WAS so rude of you, Fleassy.'

'Oh, rude, was it? I'm sorry for hurting your little squishmallow feelings by inviting you into a share of the greatest chocolate haul we could have ever got.'

'You didn't invite us. You forced us.'

'I would never force you. You could have walked off at any moment.'

'We couldn't have. We –' I started.

'Anyways,' Fleassy cut me off, 'it was a flop, wasn't it? After all that careful planning, it bombed because of Yell-O-Matic Jenkins and his weird, secret, whatever-that-was behind the cooler.'

'Yeah, what is the go with that room?' Nick asked.

'I don't know,' Jasmine responded. 'But I do wonder where it goes.'

'Well, *I* wonder how we can get back in and actually get some of that chocolate,' said Fleassy.

'Enough, Fleassy, we are not ever going to join you in stealing chocolates. Never. Ever. Ever.'

'Pffft. You're all soft.'

'Why are you hanging out with us then?' I asked her.

'I'm . . . I'm not. Nick and I were just walking past, weren't we, Nick?'

'Yeah, yeah. That's right.'

Still, she and Nick didn't get up and move on. The five of us just sat there at the table for a few more moments. A few moments that turned into the rest of lunch break.

There we were, an unlikely congregation. Like one of those party-mix lolly bags that has all the random lollies tossed in together. There was the nerdy, talkative, smart-as-anything Marlie Balooby. The master-planner, master-annoyer and master of the bad attitude, Fleassy Davies. She was joking with fun-loving Nick Delancey, whose mouth could get him out of anything. Then there was the stealthy, mysterious Jasmine Quinn, who ate her salad quietly beside me but who would occasionally whisper something teasing about Nick and Fleassy that only I could hear.

And then there was me. Andy McGee. Who was I in this weird lolly-bag mix? I wasn't really sure. What I did know, as I looked over at Marlie, was that I wanted to be a better person than I had been the day before. Or was I just being the chameleon I'd always been, doing anything to fit in and be accepted, even in this mixed-bag of lollies?

Is there a chameleon-flavoured lolly? I don't know.

Anyway, that's all WAY too deep for a Wednesday lunch, five days before a heist. So, let's get back to the story at hand.

Nick and Fleassy had been arguing for the last ten minutes about whose BMX was better. Marlie had taken off her shoe and was rubbing her foot. I had seen her doing this at different times over the years.

'Sore foot?' I asked.

'Yeah, just hurts some days, that's all. Actually, no, that's not all. It really bloody hurts a lot some days.'

'Oh. Well that . . . I don't know, that really sucks,' I said ineptly, all the while realising that I'd never really thought about the reality of Marlie being in pain sometimes because of her limp. And then I wondered why I hadn't thought about it. Because I could remember her wearing a foot-brace thing some days when we were in primary school, and she'd used a walking stick sometimes, too. But I'd just, I don't know . . . I'd ignored it.

'I suppose I didn't really realise, Marlie.'

'I don't think you realised much in primary school, Andy.'

'Hey, that is not . . .' I paused. 'Yeah, fair enough.'

'But maybe it's 'cause I didn't talk about it, as well,' she added.

Ding. Dong.

The end-of-lunch bell went and we all got up to move off.

'Heard your bro is sick today, Balooby,' said Fleassy.

'Yep, he is,' she replied. 'Or he's just faking it. Who knows?'

'Well, I heard that those two goofballs that hang off him, I mean out with him, are off sick, too. Unless they're all faking it and are actually hanging at your place, Marlie, which is certainly a possibility. But Frankie's brother said he's actually real sick. He said his brother was feverish and mumbling to himself all morning. Weird, hey? Was your bro the same?'

'Um, no. He . . .' Marlie looked over at me. 'He's just sick, is all.'

'Well, whatever. Off to class we go anyway, losers, and guess what? It's science.'

'Ughhhhh,' we all said together, dreading how Mrs Grouse was going to treat us this lesson.

7

A NIGHT-TIME SWIM

WEDNESDAY EVENING

'Son!' I heard my dad call out. 'There is a Marlie Balooby on the phone for you.'

'Ugh . . . pfluegh . . . bluegh . . .' is about all that came out of my mouth in response. Oh, and the splattering of milk I was now choking on. 'What? Whose phone?' I managed to call out.

'Marlie Balooby,' Dad repeated as he came into my room with one of those sly smiles a parent gives when they are proud of you but are trying not to show it. 'She just rang Mum's mobile. Says she got it from the old primary-school class contact list. Mum's talking to her in the lounge room.'

I had no idea why Marlie would be calling me. My parents hadn't let me get a phone yet, but why would she be desperate enough to call Mum's phone? Surely not to ask me on another date. Oh, geez. My stomach lurched inside me.

'Oh, and son . . .' Dad called from down the hallway.

I turned around. 'Proud of you, mate, for, you know, changing your attitude. I told you Marlie could be a good friend.'

'Ughhh, Dad! Enough already.'

'Yes, yes, sorry, son. Hurry up, then, she's waiting. Mum says she sounded a bit panicked.'

'You could have led with that, Dad.' I hurried round the corner into the lounge room.

'Ah yes, here he is now. I hope it's all okay, Marlie,' Mum said into her phone. She held it out toward me, her eyebrows raised to the roof.

I took the phone and walked through our chaotic cooking-laboratory kitchen and out the back door, making sure to shut it behind me. It was dark outside, and a sudden grunt out of nowhere made me jump. But it was just one of Mum's strays. A llama, in fact. An actual llama was tied up by the back fence, munching on a bale of hay.

Mum brought home Australian native animals from the zoo every other week, for whatever intensive care they needed. I kid you not, there had been emus, baby kangaroos, echidnas . . . But a llama! That was a first.

I knew that in the lock box beside the back door were vials of an animal sedation drug, in case things got out of hand. I didn't think I'd need to use them on the llama. But still, I decided to steer clear of the spitting animal.

'Um . . . Hi, Marlie.'

'Andy! Finally!' She really did sound panicked. 'You gotta help me.'

'What? Why? What's wrong?'

'It's my brother. He's worse. Way worse.'

'He's sicker than he was?'

'Well, he's not so much sick anymore as . . . I don't know, like, deluded.'

'Deluded?'

'Like, seeing things. He's really losing it.'

I could hear sounds in the background. Voices yelling. Things banging. Crashing.

'Yeah, I can hear –'

'I need you to come over.'

'What? What am I going to do?'

'It's you he's raving about.'

'What?'

'He is rampaging around and screaming for you.'

'Screaming for me?'

'Stop repeating everything I am saying and just get here now, all right?'

'I am not coming over to your house when your brother is screaming for me.'

'He's not screaming as much as . . . ah . . .'

'WHERE IS MCGEEEEEE?' I heard through the phone.

'Yeah, that doesn't sound like he's screaming at all.'

'WHERE IS HE?'

He was getting louder now. Like, REALLY loud. I could just imagine The Cleaner on steroids, firing on all cylinders. It was not a pretty thought.

'He's not coming, Henry. But you have to calm –' She was trying to soothe the raging bull that was her brother.

'NOT COMING? NOT COMING?!'

Oh, he was really going for it now.

'NOT COMING????!!!! NOT . . .'

He cut off mid-scream. Silence. I wondered if the phone had gone dead.

'Marlie? Marlie, are you okay?' I asked down the line.

'Um, yeah. Yeah.' She spoke to me, and then to her brother. 'Henry? Henry, are you okay?'

There was no response.

'What's happening, Marlie?' I asked.

'It's Henry, he . . . he's doing the same thing Jenkins did. He completely lost it and now he's, like, totally frozen and just staring straight ahead.'

'Can you wake him? Like we did with Jenkins?'

'HENRY! HENRY!' She was shouting at him now.

I couldn't hear a response.

'He won't wake up, Andy. He won't wake up. What should I do? Please, just come over, would you? Please.'

'Okay. Okay.' I figured it was safe now that The Cleaner was . . . in whatever state he was in. 'I'll come now.'

Marlie let me know her address, so next I just had to figure out what to tell my parents. I went back inside, shut the door behind me and walked into the lounge room.

'How was Marlie?' Mum asked. 'She sounded worried and said her brother was sick or something.'

'Fine. She's fine,' I lied. I'm not a very good liar. Never have been.

'Are you sure?'

'Ah . . . no. No, she's not fine. She's upset. She needs me to go over.'

'What? It's after dinner on a school night, mate,' reasoned Dad.

'Look, you're the one who wanted me to become friends with her.'

'Yes, but . . .'

'Well, this is what friends do. We be there for each other when we are going through something hard.'

Mum looked at Dad. 'He does have a point, love.'

'Yes. I know he does. Do you know what's wrong? Why she needs you?'

I certainly wasn't about to tell them that her brother, who is at the best of times aggressively ambitious, had lost the plot, hit full-on berserker mode and then imploded.

'No. She just . . . she just needs me. Her brother's sick, and she's struggling.'

'Are her parents there?'

I knew they were away somewhere. 'I don't think so, but her older brother is, and he is very . . . responsible, even if he is a bit sick.'

Okay, now I was lying.

'All right. All right. You can go. I'll drop you there myself and go do some shopping, and you can just call me when you need to be picked up. But this is not going to become a regular thing, Andy. You understand?'

'Yes. Yes. Okay. That's fine.'

Fifteen minutes later and I was stepping out of the car at Marlie Balooby's house.

'Nice pad,' my dad said, looking out the car window. 'Now remember, I'm just a phone call away. You've got Mum's phone on you?'

'Yes, Dad.'

'Well, just ring if you need me. I'll be back in an hour either way, okay?'

'Yes, Dad.'

I moved away from the car window, and Dad slowly drove off into the night. Looking up, I realised just how right my dad had been. The Balooby house was more a mansion than a house. It was HUGE and ultra sleek. Spotlessly clean glass everywhere. Unbelievable angles. Luxe finishes. It was the kind of house they feature on *Grand Designs*, my parents' favourite show.

In all the time that I'd known Marlie, I had never thought of her as coming from a rich family. And I certainly hadn't thought of The Cleaner being rich, either. I had it in my mind they must be from Struggle Town. Turns out, that was not the case. Not at all.

Actually, there was a lot that was surprising me about ALL these new acquaintances of mine. It was like, the more I got to know them, the more they broke through my assumptions of them. Or perhaps I was just realising how often I *judge a book by its cover.* Or maybe I don't even see the cover, I just go ahead and judge a book by which shelf someone else placed it on in the library.

Anyway, I walked over and knocked on the door. No answer. I rang the doorbell. No answer. My heart started pounding again. What was going on?

I waited for a few minutes. Knocked a few more times. Nothing. I didn't know what to do. But I did know that I needed to make sure Marlie was okay. So, I walked along the immaculate grass and turned down the side of the house. I looked in the windows as I went. A dining room. A lounge room. Though some lights were on, there was no sign of life from anywhere inside. I was at the back gate. It was slightly ajar, so I pushed through it and walked around the corner into the back garden. Before me was a huge pool, brightly lit, and a massive deck with palm trees scattered around. Huge boulders to one side created a little waterfall pouring into the pool. It was paradise. There was a pool house beside the deck, and movement inside. I really hoped it was Marlie.

I moved quickly across the deck, past the pool and was just about to knock on the door, my hand in the air, when . . .

SMASH!

The door slammed open toward me. I stumbled backward . . . backward . . . further back. Henry 'The Cleaner' Balooby was coming fast out of the pool house, his face in shock as much as my own. But I was the one stumbling backward. Stumbling . . . stumbling. My foot clipped a pool chair. Now I was falling . . . falling . . . falling . . .

SPLASH!

The pool greeted me. It wrapped around me and I sank into its waters, holding my breath. I really wasn't sure if I wanted to rise out of it again to face Henry Balooby. I could see the surface above. I probably should have just pushed off from the bottom and come up for air, but I was feeling the peace of floating there underneath the water after the intensity of falling in. Just a moment longer, I waited. One more moment. Just in case.

Then I saw it. A figure above me. A smudge above the water, moving so quickly and . . .

SPLASH!

The water split as first hands, then arms, then a face came into view. A face slightly blurred in the water, but a face I knew. It was Marlie. She was diving down toward me. She grabbed hold of me and swam upwards. I let myself be pulled up with her to the surface, and then she was dragging me to the side of the pool.

'It's okay! It's okay!' I shouted. 'I am okay. You can let go of me.'

She looked back and saw my still-conscious self. I gave her what I hoped was an encouraging smile.

'You're okay?'

'I'm okay.'

'Then why the hell did you not come up from the bottom of the pool? I thought you were drowning. That you'd hit your head.'

'Ah. No. Sorry. I was just enjoying the peace down there.'

Her face went from concern to violent anger. She let go of me in the water.

'I will drown you myself, Andy McGee. I will –' She stopped, mid-sentence. Her anger dissipated as the corner of her lip turned upward and a grin broke through. A grin that turned into a smile, and the smile into laughter.

'It was pretty funny,' she laughed. 'You should have seen your face when you tripped over that chair. You were like a stunned . . .'

'Llama?' I offered.

'Yes. Llama. It was, ha-ha, it was the funniest I have ever seen you look.'

'Oh, thanks for the grave concern, then.'

'Hey, I just dived in after you to save your life, didn't I?!' she said, splashing me with water and laughing even more. She turned and swam to the side of the pool and . . .

Look, there were a lot of other things I should have been thinking about in that moment, but all I could think about was that smile. Her smile. I hadn't really noticed it before. It was . . . she was . . . ah . . .

'You coming?' she asked, sitting up on the edge of the pool.

'Um, yeah. Yeah, of course. Hey, speaking of lives needing to be saved. Your brother. Where is he now?'

'He just kept on going. He didn't even stop to check you were okay. Before I knew it he'd run around the side of the house and was gone. Come on, let's get dry and talk.'

She held out her hand to help me out of the water. I grabbed hold. She looked at me. My heart did a little skip-rope jumpy thing. I told it to stop being silly. It was just Marlie, after all.

'Andy,' she said sincerely as she held my hand.

'Um, yeah?'

'Thanks for coming to help me.'

'I . . . That's . . . I . . .' But before I could even answer, she grinned and pushed me back into the water.

Twenty minutes later and I was in a pair of WAY too big board shorts, complete with way too big T-shirt. Yep, I was wearing the actual clothes of Henry 'The Cleaner' Balooby. It was a weird night. Marlie and I were on a couch in the pool house, and Marlie was telling me about her brother.

'. . . so then I got home from school and he was delirious. He was walking around the house mumbling to himself and scratching his neck and arms. I tried to talk with him. He didn't even look at me. I tried to listen to his mumbling, but I couldn't really make it out. So I grabbed this recording device my dad got me last birthday for my music, and . . .'

'You play music?'

'What? Yes. I do. All through primary school. Did you not know that?'

'Oh. Um, sure.'

'Anyway, so I recorded him and played it back, but all I could make out was, *Andy*.'

'Yes?'

'No, that was the word. Your name. Over and over. As well as rambling about chocolate. He kept on raving, and it got worse and worse, and he came out here to the pool house, and that's when I decided to call you and he lost his mind and did the shut-down frozen thing, like Jenkins. I couldn't wake him, Andy. I tried tickling him and slapping him, but he just sat there staring straight ahead. Nothing worked. I really didn't know what to do. I was thinking maybe I should call an ambulance, or even my parents, but they are halfway around the world on some business trip. I was just so scared. But then I had a weird idea.' Marlie picked up a half-eaten, half-wrapped Mars bar from the side table next to the lounge we were on.

'Is that from school?' I asked.

'No. No. Just from my fridge. I don't know why, but I thought it was worth a try 'cause he'd been rambling about it. So, I opened the Mars bar and I held it up to his nose. His eyes flickered and he took a bite and came back to his senses. But he couldn't remember anything of what had happened, and he was really disorientated. He said he needed to see Frankie and Lloyd, and we argued a bit more, and then he stormed out and ran straight into you. You had your little swim and, now, here we are.'

'Whoa!'

'Yeah, I don't know what to do, though. I did ring Frankie's brother, Josh, this afternoon, and he said Frankie and Lloyd were acting in the same weird way.'

'All three of them, just like your brother?'

'Scary, right? But why all three?'

'Ah. Oh no.' I'd just realised something.

'What?'

'The chocolate. When your brother, ah, persuasively encouraged me to give him the M and Ms from the store-room, all three of them ate them.'

'You didn't tell me that. So all three of them ate the chocolate, but not you?'

'That's right. I didn't.'

'Could that be it, then? Is there something wrong with the chocolate in the science coolroom?'

'Maybe. I mean, we know Jenkins had something to do with the chocolate, too. So it certainly seems likely.'

'Well, that's what we have to do, then!'

'What?'

'We need to steal another bar of chocolate from the coolroom.'

'Phwooooarr! What?'

'We need to steal the chocolate and see if there is something wrong with it.'

'Right, just after we swore to Fleassy today that we would NEVER, EVER, EVER steal chocolate again.'

'We must, Andy. We gotta work out what's going on. Or who knows what will happen with Henry. I know he's a bully. I do. I get it. But beneath all that, I promise you, he's a really decent person. He just . . . my parents are never around and . . . and, look, I love him. He's my brother.'

'Okay. Okay. But even if we do steal it, we are NOT eating it.'

'No. Of course not. But there must be some way to find out what's wrong with it?'

We both sat thinking for a moment until I realised I knew the exact person who could figure out what was wrong with that chocolate.

'Marlie, have I ever told you what my dad does?'

FOUR DAYS BEFORE THE HEIST

A SECOND ATTEMPT

THURSDAY MORNING

I was nervous. Chewing-my-fingernails nervous. Playing-with-a-fidget-spinner nervous. Needing-to-pee-every-few-minutes nervous. We had no elaborate scheme to steal the chocolate. On the bus this morning we worked out that Marlie would make a distraction during science class, thus allowing me time to run into the science storeroom without being noticed. Quick as I could, I'd grab another packet of the chocolates. That was it. Simple. Clean. Efficient. Or just absurd.

So there I was, in science class again, waiting for Marlie to make her distraction. Mrs Grouse droned on and on about the differences between some types of organisms.

'What are you doing, McGee?'

It was Fleassy, she was sitting next to me. Nick was next to her. Mrs Grouse had moved us to the front of the room after the incident in Science on Tuesday. Marlie, much to the chagrin of Fleassy, was allowed to sit wherever she wanted. So, she purposefully sat at a table toward the back of the room where she could make a distraction far away from me.

'What? Ah, nothing,' I replied to Fleassy.

'Then, why are you so nervous right now?'

'I'm not.'

'Oh, so this whole table is shaking 'cause it's a ruddy earthquake, is it, McGee? And not 'cause your leg's turned into a bowl of jelly on a washing machine.'

'Maybe.' I stopped my leg, and tried to block out Fleassy.

Mrs Grouse was yabbering on, and I hoped she wasn't going to ask me a question. In my head I was coming up with excuses for if we got busted for what we were about to do. I was glancing back at Marlie to see when she would make her move. Turns out, there are a lot of things to keep in mind when you're about to make a seriously questionable life choice.

Fleassy was still staring at me. She knew something was up. She'd said something to Nick beside her and now both of them were sniggering and looking at me. They were going to stuff everything up, I just knew it. I glanced back again toward Marlie. *Come on. Come on.* Fleassy saw the move and looked back, too, to see why I kept turning.

'Ah, I see now,' she whispered as Mrs Grouse wrote on the board. 'You can't keep your eyes off little Balooby, can you, lover boy?'

'What?' I said, turning to Fleassy.

'It's true, McGee. You can't keep your eyes off her,' Nick whispered. 'Got a little Balooby crush, do we?'

'Shut up. No. No. I do not.'

'Then why keep looking at her?'

'Nothing. No reason.'

This was turning out to be a lot trickier than I'd thought it would be. Maybe this wasn't such a . . .

Bang! Clatter!

I jumped. The distraction. It must be. I turned around just as everyone else did, too. Marlie had dropped a tray onto the floor. It had held a Bunsen burner and a test-tube holder with two test tubes in it, now all scattered and smashed on the floor.

'Marlie Balooby, what have you done?' Mrs Grouse was saying from the front of the room.

'Don't touch the smashed glass. We can use this.' Mrs Grouse had grabbed a dustpan and brush and was walking to the back of the class to Marlie and the mess. She had passed our table. This was it. I had to go now. This was the moment. I got up quickly. I moved. Fast. All eyes were on Marlie. Ten steps to get past the teacher's desk and I'd be through the door. I knew I didn't have much time.

One. Two. Three. I walked past Mrs Grouse's desk. Well, that's what I tried to do. In actual fact, I walked just a little too close to the desk and my leg clipped a ruler that was jutting out. The ruler was beneath one of those metal tin pencil cases and so, as the laws of physics would dictate, the pencil case was levered up into the air. I turned as soon as I felt my leg hit the ruler and watched the pencil case fly higher and higher and then lower and lower. I braced myself for the smash.

But it never came.

A hand appeared out of nowhere and grabbed the pencil case just before it hit the floor.

Jasmine Quinn. Of course. She smiled, winked and placed the pencil case back on the desk as quietly as she always did things.

I looked to the back of the classroom. Mrs Grouse was down on the ground helping Marlie with the clean-up. I turned back to make my way through the door, but Jasmine was already doing so. I quickly went after her. Five more steps and I was through, into the science storeroom.

'What are you doing?' I hissed quietly, as we both crept over to the coolroom again.

'I'm saving your butt, that's what I am doing,' she hissed back.

'But how did you know we needed to, you know, get more chocolate?'

'I was sitting behind you both on the bus this morning. Now, shhhh.'

Of course she was. Even though I checked to make sure there was definitely no one there. Oh well.

We reached the coolroom, and I stretched my hand out to the handle.

'What the hell are you two doing?' A voice from behind.

My heart, furiously pounding, now froze. I turned to face a grinning Fleassy.

'How dare you steal chocolates without me.' She tut-tutted at us.

I breathed out. 'Shhhhh! What are you doing back here?'

'Saving you twerps,' she said. 'Don't you remember the loud screech this thing made when I opened it?'

I had forgotten. But now I very much remembered. Without another word, Fleassy walked up beside us. I then saw what was in her hand. It was a small bottle of bike-chain oil.

'What are you going to . . .?'

She walked straight over to the side of the coolroom door and poured the oil onto its hinges as well as the floor, where it had scraped loudly the other day.

'Just needs a bit of lubricant!' She grinned again. 'You're lucky I keep my bike stuff in my bag.'

'Good one, Fleassy,' I encouraged, before realising who it was that I was encouraging.

'Doesn't matter either way,' whispered Jasmine, who was now looking through the little fogged-up window into the coolroom. 'The chocolates are not there. They must have been moved.'

'What? No!' I said, looking in, too. But, sure enough, the centre of the coolroom was now empty.

'Quick, we gotta get back,' urged Jasmine.

All three of us moved as quickly as we could back to the classroom. We walked through the door just as Mrs Grouse turned around with a dustpan full of shattered glass in her hand. She was staring directly at us.

'What is happening here?' she demanded.

'Ah . . . um . . . ah . . .' None of us could speak. We stood there gaping like proverbial fish out of proverbial water gasping for proverbial air.

'Mrs Grouse.' It was Nick Delancey, waving to get her attention. 'Mrs Grouse, they were just getting some more cleaning supplies.'

'Were they now, Mr Delancey? So where are those cleaning supplies now?'

'That is a good question, miss. A really good question. One I have been thinking about for a while. It seems that this school does not have the appropriate amount of cleaning supplies for a science room like this to reach, what I would say, is the occupational health-and-safety requirements.'

We were all gaping at Nick, who had turned on his uber charm and was somehow disarming and distracting Mrs Grouse away from us.

'And not for a moment do I think this is your fault, Mrs Grouse. I am sure you must feel the same, that the science department does not get the kind of budget it deserves. And all of us in this class agree, miss. Don't we, everyone?'

The class mumbled a confused agreement.

'Don't we, everyone?' he said again, rousing their mumbled agreement to a fervent, 'Yes. Yes, we do!'

He seriously had a manipulation superpower. Something that, only a moment before, no one had cared about, now felt like it was really important to the whole class. I had never seen Nick cast his magic like this. But here he was. And it was working.

'Well, I didn't realise you all cared so much,' said Mrs Grouse, forgetting about the three children at the front of the class who were now walking quickly back to their seats without being noticed.

'Yes, Mrs Grouse. We certainly do,' Nick continued. 'And we thought we should all sign a petition from us students to take to Principal Jenkins, on your behalf, appealing for more budget for the science labs. How would that be? Do you think that would work, miss?'

'Well, Nick. That is a lovely thought. And, you know, it might just do. Why don't we write that up now, hey?'

And so, for the rest of science class, we all worked on a class petition for more funding to come to the science department at the school. I looked around as we did so and shook my head at Marlie to tell her that I didn't get the chocolate. She frowned. But I also looked around at Nick and at Jasmine and at Fleassy. At any point that morning, the whole escapade should have led to at least a week of detentions, but it hadn't. Why? Because I had found the best team of heisters in the world. Okay, that may be just the slightest exaggeration. But they did each have their talents. That much was obvious.

9

THE GREAT UNDERWORLD OF DARKNESS

THURSDAY LUNCHTIME

'So, what the heck was that all about, you thieving scoundrels?' Fleassy demanded.

It was lunchtime, and the five of us were sitting down at what had somehow become OUR table in the back quadrangle of the school.

I'm sure it had been someone else's spot, but where the sister of The Cleaner sits, there she gets to stay. So there we were, five mismatched mischief-makers. Or, at least, two mischief-makers, one nerd, one sneaky sneak and me. Whatever we were, we were becoming a thing. This sitting together was becoming a thing. I really wasn't sure yet whether it was a good thing or a bad thing. But it was a thing. We were now firmly gravitating toward each other.

'Yeah, what was that?' Nick asked.

'Amazing covering by the way, Nick,' Jasmine encouraged.

Nick looked shocked. 'Yeah, it's what I was born to do,' he said, his head inflating every second.

'What, suck up to teachers?' Jasmine quipped back.

'No, manipulate them,' he said with an evil grin.

You can see why I wasn't sure if this was a good thing or not.

'Just tell us what that was about!' Fleassy faced off toward Marlie and me with a hint of annoyance.

'What, you don't like being pulled into something without knowing all the details?' Marlie threw back at her with an eyebrow raised.

I looked between them. After what Fleassy had pulled the other day, I loved Marlie giving it to her like this. An eyebrow-raise, and she had the power. Ha-ha, what a tactic!

'What? No, actually, I love it,' Fleassy replied.

'Yeah, right.'

'Look, just tell us already.'

'We just wanted some chocolate, is all.'

'Yeah, we were a little peckish. You know how those cravings can get,' I said.

'Bull. Crap. Sticks,' said Nick.

'Bull crap sticks indeed, Delancey,' said Fleassy.

'Whatever bull crap sticks might be,' I retorted.

Fleassy kept pushing. 'So you're telling us that, one day you swear you shall NEVER EVER EVER steal chocolates from the science storeroom. And then the next day you're masterminding the stealing of more, AND not telling us about it, AND doing a really crap job of it AND it was all just because you were a little peckish?'

'Yep.'

'Look, McGee, if we hadn't been there, you would either be on lunchtime detentions for a week or suspended from school right now,' Nick argued.

'All right. All right,' said Marlie. She looked at me. 'Let's tell them.'

'Ah, if you're sure,' I responded softly.

'Oh would you two just go on a date already?!' Fleassy threw down at us.

We both blushed.

'Shut up, Fleassy!' Marlie retorted. 'Unless you don't want to hear about it.'

'What, about your date? I definitely don't want to know –'

'No! About the chocolates.'

'Oh right. Yeah. That'd be good.'

And so, Marlie and I told the other three everything. Henry. Jenkins. Everything. Jasmine had heard some of it from the bus that morning, but it was all new to Fleassy and Nick.

'Phwoar, that is, that is –' Nick began as we finished.

'There is no way –' Fleassy started at us again.

'We're telling the truth,' I promised. 'Cross my heart.'

'I'll cross your heart with a sharp scalpel if you are lying to us and joking about it behind our backs, McGee,' Fleassy threatened.

'It's true,' Jasmine jumped in. 'It makes sense. I live down from Lloyd, and I saw him out on the street yesterday pacing back and forth, rambling to himself and itching at his skin like you said the others were.'

'Well, it sounds to me like they've just been smoking something they shouldn't have,' Nick said.

'What, and Jenkins, too?'

'Yeah. Probably.'

'It's not that, Nick. I know it's not,' said Marlie sadly. 'I wouldn't lie about my brother like this. It's true, something strange is happening. And now the chocolates are gone, too. I don't know what to do.'

'Well, they must be somewhere in the school, mustn't they?' Jasmine said.

'Yeah, you're right, Jaz,' I said enthusiastically.

She smiled shyly at the shortening of her name, but then grinned.

'There was a whole pallet of them,' I continued, 'and the Year Twelves haven't been given them to sell for their formal fundraiser yet. I think they get them on Monday.'

'Can't be Monday. We all have the day off that day,' said Marlie.

'Oh yeah. Tuesday then,' I said. 'But that means they must still be here.'

'But where?' Nick asked.

'It's gotta be through that back door of the science coolroom,' said Marlie. 'Wherever Principal Jenkins was taking the handful he had of them on Tuesday, that's where they'll all be. Whatever it is that's actually back behind there.'

'It's probably some teachers' hangout,' said Nick. 'Where they sit around eating chocolate all day long.'

'You're probably right,' I said. 'Well, maybe not about the teacher hangout, but there's something back there.

So then, the question is, can we get back into the science storeroom and not get caught?'

'Nope. You can't,' Fleassy responded instantly. 'That's why I had to get us all on lunchtime detention on Tuesday so that we'd still be in the building. Because the science labs are fully locked during recess and lunch. There is no way in or out of them, unless you swipe one of the science teachers' keys.'

'Well, can we do that?' Nick asked.

'Jasmine could,' I said, looking around at her. 'What do you say, Jasmine? With those stealthy skills of yours, could you get one of the keys?'

'I could, but there wouldn't be much point.'

'Why not?'

'Didn't you hear the announcement yesterday morning? No one is allowed near the science block from lunchtime today, which is right now until next week. The Year Twelve exams are happening there. The place will be filled with Year Twelve students the whole time.'

'Ah . . . darn it, you're right,' I responded. 'And Year Twelve exams means there'll also be teachers in the class, looking around intently to make sure no one is cheating. There's no way we can get through that. Not even you, Jasmine. So what do we do?'

Everyone shrugged. None of us knew. We all grew silent. Minutes passed. Marlie was looking increasingly forlorn. Someone's hand was on her back in front of me, attempting to give her some comfort.

Oh crap. I realised it was my hand. I was about to take it away when Marlie leaned back into me.

Fleassy rolled her eyes. Nick snorted. I quickly removed my hand. The bell rang.

'Well, that's that. We've got nothing,' said Fleassy. 'Your brother's a tyrranical mobster, anyway. What do we care if he's getting sick 'cause of chocolate?'

'Takes one to know one, hey, Fleassy?' I said.

She narrowed her eyes and was about to let loose back at me.

'My brother . . .' Marlie said, cutting her off.

'Yes,' Fleassy said. 'Your brother and his kooky mates. All of them are –'

'No. No. My brother. It's my brother. Look,' Marlie said, pointing.

Sure enough, Henry Balooby was walking down the other side of the quad. And, to make it all the more strange, he was walking and talking with Principal Jenkins, Frankie Dwight and Lloyd Botherton, each of them wearing sunglasses.

'Okay. Now I believe your story,' Nick said. 'The Cleaner and Frankie and Lloyd getting buddy-buddy with Principal Jenkins. There really is something highly disturbing happening here. And I am not just speaking about their weird matching sunglasses.'

We sat and stared at the four of them walking together in focused discussion through the quad.

'Quick, we need to follow,' said Marlie.

All five of us got up from the table, grabbed our bags and walked as fast as we could while, at the same time, trying to look like we weren't up to anything in particular. Just five innocent Year Seven students walking quickly through the school. I am pretty sure we looked as shifty as a pack of wolves trying to creep up on some sheep without being seen, but we followed them anyway. Through the main quad, past the old stump of a fig tree and down through the corridor into the next quadrangle.

'What are we going to do if we catch up to them? Confront them?' I asked Marlie, but then I realised she was a few paces behind. I slowed down a little. 'You okay?' I asked, taking in the quick, uneven rhythm of her walk.

She looked at me strangely. 'I've had this all my life, Andy. I do not need you to start helping me now.'

'Right. Sorry.'

'Just focus on not losing them.'

We reached the end of the quad and turned the corner at the same time as the four of them turned right between two buildings. We followed after them. They went straight into the next building. Keeping up the pace, we tried to get closer. Then I realised where they were headed. The Administration block. They were going to Principal Jenkins' office. They must be. The five of us kept following and, sure enough, we were soon back in the hallway that led to the principal's office. Jasmine led us down it as we crept closer and closer, knowing they'd already be in the room.

'What are you lot doing?' The inevitable callout from the receptionist in his nasally voice, his beady eyes not looking up once from his three computer monitors as we approached.

'Ah, um . . . we are here to see Principal Jenkins,' I said.

'Well, you are not booked into his calendar. No one gets to see Principal Jenkins without an appointment. Why are you wanting to see him?' he asked flatly, still not looking away from his computer.

'Ummm . . .'

Beside me, Marlie started groaning. 'Ugh, I'm not feeling well at all,' she said. 'Can I go to sick bay?'

The receptionist rolled his eyes as though he'd heard every excuse under the sun for a student to go into sick bay.

'Yes, just through there,' he said, still not looking up. 'But Nurse Mildred is on lunchbreak. So you'll just have to lie down and wait for her.'

'And we'll stay out in the hall and wait,' I said.

'No you will not. You lot won't be making a commotion in my hall. One of you is allowed to stay with her. The others can all leave.'

'Ughhhhhhhhh!' It was Fleassy. 'I'm not feeling well, either.'

'Nice try. Nope. You're all out besides the sick girl and one other. Now, scram.'

Nick stepped in front of us at that moment and spoke up. 'That's a nice computer you got there, Denny.'

I didn't even know his name was Denny, and I had no idea how Nick knew such a thing.

'Thanks, but I don't need YOU to tell ME that.'

'Quite a good computer for a reception desk.'

'Your point, kid?'

'Well, I just wonder . . . you don't happen to also like a bit of gaming, do you?'

'Maybe I do. Maybe I don't.'

'Are you into that new *Assassin's Creed*?'

'Pffft. *Assassin's Creed* is for amateurs.'

'Really? I thought it was great.'

'You need a lesson in gaming, young man!'

'Do I? Well, tell me, Denny, what should I get then?'

For the first time, the receptionist, now known as Denny, looked up from his computer right at Nick Delancey. He looked him over, trying to tell if he really was asking a serious question or if he was just having a go at him. Nick batted those innocent eyelids, turning on his magical charm and appeared as curious as anyone interested in gaming might be.

It worked. Denny began going through the list of his 20 favourite games, ranked in order, with at least five positives about each.

By the time I'd realised the distraction that Nick was causing, I'd also noticed that Jasmine was not with us any longer. And then suddenly, before I could blink, she was back again.

'They're not there,' she whispered to us as we stood around trying to appear interested in Denny's computer diatribe.

'What?' I whispered back while still nodding at Denny. 'Did you already look?'

'Yes. And they are not there.'

'They have to be,' Marlie spoke quietly.

'Well, they aren't.'

'But they just went in there and haven't come out,' I whispered.

'I know that. But they are not there.'

'We have to get in,' Marlie said with determination. 'We –'

DING DONG. DING DONG.

'That's the end-of-lunch bell,' said Denny, cutting off his computer-game lecture. 'Sorry, I got a little carried away there. Now, back to class, unless . . . Who was the sick one again?'

'Ah, that was me,' said Marlie.

'All right, well, into class everyone except for you and one other.'

'Andy, can you stay with me?' Marlie asked.

'Pffft! Of course it's Andy who gets to stay,' spat Fleassy.

'Shut up, Fleassy,' we both said back.

And so it was that the others walked away, and Marlie and I walked into sick bay. I wasn't sure what we could do from out here, but there had to be something. And it needed to be quick before the nurse came back and Marlie would have to really fake something.

'What can we do?' she whispered, trying not to be overheard by Denny who was focused back on whatever game he was playing at reception.

'I don't know. Surely we can think of something.'

'We need to distract Denny somehow.'

RING RING RING.

Denny picked up the phone. 'Hello, this is Bellington High School, how may I help you?'

He listened. 'Pardon, what was that? No, I . . . What?' He was getting more and more worked up. 'Well, you can't do that. No! I . . . that is not right!'

Marlie and I both looked at each other. It was Fleassy. It must be. A phone call like this had her fingerprints all over it.

'Fine!' he said, slamming down the phone.

Denny picked up his keys and bolted off down the hallway without even a look back. We didn't know what Fleassy had said, but she must have made up some whopper.

Marlie and I quickly walked past the now-empty reception desk. Out of the corner of my eye, I noticed a small key cupboard beneath the desk where Denny sat. *Good to know,* I thought. We went straight to the office door and knocked twice, just to make sure Jasmine was correct. No one answered.

I tried the door. It was unlocked. Not certain of what we were hoping to achieve or what we'd find, we both slipped inside the principal's office and quietly shut the door behind us.

The room was empty. Well, empty of people, that is. It was otherwise just as we had seen it the day before – plush and old. The memory of Principal Jenkins imploding sent a shiver down my neck. What the heck were we doing back here?

'What now?' I asked.

'Good question. I don't know. I was hoping something would present itself.'

We walked over to behind his desk. The building plans were still sitting scattered upon it, Bellington High School written at the top. They were indeed plans to the school.

I had an idea. 'Let's find the science lab storeroom and see if the plans show whatever is behind the coolroom.'

'Okay. It's a start, at least.'

We scoured the blueprints. True to their name, all the lines were in blue.

'D-block. Gymnasium. Dante's Dungeon. Not this one,' I said.

We flipped over to the next paper. Not there, either.

'Wait, here it is. C-block. Art and Science. The Correctional Centre. First floor.'

We quickly located the science storeroom.

'And there is the coolroom. That little square there,' said Marlie, pointing. 'And look, there is the symbol for steps in red going down from behind it. I wonder why it's in red?'

'No idea, but maybe there are stairs that lead up to it from that side. That's interesting.'

We flipped over to the next sheet of plans.

'Oh, this is here. Where we are, look. The Admin block. And here is the office. Wait! Look at this . . . The same red staircase symbol. And look where it is . . .' I pointed.

'Right here. Like, *right* here. At this wall. In this office.'

We both looked behind us at the book shelving, wondering instantly if it was hiding a doorway, like in the science coolroom.

'This is where my brother just disappeared, so there has to be something here he disappeared into.'

'But what? There's no door,' I said quietly, looking

back at the plans and flicking over to the next sheet, which showed B-Block's first floor. English and Maths. Blue lines. No red. Nothing there.

We flipped again.

'Ah, look. Another red symbol. What's it under?'

'Um . . . oh, that is the bell tower, isn't it? Yeah, look, there is a musical symbol there, too.'

Though the whole school bell system had been upgraded to an electric speaker system, we knew there was still the original school bell, high in a tower in the very centre of the school, left there for posterity.

'Yeah, and the red stairs symbol looks like it might be right in the tower itself.'

'Any other sheets?'

'Yeah, one more.'

I flicked it over. We both gasped.

'Lower basement level?' we both read aloud at the same time.

'But there is no –'

'There must be.'

We were looking at a sheet of plans. This one was all in red and clearly showed a lower level of our school, beneath the ground. A level that we were sure no one knew even existed.

'Ah, I wish we had a phone here so we could take a photo of this,' I said.

'Well, let's at least . . . Wait!' Marlie grabbed a pen and blank sheet of paper off the desk and quickly set about making a mock-up drawing of the underground plans. It looked like lots of winding walkways with tiny rooms coming off them, and a few large rooms at the ends of hallways. There were also three of the stair symbols.

As Marlie drew the plans, we heard a sudden *creak* from the door. Both of us held our breath and ducked behind the desk immediately. We peeked out. A moment later, Fleassy's head poked around the corner, followed by Jasmine's, followed by Nick's. All three tumbled into the room.

'Oh, it's just you,' I breathed out.

'Don't sound so excited, McGee. Of course it's us, you nitwit. I got rid of Dense Denny, didn't I?'

'Good work, Fleassy. Thanks for that,' I said with sincerity.

'Ah, that's okay,' she replied, looking slightly embarrassed at the sincere compliment.

'So, what do we have here then?' asked Nick, looking at Marlie, who was continuing to scribble down the map.

I quickly explained to them what we had found.

'No way!' all three said at the same time as I finished. They crowded around Marlie to see the map.

'So, there seems to be only three ways to get down to the secret lower basement level of the school,' I explained, just as Marlie finished copying the plans. It wasn't quite exact but it would have to do. 'From the back of the coolroom. From the bell tower. And from this very office.'

'Yep, looks that way,' Marlie agreed. 'I think Jenkins must have rigged all of them to open in some way that only he knows, because I can't see a door anywhere in this office.'

'Why is it even there? Like, what is it? The basement, I mean,' Jasmine asked.

We all shook our heads.

'Do you think . . .?' I said, looking around. 'Should we try to find this door, and how to open it?'

'Hell yes!' exclaimed Fleassy and Nick.

'Definitely,' said Marlie. 'My brother is down there, and I have to help him.'

We all started searching around the bookshelf, trying to find something that might open a door leading to the stairs shown on the map.

'I don't know what I'm looking for,' I said.

'A switch? A lever? A button, maybe,' responded Marlie.

'Bah! There must be something,' said Fleassy, getting frustrated.

But there was certainly nothing obvious. We all pulled out a few books. Nothing.

'Don't make it look like we've been here,' I said, as Nick and Fleassy tossed books down onto the floor. 'We don't want it to look like someone ransacked Jenkins' office.'

'Why? What does it even matter?' Fleassy retorted.

'Because we don't want him to know that we are onto him.'

'He's right,' said Marlie, backing me up. 'Put everything back exactly as you found it.'

'Oh, of course you side with lover boy,' said Fleassy.

'No! It's just smart,' Marlie replied angrily.

'Pah! We don't even know what we are supposedly onto him for.'

'Whatever it is, it can't be good,' I said. 'So just put the books back where you got them from.'

Fleassy rolled her eyes but started to put back the books, regardless. Nick followed suit. Jasmine opened some of the drawers of the desk to see if there might be a button in there. Again, nothing. After a few minutes, we all took a step back around the desk, so we could look up at the wall of books from a distance.

'Can anyone see anything?' I asked.

'A bookshelf,' Nick said.

'Good one, genius, anything else?'

'Nahhhh . . .' Fleassy said despondently. 'It's useless.'

'Wait, wait a second!' I had realised something. 'Isn't the head on that silver eagle turned the other way from what it was yesterday, Marlie?'

'Um, I don't know. I can't remember.'

'I'm pretty sure it is.'

'Yeah, but can any of us reach –'

Jasmine was already on her way up before Nick could finish his sentence. She deftly moved from one shelf up to another, one more and one more.

'Nice one, Jasmine,' encouraged Nick.

She was high enough now to reach the silver eagle statue. It was perched high, looking out over the office. She grabbed hold of its head, took a breath and twisted.

Nothing. I sighed. 'Ah, so much for –'

Click.

We looked around. The sound of a door opening. But not just a door. In a second, a whole section of the bookshelf swung open to reveal concrete steps leading down.

'My goodness!' said Jasmine.

'Bugger,' said Fleassy.

'Incredible,' said Marlie.

'Flippin' heck,' said Nick.

'Tell me about it,' I said.

All five of us stood staring at the open door. But none of us moved.

'Shall we do this, then? I need to help my brother.'

Marlie's worry jerked us into action.

'Of course we should, you bunch of wusses,' said Fleassy, pushing ahead.

Marlie stepped cautiously behind her, her hand finding the concrete wall in the absence of a handrail, followed by Nick and Jasmine, and then I was at the back.

'Hurry up, you lot. Marlie, quit slowing everyone down!'

'Shut up, Fleassy,' we all said back.

So there we were, five intrepid explorers beginning our descent into the great underworld of darkness. Or, as some might call it, the basement of Bellington High School.

10

WILLY WONKA

STILL THURSDAY LUNCHTIME

Our descent into the great underworld of darkness lasted all of ten steps. It was not a long descent. Turns out, the underworld isn't too far away, at all. But those ten steps, they felt like an eternity. Each one accompanied by the weight of our fear, our fear accompanied by sweaty hands, our sweaty hands accompanied by panicked breaths.

'Who the heck is breathing like a foghorn?' Fleassy's voice echoed in the cold concrete of the empty corridor.

'Shhhh!' we all shushed back. Although I quickly realised it was, in fact, me doing the heavy breathing. So I decided to stop breathing all together. As you can imagine, that lasted only a few more steps until I had to take a huge breath, lest I faint. Look, I wasn't the chillest explorer into those murky depths.

At the bottom of the steps was a dank concrete stairwell with one door leading out. A light was coming through a little window in the door from the hall beyond.

Fleassy peeked through the little window. 'Looks clear to me,' she whispered, before pushing the door open quietly. We all scampered through after her.

We were now in a concrete hallway. As much brutalism below as above. At least it kinda fit the vibe of the whole underground lair thing. It felt like some guards would swamp us at any moment. We waited.

'What now?' Nick asked too loudly, his voice echoing down the hall.

'Shhh . . . would you whisper already, Nick?' Marlie whispered back, annoyed. She pulled out the scribbled map she'd drawn and, through another minute or two of whispered arguing, we figured out our way forward. Straight to the end of this corridor. Turn right. Turn left. Past two doors, which looked like they just opened onto tiny rooms. Then we'd go into the third door to another small room, but this room looked like it connected to one of the massive rooms on the map. If we could get into that little room connected to the large one, we might be able to figure out what was going on.

As quietly as we could, the five of us crept straight down the corridor and turned right. Maybe we'd all seen too many movies because, like a crew of bumbling bank robbers, we crept along with our backs hunched and our hands slightly out in front of us.

Maybe this was a movie. That's what it was starting to feel like. I just didn't know if it was a crime story, a thriller, a heroic tragedy or a comedy of errors.

Fleassy stopped to peep around the corner where we were to turn left. The others slowed behind her. But I, being distracted in my thoughts, ran straight into the back of Jasmine, who fell straight onto Nick, who fell onto Marlie, who fell onto Fleassy, who fell straight out into the hallway.

Definitely a comedy of errors, then.

'Who the hell –?' Fleassy whispered in a rage as she got up from the ground and seethed back at us. Thankfully, no one was around the corner.

'I . . . I . . . sorry,' was all I could say while looking highly embarrassed.

'McGee,' Fleassy said through gritted teeth. 'If I'd been shot dead by a guard or eaten by a monster just then, I would haunt you for the rest of your miserable –'

'All right, all right, come on, Fleassy, I'm sure he didn't mean to.' Once again, Marlie was defending me.

To her credit, Fleassy just shook her head and carried on. We crept along and came to the first little room on the left. The door was locked. The second little room. The door was also locked. We had just come to the third door when we heard, from around the corner ahead, the clearly recognisable and loud voice of Jenkins.

'ALL RIGHT, LET'S HEAD BACK.'

Fleassy and Marlie looked back at the rest of us and we all panicked about what to do. Jenkins and the others were going to come around that corner any moment.

Marlie reached out toward the third door that we were all standing by. I prayed it would be unlocked.

Phew! It was. And dark. No one was in there. As quickly and quietly as we could, we all piled into the room. I turned back around and shut the door, glimpsing two legs coming around the corner as it shut soundlessly. Just in time.

We all crouched down to the floor. Hearts thumping. As I sat in the dark, I made a split-second decision to reach up and flick the lock on the door. I couldn't quite believe what was happening. Above us, our fellow students were going about their normal school life, while we were here, hiding in a room in a secret part of the school facing what felt like life-or-death decisions.

'COME IN HERE FIRST, SO WE CAN TALK IT THROUGH.' We heard the voice of Principal Jenkins from just outside the door. The handle above my head jiggled. I'd made the right move in locking it. But surely he had a key.

'WHY IS THIS DOOR LOCKED? IT SHOULD NOT BE LOCKED!' came the annoyed voice of the principal.

'No idea!' It was Henry Balooby's deep voice.

Marlie, who was right beside me, leaning against the wall, took a sharp intake of breath.

'ALL RIGHT, WELL, LET'S TALK HERE IN THE CORRIDOR QUICKLY. WE MUST GO AND PREPARE. THE WHOLE SHIPMENT HAS TO GO TO THE STUDENTS ON TUESDAY AND WE STILL HAVE SO MUCH TO DO. THE TRUCK MUST BE FULL, IF WE ARE TO GET IT ALL OUT TO THE OTHERS AROUND TOWN.'

'That is exactly my point,' said either Frankie or Lloyd. I couldn't tell which. 'We need to bring in the rest of us this weekend and just get it all done in one hit.'

'What? All of the school's chocolate in the whole area done this weekend?' questioned Henry Balooby.

'YES! THIS IS WHERE IT ALL BEGINS. YOU KNOW THAT.'

'Yes, but . . .' Henry interjected again.

'BUT WHAT?' Jenkins fired back. 'THE COCOA, IT IS THE BEST WAY TO TAKE OVER THE BODIES, THAT IS WHAT THE SCIENTISTS HAVE SAID.'

Okay, this was getting *really* weird now. Marlie gripped my hand. I squeezed her hand back in what I hoped was a squeeze that said . . .

Did he just say what I think he said? This is getting really weird now. What does that even mean? Whatever it is, I am here for you, Marlie Balooby.

I don't know if she quite picked up the nuance for all of that in one squeeze of a hand.

'WE HAVE BEEN PLANNING FOR IT FOR YEARS,' Principal Jenkins continued. 'YOU SAW IT IN THE LIBRARY IN THE NEXUS. YOU THREE AND THE OTHERS ARE PROOF THAT IT IS NOW WORKING. NOW IS OUR TIME! YOU MAY NOT REMEMBER WHO GAVE YOU THE CHOCOLATE, BUT YOUR THREE HOST BODIES ARE WORKING FINE, AREN'T THEY?'

'Yes, yes they are. But . . .' said Henry.

'NO BUTS! I KNOW YOU HAVE YOUR RESERVATIONS. YOU ALWAYS HAVE. BUT THIS IS THE ONLY WAY. AND NOW WE KNOW IT IS WORKING. WE GET IT ALL OUT ON TUESDAY TO THE WHOLE CITY. AND THEN, FROM THERE, WE SPREAD OUT TO THE WHOLE COUNTRY AND WITHIN THREE MONTHS WE WOULD HAVE SPREAD OVER THE ENTIRE WORLD. WE WILL FINALLY BE SAFE.'

'But at the cost of . . .' Henry argued again.

'ENOUGH!!!!!' Jenkins yelled at him. 'IT IS DONE. EVERYONE WHO HAS A HOST ALREADY, WE GET THEM IN THIS WEEKEND. ON TUESDAY, WE SHIP THE CHOCOLATE OUT. NOW, COME BACK TO THE LAB. I FORGOT MY KEYS. WE HAVE A LOT OF CHOCOLATE TO MAKE THIS WEEKEND, MY FRIENDS. THE C-V-W CONSTRUCTION COVER IS ALL ORGANISED. IT IS TIME, WE SHALL . . .'

As they walked down the hall, back in the direction they had just come from, we couldn't hear any more.

Marlie was shaking. Visibly shaking. I realised that I was, too. My eyes, now adjusted to the low light of the room, took in the others. They were also shaking. We all were.

You can never be prepared for what we had just heard. Ever. This wasn't real. It couldn't be. What had we just uncovered? Whatever it was, it had just exponentially exploded from 'something strange is happening around here' to 'something globally catastrophic is happening around here'. It was quite the leap in importance.

'What the actual?' Fleassy whispered, the first of us to speak.

'I know,' Marlie whispered back. 'I don't know what this is.'

'We gotta get out of here before they come back, then we can talk it through,' I whispered, glad I had kept something of a level head, even though I was shaken to the core.

'Agreed,' whispered Jasmine.

The others all nodded. Everyone knew we had to get out of there.

Slowly, we got up from the floor.

'Hey, look at this,' said Nick. It was a small table in the corner of the room with a block of chocolate upon it. 'Do we take it?' he asked.

'Definitely,' said Marlie, walking over and picking it up. Then she gasped. 'What is this?' she asked, pointing to the wall she was now facing above the table. We all joined her. It wasn't a wall at all, we realised as we got closer. It was a tinted window. It had just been hard to see in the dark.

The five of us were looking out onto one of the large rooms from the floor plans. It looked like a factory warehouse, mixed with a laboratory, mixed with a chocolate-making kinda kitchen. About five people were down there, stirring brown liquid in one of five huge vats. It certainly looked like liquid chocolate.

Another section of the warehouse seemed to be for moulding that chocolate into its final product. And then another area for wrapping it with boxes of different product wrappings. I could see labels for M&M's and Mars bars. The section just below us had at least five pallets of wrapped chocolates sitting side by side.

'Ruddy Willy Wonka's is what it looks like,' said Fleassy.

'If Willy Wonka's was a . . . a . . .' I couldn't finish my sentence. All I could do was point to the right as, out of a door walked . . . No, 'walked' is not really the right word. Out of the door crawled . . . No, not even crawled. Out of the door slid, slimed, oozed a large purple, almost jelly-looking . . . well, I gotta tell you, it was an alien. There was no doubt about that. We were looking at an actual alien.

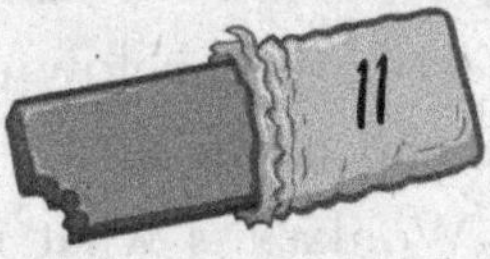

FOOD TECH WITH MR MCGEE

THURSDAY AFTERNOON

What do you do when EVERYTHING you held to be true is irrevocably smashed in a single moment? You flee. That's what you do. You bolt, as fast as you are able, away from that thing. Out the door. Stumbling along the corridor. Turning right. Turning left. Up the stairs. Slamming shut the secret door. Through the office. Past the astonished receptionist, back at his desk. Down the corridor and out into the school yard. Out into the fresh air. Out into freedom.

'Excuse me, you lot!' a loud voice yelled.

We all froze, petrified. We looked back. It was Mrs Grouse.

'I don't know what you are up to, but you five had better get to whatever class you are meant to be in right this moment or I will march you straight to Principal Jenkins' office.'

That was, quite literally, the very last place in the entire universe we wanted to go back to right now.

'It's okay, miss. We were just doing a job for Principal Jenkins. We are off to class now,' Nick spoke up.

'I'm sure you were, young Nick. Now, why don't I just walk with you all to make sure you get to where you are meant to be.'

What could we do? We all walked to maths class in silence, splitting into two when we got to the maths building. Grouse watched us all the way to our separate classes.

Inside the classroom, the teacher instantly separated Nick, Jasmine and me to opposite corners for coming late to class. I sat there, not listening to a word of whatever *algebra* meant. How could I? The fundamentals of the very fabric of the entire make-up of the universe had just been flipped. It was not a productive maths lesson.

The last school bell finally rang. I walked out of school with Nick and Jasmine. None of us spoke. Out the front of the school, we were expecting to connect with the others, and there was Mum . . . *Crap!* I had forgotten I'd promised her that I'd help her clean some of the zoo that day. She had a bunch of staff away sick, so I'd said that I'd give her a hand. So, just as Marlie and Fleassy came running up to us, eager to talk through what we had experienced, so, too, my mum got out of the car.

'You ready, Andy?' she called to me.

'What? Are you going? Where are you going?' Marlie asked, exasperated.

'I gotta go help Mum at the zoo. Clean a few of the enclosures. There's been a bunch of sick staff and they need help.'

'After what we just saw, you have to go clean up a zoo?' Fleassy hissed at me.

'I know. I know. But Mum . . .'

'We really gotta go, honey, it's going to take a while. Unless your friends want to come and help? That'll make it quicker.'

I looked back at the four of them. Friends? That may be taking it too far. Accomplices in uncovering a terrifying world-changing secret, that was more like it. I raised my eyebrows at them.

'You have got to be kidding,' hissed Fleassy.

'It'll mean we get through it super-quick, and then we can work it all out from there,' I said.

'Oh, and we can get your dad to look at the, you know, sample afterwards,' said Marlie, patting the pocket where she'd stashed the chocolate we'd taken from the underground room.

'Yeah. Good idea,' I said.

'I can't believe this. Ah. Yes. Okay. Whatever,' said Fleassy.

'Yep, let's do this,' said Jasmine.

'If we must,' sighed Nick.

'Yes, Mum,' I turned back toward her. 'My . . . ah . . . *friends* are going to help us.'

'Oh, well that is just lovely of them. Really it is.'

'That wasn't so bad, was it?' Mum said two hours later to five VERY exhausted kids as we all tumbled out of the car at my house. 'I truly appreciate your help, you kids.'

'Not so bad?' whispered Fleassy, out of earshot of my mum. 'I smell like actual animal poop.'

'You were just lucky that skunk didn't get you in the mammal enclosure,' Marlie said to her.

'Yeah, then I would have smelt like you, Balooby.'

'Don't mention it, Mrs McGee,' Nick said sweetly to my mum. I was instantly nervous with Nick talking to my mum, as though he'd be up to some kind of swindling that would not end well for her, without her even realising. 'Perhaps if you –'

'Yeah, Mum. No sweat,' I cut him off. 'We're all just going to go to my room, okay?'

'Okay, honey. Have fun with all your friends,' she said with the kind of proud-mum smile that made me instantly embarrassed.

'Yep. Yep. We will. Hey, is Dad home?' I asked.

'He will be soon, I think.'

And so, with that, I took these four 'friends' into my room. It was the first time I'd had anyone from school come to my house. And, I must be honest, it felt . . . nice. Even if the fate of the whole world was at stake.

'FINALLY!' Fleassy yelled as the door to my room shut behind us. 'How long does it take for us to be able to talk about the end of the frigging world?'

'Yeah . . . sorry about that,' I mumbled.

Marlie and I were on the bed. She was stretching out her sore leg, reaching her fingers towards her toes. Nick was in my desk chair. Fleassy cleared my desk with a sweep of her hand and sat on it. Jasmine sat on the floor. We looked at each other. But no one really knew where to start. No one knew what to say. So we kinda just sat there for a few moments in silence, not even sure where to begin. I mean, how do you talk about such a thing?

'Why is your wall covered in red spots, McGee?' Fleassy finally broke the silence.

'Yeah, I was wondering that, too,' joined in Nick. 'It looks like Banksy's extremely less-talented artistic cousin lives here.'

'Oh. I just was taking some anger out the other night with a red ball.'

'The poor ball,' said Jasmine.

'What were you angry about?' asked Marlie.

I froze.

'Ah, who gives a stuff?' Thankfully, Fleassy interrupted the question.

'Yeah,' I agreed. 'We need to talk about . . . you know, what we saw today.'

'Was that really a . . . a . . .?' Nick spoke up.

'Yep,' we all chorused together.

'Right. Right. And . . . um . . .' he mumbled off into silence. Nick not having the right words . . . Now, that was a strange thing.

A few more moments passed.

'So, there is no way that it wasn't a –'

KNOCK! KNOCK! KNOCK!

'Just seeing if you and your friends want some food and drink, love?'

'No, Mum. No thanks.'

'You're all pretty quiet in there. You okay?'

'Yes, Mum. We are just playing a quiet game, is all.'

'Oh. Well, just yell out if you need anything.'

'A quiet game?' Fleassy laughed, raising an eyebrow. 'What kind of quiet game are we playing, McGee?'

'I don't know. Sleeping lions. Dead fish. Whatever you call it.'

'You're a dead fish.'

'Shut up, Fleassy,' Marlie cut in. 'You're a really annoying fish.'

'Good one, Balooby, standing up for your boyfriend again.'

'At least I have a friend!'

'Oh, what am I then?' Nick cut in. 'I'm her friend.'

'You two are as bad as each other.'

'All right, stop it!' I said forcefully, maybe slightly taken aback at my own forcefulness. 'Just stop fighting and listen. This is where I think we are at. Tell me if I'm wrong. We have just witnessed the very existence of an alien life-form. And it is not out there amongst the stars. The alien is here. Living here, on this Earth. All those who have questioned the nature of our existence in this world, whether we are the only ones who inhabit life as we know it, all of those have just had their question answered right here in Bellington. The world is grander and more diverse than we ever thought possible.

'But this race of alien creatures seems to want to take over this planet that is our home. To take over these very bodies of ours. They have already taken over Principal Jenkins, Henry Balooby – sorry, Marlie – and Frankie and Lloyd, and any number of others who are already hosts of this alien life-force. Hosts against their will.

'The aliens have discovered that they can spread and make hosts of more humans through chocolate, which we can get my dad to look at when he comes home. So now, these aliens are beginning their plan to take over this entire world from right here in Bellington, within our very own high school, by starting with the Year Twelve school-formal fundraising chocolates.

'These chocolates somehow transfer an alien into the human's body, and from there the alien takes over the cognitive abilities of the host human, causing them to mumble erratically and scratch their skin. Which means, if we are to stop this alien race from taking over Earth, then we have to go back into the basement of the school and get rid of all the chocolates that they are planning on using to start their mass subjugation of the human race. As well as get rid of the formula they have discovered to make it happen.

'And, if we are lucky, get rid of the aliens themselves. And, if we are even luckier, save Henry, Frankie, Lloyd and Principal Jenkins. And should we be extremely lucky, maybe we won't die by the time we do so. Is that about it?'

Silence.

'Well, you're not wrong, McGee,' Nick finally said.

'Yeah, I followed about half of what you said,' quipped Fleassy. 'But the general gist I am picking up is: The whole world is doomed unless we steal the chocolates and kill the aliens. Is that about right?'

'We are not killing them. We have to save Henry,' pleaded Marlie.

'Yeah, and we gotta do it by Monday, 'cause on Tuesday all that chocolate is going out into the world.'

'So, we have three days to save the entire human race?' Jasmine asked.

'Yep.'

'Easy,' said Fleassy.

We all stared at her.

'We just call the government. Nuke the whole place.'

'Once again, we are not *nuking* my brother,' said Marlie. 'Besides, are we just gonna ring that handy governmental alien hotline, tell them what's happening and then they'll just get right to it, will they?'

'Maybe.'

'No, Marlie is right,' I started to say.

'Of course she is,' interrupted Fleassy.

'Shut up, Fleassy!' we both yelled back.

'It's true, we gotta do this ourselves.' Jasmine spoke into the silence after our yelling. 'No one will believe us. They never do. We must be the ones to save this world.'

'No pressure then,' said Nick.

'So, what we need to work out,' I responded, 'is a plan of action. And we all know who is the very best at planning things out.'

'No. Who are you talking about?' Fleassy said.

The four of us looked at her without saying a word.

'What? Me?' she choked.

'Of course YOU! As much as we hate to admit it, you're brilliant at planning heists, Fleassy. And this is going to require a heist of the most EPIC proportions. We need you.'

'Shut up. Stop stirring me.'

'No, it's true, Fleassy. It *really* kills me to say this, but you are really very good at it,' Marlie managed to squeeze out of her mouth.

I'd never seen Fleassy embarrassed before. But this was the moment. She didn't know how to take such a compliment. Her cheeks reddened. She looked away. She was speechless. And, I gotta admit, in that moment, my heart softened for her. Just a little.

'It's just, we'd rather not be the ones being manipulated in your fiendish plans,' I told her, so as to distract the mood.

'Fair enough,' she said. But it sounded like she was choking back tears.

KNOCK! KNOCK! KNOCK!

'Mum, what do you want now?'

'Calm down. Calm down,' said my dad as he opened the door.

'Oh, sorry, Dad, didn't realise you were home.'

'Yeah, I gathered,' he said. 'Look at you, hanging with your friends in your room.'

'Daaaaad . . .'

'Sorry. Sorry. Just came up to say hello to you lot. I'm Jasper, Andy's dad. Good to meet you all.'

'You too, Mr McGee,' Nick said with a smile, holding out his hand to shake my dad's. Always the greaser of palms.

'Ah, thanks,' Dad said, taken back by the warm welcome. 'Oh, and hello, Marlie, nice to see you are part of this crew.'

'Of course, Mr McGee. I wouldn't be anywhere else. Actually, we were wondering something.'

'Yes?'

'Well, we have a class assignment, a group assignment where we have to analyse the properties of this bar of chocolate for . . . for . . .'

'Food tech.'

'Science.'

Nick and Fleassy spoke at the same time. Dad looked confused for a moment.

'Ah . . . it's for both, Dad. A combined assignment between classes.'

'Oh yes, sounds good.'

'And we were wondering if you could maybe help us, you know . . .' Marlie said. 'What, with all your special chef equipment. Andy said you would be able to.'

'Oh, I don't know . . .'

'Mr McGee,' Nick interrupted with a smile. 'We heard from Andy that you are the most magnificent food-tech-type person and, well, it would be an honour to see you in action, sir.'

'Well, okay. Yes, that's fine. Why don't you all come through to the kitchen now, and we can see what we find.'

'Thanks, Dad. That'd be great.'

'Yeah, thanks, Mr McGee!' the others chorused.

And so down we went to the kitchen. Marlie grabbed a paper and pen, and jotted some notes to try to make it seem more like an assignment.

'First thing we gotta do . . .' said Dad, lifting the chocolate to his mouth as we arrived in the kitchen.

'NO!' we all shouted at once.

Dad dropped the chocolate in shock.

'We are not allowed to taste it, Dad. That's . . . that's part of it.'

'Okay. No tasting. Weird, but that's fine. You guys didn't have to scream at me about it.'

'Sorry, Dad. We just want to follow the rules, is all. And we need to work out what the . . . um . . . secret ingredient is within it.'

'Oh, a good old food mystery. I love it.' Dad beamed as he walked over to his equipment, eager to get underway. 'Well, we will have to melt it. See if we can break it down to its base elements. Have a look through the microscope. We will work out the mystery yet, my young Sherlock chefs.'

I rolled my eyes. Dad took a saucepan and melted the chocolate while the rest of us looked on.

'What do you call melting chocolate?' he asked. 'A choc-tastrophe.'

None of us laughed. Dad frowned. Then Superchef Dad took over and he lost himself in the work. Heating and reheating. Looking through the microscope. Using various instruments to test for who knows what. He loved working out exactly why different flavours worked with each other, and what just the slightest additions might do to his creations. This was my dad in his element.

'All right, I've managed to separate out the cocoa butter from the other ingredients, and now I'm just using a diffraction experiment on the shear-induced behaviour of the cocoa. And there seems to be a two-dimensional diffraction pattern at crystallisation temperatures of seventeen-point-five, twenty and twenty-two-point-five degrees Celsius. The crystallites grow layer upon layer at slightly differentiating compositions as to the shear-rate and temperature of the compositions. And it's the temperature, too, that defines the crystalline interface area available for secondary nucleation by affecting the size distribution of the crystallites. Oh, and look! There are the triacylglycerols deriving from the milk fat. That's good. Oh, and the sugars are . . .'

My dad was really worked up now. He looked up at us like it was Christmas. We looked back at him with *very* confused faces.

'I literally understood not a word of what you just said, Mr McGee,' Fleassy told him.

'Oh, right. Sorry. A bit advanced for your assignment, hey? Ummm . . . the chocolate looks normal. Cocoa solids. Cocoa butter. Sugars. Milk. But let me just turn up the temp here more and see what this secret thing . . . WHOA! WHOA! WHOA!'

'What? What is it?'

We all crowded around, Fleassy pushing us out of the way. We couldn't see anything.

'It just looks like slightly bubbling chocolate, Dad. I can't see –'

'WOW!' we all said together as we saw a weird movement appearing in the chocolate, like a wave. Like the chocolate was moving of its own volition. It disappeared again.

'Does chocolate normally do that when melted?' Marlie asked.

'No chocolate I've ever seen,' Dad replied. 'Oh, it's doing it again.'

But not only was it doing it again, something more began to happen. As the chocolate got hotter and hotter, the movement in the brown liquid became more apparent. It rippled faster and faster. Now it was almost violently thrashing. As though there were something in the chocolate that was really finding this temperature very uncomfortable.

Then, as if on cue, as if this were a horror film, the chocolate gathered together into a shape. A long lizard-like shape. A shape with a face. It was some kind of alien creature that had come back together in the dark goo. Its face was ferocious, and one long tentacle started reaching out of its head towards us. It was getting higher and higher. We were all speechless.

'What is happening?' Dad questioned, utterly perplexed. He thrust a glass saucepan lid on top of the thing that was now trying to get out. The heat grew and grew.

'Ummm . . . should we turn it down? Is it getting hurt?' asked Marlie.

'Who cares?' shouted Fleassy. 'Kill the thing.'

'But what if it . . .?'

Too late. There was no time for discussion. The ferocious little alien creature must have hit a peak. It thrashed wilder and wilder for a few seconds and then suddenly combusted. It burst into flames right there under the lid.

We were speechless. All of us. In a moment, the fire was gone. The saucepan held only gooey ash inside it. We stood there, gaping at what we had just seen.

'Ah. That was . . . unexpected.' I broke the silence, not really knowing what to say.

That was when Dad turned on us.

'All right, out with it,' he said, very seriously.

'Out with what, Mr McGee?' Nick innocently protested.

'Out with where you got that chocolate from, for starters, and what that . . . that thing was!'

'We got the chocolate from school, Dad,' I said, telling the truth. 'We really did.' Yes, I may have skipped over the part about getting it from the secret alien laboratory beneath the school, but it was still the truth.

'It's true, we did,' the others said in unison.

'It must have been the . . . the secret ingredient, Mr McGee,' said Nick.

'Yeah,' Marlie joined in. 'That's why it was a combined science and food-tech assignment. Because they had put some chemical in it that, when heated to a certain temperature, has a massive chemical reaction.'

'Massive is one word for what just happened,' said Dad.

'I'm just writing down a report on what happened right here, Mr McGee,' said Marlie, holding up her writing pad. 'How would you all, um, describe the chemical reaction we just witnessed?'

'Sick as,' said Fleassy.

'Disturbing,' I said.

'Extra-terrestrial,' said Nick with a smile. Marlie kicked him in the shins. 'I mean, extra . . . special and weird,' he corrected.

'All right, good, um, observations. I think that is probably all we need. Thanks, Mr McGee. Thanks for that. Well, look at the time, it's best we all got off home.'

Dad still looked completely shell-shocked. He just stared down at his saucepan, then nodded at us as we left the kitchen and headed for the front door.

We piled out of the house and onto my lawn.

'Well, that settles it,' said Marlie. 'If one of those things is in my brother, then we *really* gotta get rid of those chocolates under the school by Tuesday.'

'Agreed,' we all said.

'But we have to be smart about it, too,' I said. 'This is, like, literally life and death. So, what if tomorrow, at school, we all do as much reconnaissance as we are able. Then, over the weekend, under the expert guidance of Fleassy, we work out how we can pull this thing off. We prepare what we need to do and then, come Monday, when there are no students at school, and the teachers are off at their PD day, we save the world. It'll be the greatest chocolate heist against an alien race that this world has ever seen.'

'McGee,' Nick said, with the air of someone who was about to call me deluded. 'You are, sometimes, impressive.'

'Ah . . . thanks. All right. Well, let's do it!' And with that, I put my hand into the centre of our gathered circle. They all stared at me weirdly.

'Notice how he said "sometimes", McGee,' mocked Fleassy, rolling her eyes. 'We are not doing a group hurrah.'

'Oh. Sorry. Right. Of course not,' I said, embarrassed, quickly removing my hand.

THREE DAYS BEFORE THE HEIST

12

SCOPING THE SCHOOL

FRIDAY MORNING

The walk into school the following morning was a particularly harrowing experience. The great prison of Bellington High loomed larger than normal. Its impenetrable walls seemed doubly strong and twice as thick. The iron gates towered above us. Their sharp tips looked like they were made for skewering an orc.

And there, standing tall beneath those gates, was the alien warden himself, Principal Jenkins. Or, more true to say, there stood the man who was symbiotically hosting an alien life-force that had taken over his autonomous volition. I wasn't sure how exactly to describe it.

I gulped as I saw him (or it) with dark sunglasses. Body shaking, I felt like turning and running straight back the other way. But the feeling of a hand grabbing hold of mine soothed the worry. Just for a few seconds, and then it was gone. I looked over at Marlie. Of course, I knew it would be her. She was looking straight at Principal Jenkins, and she looked even more worried than I was.

Actually, she looked pretty terrible, like she hadn't slept a wink. Which she probably hadn't. Her brother was obviously on her mind. The quick squeeze of her hand, though, was enough to . . . Oh, I don't know. It felt good, all right? So what? Don't go getting all mushy about it! It was just . . . nice. And what was perhaps even stranger was that I hadn't freaked out about others seeing such a thing. That was new.

'WELCOME TO SCHOOL THIS GLORIOUS FRIDAY, KIDS!' Principal Jenkins spoke loudly as we went through the great gates. I wasn't sure, but he certainly seemed to be looking more intently at each of us entering on this day. As though he knew we were onto him (or it). He/it ushered Marlie and me through with the rest of the students.

'AND MAKE SURE YOU STAY AWAY FROM THE C-V-W CONSTRUCTION SITES BEING SET UP INSIDE!'

It seemed his mind meltdown two days ago meant he really didn't remember Marlie and me from the science coolroom. And, in the corridor under the school yesterday, he'd said that Henry and his two henchmen couldn't remember who gave them the chocolate, either. So, aside from the alien-taking-over-one's-body thing, the chocolate seemed to mess with your memory in some way. Luckily for us, it meant we were in the clear, as far as Jenkins was concerned.

The first thing we noticed once we came into the school grounds that day was the influx of people. The morning announcement told us that building works were beginning today, and so there would be lots of builders around, and sections of the school would be off-limits to students. Namely, the science block, the admin block and the old bell tower.

Of course! Every place where there was an entrance to the secret underground level of the school. The scheduled exams in the science rooms had been moved. Administration would be moved next week, but was closed today. The school was a construction site.

Marlie and I walked past the science and art block. Big building site fences were in the process of being constructed around the area with 'DO NOT ENTER – CVW Construction site' signs stuck all over them. It was clear that whatever was happening in there, we were not invited. Two of the supposed 'builders' were just standing beside the door into the science rooms wearing sunglasses, staring into the distance.

'Alien guards?' Marlie whispered when we were far enough away.

'Must be. And I bet you it'll be the same at the bell tower and the admin block, too.'

We walked quickly, eager to see each place before the bell for first period sounded. Sure enough, they were all the same. Construction fences. Big signs. Two guards in sunglasses at each.

'Geez, they worked quickly after we left yesterday,' said Fleassy, coming up loudly behind us as we passed the bell tower.

'Shhhh!!!' We both turned, whispering, 'Don't talk about it out loud.'

'Okay, okay. Don't get your knickers caught on fire.'

'I don't think that's the saying, Fleassy.'

'Oh, and you'd know, wouldn't you, Balooby?'

'All right, you two. Come on! Let's get to class.'

We all went to our classes as normal, so as not to arouse any kind of suspicion. But in every class, each of us would take a toilet break to do the reconnaissance rounds, making observations as we went. Of course, Jasmine was the best at such things. It was she who reported that the science storeroom entrance, the principal's office and the bell tower all had not just the two guards outside, but also two more inside. Four guards all up.

At lunchtime, we gathered together at our usual table in the back quad of the school.

'I can't work out how we do this,' Fleassy said, throwing a stone as hard as she could at the bin near us. Her frustration was bubbling.

'Why not? What's wrong?' Nick asked.

'There's too much unknown. I can't plan diddly-squat. I don't know what we need. It's impossible.'

I could see her point. Marlie couldn't.

'It can't be impossible, we have to do it,' she declared.

'Well, we darn well can't, Marlie!'

'Come on, you're meant to be some hot-shot heist planner, and yet you can't work it out? What does that say about you, Fleassy?'

'What does that say about *me*?! You little slowpoke of a snail!' Fleassy stood up. Things were starting to get out of hand. 'What does your staggering –'

'Would you two stop it?!' I interjected loudly. 'This

is not gonna help anything. And you need to stop talking to Marlie like that, Fleassy. Seriously . . .'

'Oh shut up, McGee.' Fleassy turned on me, hackles raised. A wolf ready to pounce. I did not want to be on the receiving end of that. I ignored her. Or tried to.

'Look, we just have to be able to find out more. Jasmine, do you think you can get in through one of the doors and suss out more about what's happening underground?'

'I'm not sure even I have the abilities for that, Andy. I'll try to keep sneaking around next period and see what I can do. I can't promise anything. But maybe I'll notice something else.'

'All right, all right, it'll have to do,' I said. 'I guess we all just need to keep our eyes open for anything that might be of use to actually get us through the guards and make this heist happen.'

'Yeah,' Nick interjected. 'Like, C-V-W is where my brother works.'

'Yeah, like . . . what? What did you just say?'

'C-V-W, the building company, it's where my bro works.'

'Oh gosh, Nick! Yeah, crucial information that maybe, you know, you could have told us earlier.'

'Sorry.'

'All right,' I continued, 'write that bit of information down, someone. And let's go! We aren't going to work it all out sitting around here arguing. Let's say, Marlie and I go off together and make a round.'

'Ha!'

'Shut up, Fleassy.'

'Go to hell, you two.'

'You and Nick can go together. And then, Jasmine, you do better on your own sneaking around in the shadows. Come on. Let's go save the world, team.'

The last line came out of my mouth with absolutely no confidence. My voice was even shaky. So, in reality, it had the opposite effect of inspiring them. Everyone walked away from the table feeling even more despondent and more dubious about our ability to actually pull this off. Whatever 'this' was going to look like. For now, we didn't have a clue. Our scoping was a failure. We were up a chocolate creek without a paddlepop stick.

COMMANDEERING FOR THE SAKE OF THE WORLD

FRIDAY AFTERNOON

The rest of lunch was no better. Nor the afternoon. Our supposed class-time 'reconnaissance' uncovered less information than a Sherlock Holmes impersonator. And that's what we felt like. Impersonators. And, to make matters worse, by the end of Science, Mrs Grouse was convinced I needed to see a doctor about my weak bladder.

'And you, Marlie. And Nick, too. You both seem to be no better than McGee here. Did you lot have a water-drinking competition at lunch or something?'

Final period of the day, and Marlie had her theatre production class while the rest of us had PE in the gymnasium. Marlie always said that she didn't do PE because she hated it. Maybe it had something to do with her leg, I'm not sure. It was my absolute not-favourite class, too. But it did give us a chance to notice something about the gymnasium that we hadn't seen before. I wrote it down, hoping it might come in handy.

Still, there really was *not* enough to go on. We were getting desperate. It wasn't until after school had finished that we finally made a breakthrough. Though, not in a way any of us would have expected.

All five of us heisters were standing around in a circle out the front of the school, debating whether we should meet tonight and begin to work out a plan or whether we should just meet tomorrow at Marlie's house. Or, to be honest, whether we shouldn't just give up on the whole thing.

Ah, the whims of choice when it comes to saving the world. Should we? Shouldn't we? Should we? Shouldn't we? Like picking off the petals of a daisy. If only it were that easy. We knew we had to, even Fleassy knew we had to, it was just a matter of working out how.

Suddenly, above the noise of the rising argument, we heard a crash. A scrape. Metal on metal. We all turned to the street. A banged-up green sedan had just scraped along the side of a 'NO U-TURN' signpost as it swerved along the road, narrowly missing some of the things in its path and ploughing down all the other things. It looked more like the banged-up antics of someone playing Mario Kart than somebody driving a real car down a real road. Especially out the front of a school.

We watched in horror as it passed by. The world slowed down for a split second as the face in the passenger seat, pulling up his sunglasses, turned to stare at us. Or, more specifically, to stare at Marlie. The face . . . it was Henry Balooby.

It is hard to say what transpired between them in that moment. Whatever it was, Marlie swore that it was not just the body of Henry taken over by aliens that was looking at her, it truly was Henry. He mouthed something, which Marlie took to be 'HELP!'. The crying out of someone trying to escape from his alien overlords. The rest of us took it to be the contorted face of an alien screaming, 'Death to all humans!'.

Either way, the moment ended. But it made Marlie desperate. Really desperate. She looked around with a wild look in her eye. A group of Year Eight students were nearby. They were walking and talking beside their bikes, pushing them along by the handlebars. Without hesitation, with the rest of us looking on in shock, Marlie snuck up behind the very last one, pushed him to the side, grabbed the handlebars, jumped onto the bike and simply rode away. I couldn't believe it. Goodie goodie gumdrops Marlie Balooby. She *was* just like her brother, after all. Okay, not exactly. This was more like a commandeering of a vehicle for a matter of universal importance. But still, I was pretty impressed.

'Hey! What the hell?!' the boy who she stole the bike from screamed after her. 'You better come back, you –' At this moment, he realised who he was yelling at. The sister of The Cleaner. The boy hesitated. It was a life-or-death decision for this Year Eight student. One wrong move, and his head would be the next to investigate the quality of the porcelain in the boys' bathroom toilets. His mates stared after the fast-pedalling girl, all of them uncertain as to whether they wanted to get involved in anything that involved Henry Balooby.

This hesitation gave the four of us our chance. Five of them. Four more bikes. Exactly the right number. Look, I don't condone stealing bikes from people. But when it comes to saving the world, sometimes you just gotta weigh up your options. Let the world be taken over by aliens or *borrow* a few bikes. I looked at Fleassy. She looked at me and nodded. I couldn't believe what I was about to do.

'Argghhhhh!' Fleassy bellowed as loudly as she could, right behind the bike owners. Nick and I followed suit.

'ARGGHHHHHH!' we all hollered, hoping that a little fright might give the edge we needed. Fleassy pushed one of the kids to the side and was off. Somehow, Jasmine was already cycling away, her bike's owner only just realising he was no longer holding the handlebars. Nick was wrestling away another. I veered for the smallest of the lot and, thankfully, took him by surprise, too.

'Stop it! What are you . . .?'

'Bugger off, Fleassy Davies!'

'No way, McGee!'

The boys whose bikes we were taking erupted in a barrage of abuse, but we were already pedalling away.

'We're sorry,' I called out. 'We're just borrowing them. It's a matter more important than you can ever imagine. We will take them to the bike park. One hour. They'll be there. Promise.'

They were not convinced. The shock of what was happening was wearing off and they were starting to give chase. I was the last of our group. They were right behind me, their hands reaching out, when Nick turned and yelled, 'We'll make sure we say hi to Henry Balooby from you.'

They slowed.

'Otherwise,' Nick yelled, 'he might want to join us at the bike park in an hour.'

That stopped them.

'You better bring them to the bike park, then!' the biggest boy in their group shouted after us.

'We will!' I shouted back. 'Promise!'

But by now my attention had moved from the Year Eight boys to the girl who was just disappearing around a corner far ahead. We were chasing after a Balooby, who was chasing after a Balooby, who had been taken over by an alien and was currently in a green sedan smashing down letterboxes along the street like an alien arcade game. Ten points for a letterbox. Twenty points for a stop sign. I did not want to think how many points for a human.

The four of us had a lot of ground to make up, me and the BMX bandits, pedalling as hard as we could, swerving around people, swerving around dogs, chasing after the Balooby siblings. As we came around the corner we could see the green sedan far ahead, still dangerously careening down the road. Turns out aliens are not the best drivers of human automobiles. Behind them was Marlie, fuelled by love, a blur of bike and limbs. Fleassy was out the front of our pack. Next was Jasmine. Then Nick. And I was last. Last, and falling behind. Let's be honest, I am not the most athletic of people.

Far ahead, we saw the car screech right, taking out another sign and heading down toward the shops. My legs were burning, my heart beating, sweat gathering. We kept going, not sure whether we were trying to catch the car or just catch up to Marlie.

Suddenly, Fleassy peeled off to the right. I really hoped she knew where she was going and this was a quicker way to get to the shops. The others followed her, so I did, too. Down the street before cutting across an abandoned lot and then through an alley.

'What the –?' I skidded around a blue buggy car as it cut me off. The driver's long hair blew breezily from the car window, mine stuck sweatily to my head. Around the car and over the train tracks I rode, and then down alongside the creek. The bitumen path turned into a dirt track as I started to catch up to the others.

This better be a shortcut, I thought as I curved dangerously around the bank of the flowing stream.

'Come on, you slug-headed snails!' Fleassy yelled back at us, looking around to see where we were. The comment was definitely aimed at me. She looked to her front again, just in time to dodge a biker coming the opposite way.

'Watch out!' he yelled, but he was soon past all of us in a blink.

We cut around another corner and then up and over a wooden bridge that spanned the creek. Thankfully, the way into the shops was relatively downhill, or there was no way I was going to make it.

A moment later and the path turned back to bitumen, and a moment after that we all swung around the corner, almost crashing into Marlie. Fleassy's shortcut had at least caught us up to her.

'Marlie!' I yelled. She was shocked to see us, but soon smiled, realising that we weren't going to let her do this on her own. We had her back.

'What the hell are you doing?' Fleassy yelled violently at her. Well, in one way or another, we all had Marlie's back. Fleassy's way was more of a punch in the back than a supportive hand, but still.

'I have to get to him, Fleassy. I have to. He's still in there. I saw him.'

'We all saw him, that doesn't mean . . .'

'It does! I know it! He's fighting the alien, I know he is. Now, come on!'

The green sedan turned left, still far ahead of us. We all pedalled as furiously as we could down the main road of town, flying past shops, dodging pedestrians, being yelled at by shopkeepers, being yelled at by . . .

'Andy McGee . . . what are you . . . where is your helmet . . . whose bike is . . .?'

'Sorry, Mum!' I yelled back. 'I'll explain laaatttteeerrrrrrr.'

And with that we were past the shops where Mum had been standing with a bag of groceries. I knew I would have to come up with something later, but for now, nothing else mattered. Five adventurers. Five world-savers.

SCREECH!

I slammed on my brakes. Marlie had pulled to a stop in front, and I'd been half-daydreaming about saving the world. But now the sedan was nowhere to be seen. We'd lost it.

'Damn it!' cried Marlie, hitting the handlebars on the bike. 'How will we find them now?'

'Let's NOT find them,' said Fleassy, annoyed.

Marlie turned toward her. Anger in her eyes.

I jumped in before a fight started between them. 'Look . . . we . . . are going . . . to have . . . to split up,' I managed to get out between all my heaving and wheezing. 'There are . . . three ways from here . . . that Henry could have gone . . . right?'

'Fleassy is right,' Nick ignored me. 'What are we going to do if we *can* catch up to him?'

'I don't . . . I just . . .' Marlie's anger quickly turned to defeat. Her shoulders slumped. 'I guess I don't really know. But, I have to try. WE have to try. Please! It might be through Henry that we can stop this awful thing happening to the whole world.'

'Wait!' It was Jasmine. 'Listen.'

We all listened. A screech. A scrape. A bang. A shout. It was definitely a car making chaos. And it was coming from down the road that veered off to the left.

'Do we follow?' asked Jasmine.

'I can't believe I'm saying this,' said Fleassy. 'But I suppose even The Cleaner needs someone to care about him.'

Marlie looked at her in shock.

'But Balooby, if you get us killed, I'm going to beat your ghost to a pulp.'

'Thanks, Fleassy.'

'Shut up and ride,' was all she said back.

We took off down the road toward the continued noises of a car driving wildly. As we did, another blue buggy car came too fast around the corner. I wondered if it was the same one as earlier. It was gone too fast to tell. Way too many bad drivers, including aliens, on the road that day.

Down the street we turned left, following the sounds of chaos over a bridge and around the corner until the noises stopped. Either the alien had taken a quick lesson and learnt how to drive properly, or the car was stationary. Veering right around a bend, on the lookout for any clue as to where the car had gone, we passed a street on our left.

'Stop!' Fleassy yelled. 'There it is.'

I caught up a moment later, still heaving and wheezing like a deflating balloon. But sure enough, down the road, right toward its end, was the sedan, now parked. Well, not so much parked as – stopped. Its front wheels were against a gutter, the back of the car butted out into the road.

'Quick,' said Marlie. We pedalled down the road, cautious now as to what we were about to find. But when we got to the car, there was no one there, and the house they'd parked out the front of was a derelict mess. A what-once-might-have-been-white weatherboard monstrosity. It was double storey with windows either boarded up or covered with sheets from the inside, and a literal junkyard for a garden. It was a hoarder's paradise. Tyres stacked up in the yard. Old piles of wood. Scattered boxes full of who knows what. A few old cars. Knee-high grass and weeds all over.

'Anyone know whose place this is?' Nick asked.

We all shook our heads. Nope.

'Let's take a look. They must be in there,' said Marlie, even while she was clearly in some pain from that ride. She had been stretching out her leg, which was shaking, like it was spasming or something. Now, she was limping across the garden on her tiptoes.

We followed, and the five of us snuck over to behind one of the cars, keeping an eye out for any movement. There was nothing. We watched and waited. No movement. Until someone stuck their head around the corner of the house and gestured to us.

It was Jasmine. We hadn't even realised she'd left us. But, as was her sneaky way, she'd already snuck around the side of the house and scoped it out. We followed her lead, quickly moving from behind a wheel-less car to behind an old broken fridge until we'd reached the front corner of the house. We waited for Marlie, who was looking tired now, and her limp had intensified. She caught up to us, and we crept, as quietly as we could, down the side of the house and out to the backyard where the dereliction continued. Overgrown bushes. Branches on the ground. A fence, which once might have been vertical, now fallen and rotting away. All the windows were boarded on this side. Jasmine, however, pointed up to the second storey. Finally, a window without a cover.

Before any of us could even speak she had leapt onto a stack of discarded pavers that were leaning against the weatherboard house, and was reaching for a vent sticking out of the wall.

'Jasmine,' I hissed. 'What are you doing? You'll slip.'

She turned and put her finger to her lips.

'Sometimes, I like Jasmine,' whispered Fleassy. 'Especially when she turns into a stunt woman with zero regard for personal safety.'

'She can't make it up that, though,' whispered back Marlie.

'You just watch,' answered Nick, something like admiration in his voice. Fleassy gave him a side-eye glance of annoyance. He didn't see it.

Up Jasmine went. I honestly couldn't even see where she was finding grip, but she was. She scaled up the weatherboard using whatever she could. Her foot against some kind of pipe. Her hand gripping a window-sill. All of a sudden she leapt into the air. Below her, our four jaws hit the ground. Marlie gripped my hand as Jasmine soared. She grabbed onto the top of the window frame she'd been aiming for and, in a single movement, pulled herself up.

'Did she really just do that?' Nick whispered.

None of us could even speak as Jasmine sidestepped along the narrow ledge and reached for another drain-pipe. She gave it a pull. There was a creak. A larger pull. Another creak, but it didn't budge.

Calm as day, she put her weight on the drainpipe and shimmied up. A stealth ninja if I ever saw one. She was high enough now to reach over to the uncovered window. With one foot on the drainpipe and one on the window frame, Jasmine peeped around the edge. We waited.

A moment later and she turned around, shaking her head. There was nothing she could see.

'Damn it!' whispered both Fleassy and Marlie at the same time.

Nick didn't say anything. I think he was still in awed shock. I was just giving her the thumbs up, to tell her we understood, when I was grabbed from behind and pulled backward. A hand came over my mouth. I'd been caught. I wrestled. I tried to scream. I kicked and shoved and lashed out. Nothing. The figure hauling me was too strong. Whoever, or whatever, it was dragged me behind one of the large bushes by the side of the house. I wrestled and wrestled until finally I was loose enough to at least look around, straight into the bulging eyes of a frothing Henry Balooby.

This was it. I was looking death in the face. My death. The Cleaner was about to clean me off the face of the Earth. He lifted a hand holding a hammer high into the air. I closed my eyes.

'Henry! Stop!'

It was Marlie. I breathed out, slightly opening an eyelid. The alien-human hybrid that was now Henry Balooby looked over at his sister. His eyes flickered back and forth between hostility and recognition. Maybe Henry was actually in there – somewhere.

'Henry! Please! Please! It's me, Henry,' Marlie pleaded.

'Yeah, yeah, it's your sister!' I pleaded, too, though my voice sounded more like the squeak of a terrified mouse. The alien growled at me. Well, that also could have been Henry, but I think it was the alien. Henry, though, he looked at Marlie. I could definitely see it now. Henry Balooby was fighting inside his own body for his very self.

'M . . . M . . . Marlie,' he stammered, through gritted teeth and sweating face.

'Yes! It's me! I –'

At that moment, Henry Balooby dropped the hammer in his hand and grabbed his head. He thrashed around. It was the fight of his life. I stumbled away from him as Marlie stepped right up in front of his face. She held out a hand.

'Marlie, don't . . .' I began to say, but Henry Balooby stopped his thrashing and looked straight up.

'Marlie . . . I don't . . . have long.' He pushed the words out of his mouth like he was straining for every syllable.

Marlie burst into tears as she looked at her brother.

'You . . . need to . . . help me. Something . . . taken over me. Alien.'

'You can fight it, Henry. I know you can.'

'No . . . it's bigger than me . . . whole Earth . . . in danger.'

'We know, Henry. We know. But I have to do something to save you,' Marlie cried.

'No!' Henry yelled, still fighting. 'Don't worry . . . about me . . . You must . . . save the world . . . not me.'

Personally, I couldn't quite believe the selflessness

I was hearing out of the mouth of The Cleaner. I guess, being taken over by an alien and fighting for your very soul gives you a new, more empathetic outlook on life.

'Listen,' he stammered. 'The chocolate . . . It's how they do it . . . Beneath the school. You must . . . destroy chocolate.'

'We know,' Marlie told him. 'We snuck down behind you into the basement tunnels the other day. We are planning on destroying the chocolates, but we don't know how. How can we do it?'

Henry held out his hands. 'Tie me up first . . . It'll be back soon . . . Can't fight . . . for long.'

Within a moment, Fleassy had grabbed an old rope that was lying on the ground and was lashing it around Henry Balooby's wrists. Jasmine had somehow gotten down from the second-storey window by then, too, and they both worked together to tie a knot as tight as they could. All five of us gathered around Henry. He pulled at his wrists but couldn't break free.

'Good. Now . . . Jenkins knows someone,' he began, still visibly fighting for control over his own body. 'Jenkins knows people . . . got into his office . . . and science room, too. Both heavily guarded. In tunnels . . . Chocolate going out Tuesday . . . You destroy on Monday . . . Too many aliens on weekend. Must . . . disable cameras . . . reception . . . now security room . . . You must get in . . . through . . . bell tower . . . two guards . . . but best way in . . .' Henry groaned again, thrashing his head around. He glanced up with a desperate look on his face. He was slipping away again.

'T . . . traps . . . set in . . . tunnels . . . all of them . . . motion . . . sound . . . heat . . . don't . . . gas . . . death . . . ugh . . . ahhhhhhh!'

His eyes were rolling back into his head. His face was an off-green.

'Henry, is there anything else you can tell us?' I asked desperately.

He pointed at his eyes. 'Choc . . . room three . . . door . . . Alien . . . don't like . . . don't like bright . . . go berserk . . . Really bright . . . and they break down. Hours to reboot. Angry . . . brain shut down. Smell . . . hate . . . bad smell . . .'

'Okay,' I said, trying to piece together what he was saying.

'And make sure . . .' Henry was just about to lose control again, we could see it. 'Make sure . . . destroy . . . ugh . . . aaahghhhh!'

'Destroy what?' Fleassy demanded. 'Make sure we destroy what?'

'Plans . . . choc recipe . . . formula . . . DNA . . . ARRGHHH! . . . inside the chamber . . . Middle . . . chamber room! Nexus! ARRGGGHHH!' Henry was screaming. But it wasn't Henry.

'Henry!' Marlie yelled. 'Henry!'

Nothing. It was too late. Henry was gone. The alien inside him was thrashing around, struggling against the ropes around him and screaming through Henry's mouth.

'We gotta go,' urged Fleassy. 'If there are others nearby, they would have heard.'

'No!' Marlie yelled.

'Marlie, we must. Come on!' shouted Nick as we dragged her away from the thrashing figure of her brother. She was thrashing almost as wildly, trying to get back to him.

'Let's go. Let's go!' screamed Fleassy.

We pushed her and hauled her and urged her on as she hobbled down the side of the house, through the front yard and out to the bikes. Her whole leg seemed to be giving her hell now, her face a grimace as she struggled onto her bike and started riding. Yet, without even a look back, we all pedalled away from Henry Balooby and the alien that had overtaken him. Once around the corner, we slowed down. It felt like a long ride back to the bike park. I'm sure it felt longer for Marlie. None of us spoke as we rode. I think we were all pretty shell-shocked from the experience.

A group of angry Year Eight boys were waiting for us. But as we got closer and they saw how harassed we all looked and how distraught the sister of Henry Balooby was, they calmed down and quietly took their bikes back. None of them wanted anything more to do with it. They scattered. We sat down on the grass.

'I'm sorry, Marlie,' I consoled her.

She didn't respond. Just stared blankly ahead, leaning forward over her sore leg as if she were doing a hamstring stretch, while rubbing the top of her leg and her hip.

'At least he gave us the way in,' said Fleassy.

'Yeah, your brother, he's . . . well . . .' started Nick.

'He's a hero, Marlie,' finished Jasmine.

Marlie looked up at us with a do-you-really-mean-it look.

I nodded and took her hand in my own. 'It's true. As weird as it is to say. Henry Balooby is a hero. He's fighting those aliens just like we are.'

Marlie sighed. 'Okay. Well, we can't let his fight go to waste then. Tomorrow, we gotta plan all this out. Come around to mine as early as you can. It's going to be a BIG weekend.'

TWO DAYS BEFORE THE HEIST

GREASE MONKEYS

SATURDAY MORNING

'Can you see anything?'

'Shhh, would you stop! I'm trying –'

'Let me look, you buffoon.'

'Stop grabbing them off me, Fleassy.'

'Ah, you're useless, McGee.'

It was Saturday morning, and things were going as well as you would expect when you're on a stake-out with Fleassy Davies. We were perched up on a hill above Bellington High School, and she was being her usual snide self. Actually, she was a little more impatient and vicious about everything than usual. She had been the same all day. But, as cynical and snide as Fleassy could be, watching her that morning in our planning of the great heist had been like witnessing a criminal mastermind at work.

We had all shown up at Marlie's by 8am. Okay, Fleassy and Nick were more like 8:30am, but that's pretty good. I'd told my parents I would be at Marlie's most of the weekend. So, of course, as is the way with parents, they had gone from telling me I needed more friends and needed to be nice to Marlie to now wondering if I should be spending *so* much time with her. Ah, you can never win.

Anyway, we were now all out on the back deck, overlooking the pool I had previously adventured into, trying to decipher what it was that Henry had told us the day before. After much arguing and fighting about what his warnings might actually mean, I'd managed to settle everyone down and focus in on planning the heist.

We knew there was only one chance to do this. Though the question remained, *How?* How does one go about breaking into an impenetrable fortress of a school that is swarming with alien guards, and then get all the way down into the basement to steal and destroy a tonne of alien-infested chocolate as well as the DNA-splicing formula held in something called a Nexus, whatever that was? Jenkins had said the same word in the tunnels the other day and referred to it as a library, or something like that. Marlie looked it up and tried to research it, but said she hadn't found anything at all. This whole thing was no easy task. Sheesh, it was impossible.

'All right, dorks, the first thing we gotta have is some flippin' maps,' Fleassy said.

So, some flippin' maps is where we began. We already had Marlie's hastily scribbled-down copy of the underground level of Bellington. So, next we grabbed Marlie's laptop from inside the house and Googled Bellington High School to see if there were any site maps we could use. But nothing much at all came up. Just the generic school kinda website. But no school building plans or anything. So, from memory of our time there, we all pitched in and made rough drawings of the rest of the school. Definitely not to scale, but pretty accurate.

Then, Fleassy got to work. She pored over the maps and configured an entry plan A, then a plan B. And, by the end of the hour, she was up to plan F. And that was just to get into the school.

'Plan F can stand for "flippin' done for",' she said, 'because if we get up to F, we are flippin' done for.'

Fair enough.

Next, she got working on the plans for getting past the guards and into the basement and, by the end of that session, we were at Plan X. You don't want to know what that one entailed. Needless to say, if we got to Plan X, we'd pretty much all be Xtinct.

Fleassy doesn't deserve all the credit for our plans, though. The rest of us pitched in ideas, too. Granted, Fleassy would huff and puff and call us chumps and dorks with every suggestion made, but she would still incorporate them if she could.

'Okay, so if we get Jasmine to the security room,' I pondered, 'she still isn't going to know what to do to disable the cameras or anything.'

'She can just unplug it, you bonehead,' groaned Fleassy.

'Yeah, and they wouldn't notice that in a second, would they?' said Marlie.

'All right, so we need someone who knows tech to deal with all the electronic security stuff,' I put forth.

'Yep, we really do,' agreed Jasmine.

'Any of you geniuses also tech geniuses?' asked Fleassy.

'I know a little,' said Marlie. Really, she knew more than a little. Marlie had been working hard in any spare time she had on computers and programming and coding and all that kind of stuff over the past few years. It came naturally to her. But, would it be enough? I had no idea. Fleassy certainly didn't think so.

'Well, a LITTLE is gonna get us NOWHERE, Balooby!' chastised Fleassy. Marlie looked down at her toes. 'I'm adding it to the list.'

We had started making a list of the things we needed and the holes in our plans that we had to figure out before Monday. Fleassy had titled it, *The Clueless Checklist*. And it was growing. Long.

'One tech nerd to install into the security room,' Fleassy said as she added it to the list.

'That,' I worried out loud, 'is not an easy fix if Marlie can't do it.'

'There's something else I don't get,' said Marlie, changing the subject.

'Ha, that's an understatement,' shot back Fleassy.

Marlie rolled her eyes. 'How are they getting the chocolates out?'

'Huh?'

'Well, if they are making a *huge* shipment of chocolates in the basement, then they've gotta be able to actually get it out.'

'Jenkins mentioned a truck,' Jasmine suggested.

'That's right, he did. But how does the truck get in there to the underground?' asked Marlie.

'Add it to the list.'

'Wait, you guys,' I interrupted. 'Look at this map of Marlie's.'

'Yes, we've been looking at it, McGee.'

'What does it look like?'

'What do you mean? It looks like a lair for a bunch of aliens.'

'Right, but what do you notice about the layout? Where have you seen this before?'

'Huh?'

'Look. There are the three rooms. And then these tunnels all have tiny little rooms coming off them. Remember, they were all along the corridors we went down.'

'Yeah, they were all locked,' noted Marlie. 'Except for the one looking onto the big main room.'

'Right. Now, where else do you see a corridor, with lots of tiny locked rooms and a few large ones, that you can look into from up high through a window?'

'Oh, just freakin' tell us already, McGee.'

'A prison. Can't you see? It's a prison. An actual prison.'

'Oh yeah,' they all said in unison, each of them now able to see it. It's amazing how once you notice something it seems so obvious. The layout really did look exactly like a prison's would be.

'Don't you remember they told us that the school was designed by a prison architect? Well, what if it was actually a prison, before it became the high school?'

'No way!'

'We would know, though. Everyone would know.'

'Unless it was like a secret underground prison? Why else would there be underground tunnels below the school? The architect must have known about it and built the rest of the school directly over the top.'

'Andy, you genius!' shouted Marlie with a beaming smile.

I blushed.

Fleassy and Nick mimed vomiting.

'I mean . . . good, *cough*, work, Andy.' Marlie quietened herself down.

Fleassy rolled her eyes.

Marlie quickly opened up her computer and Googled Bellington High School history. But there was nothing. She Googled gaols in Bellington. Nothing. Marlie kept clicking through to the next Google pages. Nothing. Nothing. My idea instantly deflated. Until, about ten pages down, there was a link to an old newspaper that read:

Cover-up in Bellington? The underground prison you've never . . .

Bellington Library Resource 12:135b

And that was it. Excited, Marlie clicked on the link, only to read, *This page is unavailable.*

'Ugh, it's not there,' I moaned.

'But it shows that you might be right,' Marlie consoled.

'Well, we've gotta check it out,' I replied. 'I mean, it may tell us how the truck for the chocolates can get in. They would have needed a way to deliver the prisoners directly underground. So, what if . . .? Marlie, you head to the library, there's a history section there. See if you can find this article, or anything at all in the history books of Bellington. Fleassy and I will stake-out the high school and –'

'Do I have to go with you, McGee?' Fleassy protested.

'Yes. You are the planner, you might notice something I don't.'

'All right, all right.'

'As I was saying, Fleassy and I will go and see how many aliens, I mean people, I mean . . . whatever they are. We will see what we can see at the school. Nick and Jasmine, you go to C-V-W on Clyde Street like we talked about. And get . . . what do they need to make sure they get, Fleassy?'

'Aside from the C-V-W pick-up,' began Fleassy to Nick. I noticed a slight sneer in the way she said it to him, although a sneer from Fleassy is not something out of the ordinary. 'We need walkie-talkies. Marlie said she has a few torches here, so find those and grab them, too. And we also need a long rope with some kind of hook, and instant-drying superglue and . . . ah, here's the list, just take it.'

'Yeah, but where should we get the walkie-talkies from?' asked Nick.

'How am I meant to know? Just figure it out, would you?' Fleassy snapped back.

'Okay. Okay. Calm down,' protested Nick with his hands up in the air.

Something was up with those two.

Nick and Jasmine's visit to the CVW offices on Saturday morning indeed proved fruitful, or so they recounted to us later. They'd entered on the pretence of surprising Nick's brother for his birthday. Nick was able to put his charm to good use, and quickly talked the receptionist into letting them through. Then, avoiding his brother's office, they'd gone in search of the storeroom. It hadn't taken them long to find, nor had the boxes of orange overalls that the CVW builders all wore. Nick grabbed a box, and they quickly headed for the backdoor exit, which was when they heard, 'Oi! What are you doing here, twerp?'

Jasmine froze. Nick yelped. They were busted.

'Nick Delancey, my little bro. Why is it that I was just given a rousing rendition of *Happy Birthday* by the receptionist a moment ago? Especially seeing as my birthday is not for a few months? And now I find you here? And what the hell are you doing with those?' Jerry asked, pointing at the partially open box of orange overalls.

'Oh. Ah, yeah. Hey, Jerry.'

'You are so dead, you little –'

'We just . . . It's just . . .' Nick stumbled over his words while trying to think. His charming ability had never really worked with his own siblings. It jammed up on him. They knew him too well. So, Jasmine had cut in with some charm of her own.

'We have a dress-up party tonight. It's a Village People theme.'

'Is that so? And who are you?'

'I'm Jasmine.'

Jerry raised his eyebrows at his little brother. 'So, what? This is some attempt to charm a lady, Nick?'

'Um . . . yeah. Yes, that's exactly what it is. Sorry. You caught me. I was just . . .' And with this he turned to Jasmine and put on the most pathetic puppy-dog expression he could. 'I was just trying to impress you, Jaz. Ah, I feel like such a dope. I told you we could easily get these for tonight, 'cause I just wanted to go to the party with you, 'cause I,' he took her arm, 'I like you. And I . . .'

'Oh, STOP IT!' exclaimed his older brother. 'You're just embarrassing yourself, Nick. I personally apologise for my little brother, Jasmine. I taught him NOTHING he knows. Look, why don't you two use them? Just for the weekend. I'll be back at the folks' on Wednesday, Nick. If they are not there, clean and folded, I will rat you out to the parents and to C-V-W and the police and anyone else I can think of. Actually, it wasn't you who's been taking the others, was it?'

'No. It wasn't us. What others?'

'There's been a bunch of boxes of the uniforms go missing over the past few weeks.'

'It definitely wasn't us, Jerry. I promise. I've never been in here before.'

'Okay. Okay. I believe you. So, back by Wednesday. You agree?'

'Yes. Yes. I agree.'

'All right. I'll see you then. Now, go through the back door. I gotta go keep pretending it's my birthday. I hope they buy me a cake for lunch.'

'Thanks, brother.'

'Yeah. Thanks, Jerry,' Jasmine said sweetly.

'Don't make me regret it,' he growled, before adding: 'Oh, and Jasmine . . .'

'Yeah?'

'You can do better than that twit. Trust me.'

Whilst Nick and Jasmine were off at CVW, Fleassy and I were on top of the hill behind the school, fighting over the binoculars. I looked at my watch. All of five minutes had passed. Only two hours minus five minutes to go until we'd told the others we'd be back.

'What is wrong with you, Fleassy?' I asked after another antagonistic comment. 'You've been difficult all morning. Like, even more difficult than usual.'

'Oh, that's flattering, that is. Nothing is wrong. What's wrong with you, Jerky McJerk McGee?'

I shook my head and held the binoculars up to my eyes.

'Fine, you look first then, shall you?' Fleassy sneered, before rolling onto her back and staring at the clouds.

I ignored her and looked to see if I could count how many people/aliens were visible. Or to see if there was any kind of pattern to those who were walking around the roof. We knew they were all alien-infested humans. But we didn't know how many we were dealing with, or how organised they were. There wasn't much of the school that we could see, though. The high, windowless walls that went around the whole school, as is stylish with any prison, blocked our view of pretty much everything but the roof.

'They do seem to be on a repeated pattern,' I told Fleassy after about 30 minutes of watching.

There was no response.

'I said, they do seem to be on a repeated pattern.'

'Feed them the sheep, then,' said Fleassy. 'That'll teach 'em to come crawling back.'

'What?!' I said, entirely confused. I looked over at her.

She was sound asleep and mumbling. I should have noticed the disparaging remarks had ceased.

'And if the dog bites, then we'll go ahead and feed it to the wheels of the monster truck. Ha-ha. It'll never know we even did it. Dead dog.'

Geez, Fleassy's unconscious self, though entirely incoherent, seemed to be just as mean as her wakeful self. She was lying on her side, drool dribbling down her cheek. Actually, she looked quite peaceful, even if she was mumbling about squishing a dog. I wasn't used to seeing her like that. Not asleep, I mean, that would be weird if I was used to seeing her sleep. Creepy. No, I wasn't used to seeing her peaceful. But she was. Her face relaxed, and she was slightly snoring.

'Fleassy!' I said a little louder. Still no response. I reached over and touched her arm. 'OWWWW!' She had jolted awake, grabbed my arm and was twisting it. 'Ah, let go! Let go!'

'Don't touch me again.'

'I had to wake you.'

'I don't care, dweeb. This is what happens if you get in my space, McGee.'

'All right, all right. Calm down. Look, I just want you to see the pattern.'

And with that she let go of my arm and picked up the binoculars.

'So, there seems to be two sets of two people walking in a circle around the various roofs of the different school buildings,' I started explaining. 'They walk from the gym roof across the roof of the walkway to the C-block roof, then across the walkway roof to B-block, then they do a loop of the old bell tower, go down to A-block before heading across the roof of the walkway to the gym again. When one of the pairs is at the gym, the other is at the bell tower. It takes them about ten minutes to walk the loop.'

'Okay, now, let's see . . .' Fleassy immediately kicked into planning mode. 'So, once they pass the gym roof, *now* . . .' She clicked a button on her stopwatch and looked back through the binoculars. 'We would have . . . twenty . . . forty . . . sixty . . . eighty . . . one hundred and . . . *stop*. One hundred and twenty seconds where neither of the pairs would be able to see the gym roof.'

'Is that enough time?'

'It'll have to be. Wait!' Fleassy had moved the binoculars' gaze away from the school toward the town. 'There are some of those orange C-V-W uniforms over there, too.'

'Where?'

'At Grease Monkeys mechanics.'

'Oh, that's where we get our car fixed.'

'Fascinating, McGee. Really fascinating.' Fleassy watched for a bit, refusing to give me the binoculars.

'What are they doing?'

'They are just standing around talking. But that's weird. They . . . oh, and it looks like a big truck, like a semi, just pulled up there. That's got to be something. It's reversing into the mechanics'.'

'I hope it doesn't flatten a dog.'

'What?'

'Nothing . . . But look, the mechanics' is, like, two hundred metres from the school, and there is that whole hill between them and the school.'

'I realise that, McGee. I'm just telling you what I am seeing.'

'But it's not even a big mechanics'. It couldn't fit a semi-trailer like that in there. Impossible. Unless . . . That's it! That must be it.'

'What?'

'How they are going to get the chocolates out! If it was a secret underground prison and they had to get the prisoners in there in a truck, then they'd need a tunnel out of there that leads, my guess is . . .' I grabbed the binoculars back from her, '. . . to what is now the mechanics'. See how Grease Monkeys is tucked into that side of the hill? It looks like it pretty much backs into it.'

'That's ridiculous! What a stupid . . .' Fleassy grabbed the binoculars back from me. 'I can't believe that . . . ah . . . actually, you might be right.'

'Thanks.'

'For once in your life.'

'Come on,' I said. 'Let's go down and see if we can get a closer look. I think we've seen all we are going to of the school from here.'

'Sounds good,' smiled Fleassy, before catching herself and growling at me. 'I mean, if we must, McGee.'

THE LIBRARY

SATURDAY AFTERNOON

A while later, Fleassy and I walked through the doors of Bellington Library looking for Marlie. Our scouting of the mechanics' had proved all but useless. By the time we got there, the big garage doors were shut up and no one was around.

Fleassy, being the impulsive person she is, took off before I could stop her. She walked straight up to the locked doors and knocked while I hid behind a big rubbish bin. I watched as the door opened, and Fleassy exchanged some words with a man in orange overalls. The door was quickly shut and she was coming back toward me.

'Well, turns out the mechanics' is shut for the week. Or so the alien just told me.'

'I can't believe you did that.'

'It was nothing. And I got a glimpse inside. There were, like, twenty of them all standing around. There's no way we are getting in that way. And, Andy . . . there was no sign at all of the truck that just reversed into there.'

We scooted around the back of the mechanics' to confirm that, yep, the back wall sat snugly against the hills. And so we sat at the bus stop for a while, pretending to be waiting for a bus as we watched. But nothing else happened, and so off to the library we went.

'Let's check out the history section first,' I said, thinking that was most likely where Marlie would be. But there was no Marlie. Hmm . . . We walked the aisles and rooms of the library, looking for her. Nothing.

'Maybe she found what she needed and went home?' Fleassy suggested.

'Must have. All right, let's –'

'**Arrghhhhh!**'

'That's Marlie,' I gasped. 'Come on, it sounded like she's through that door.'

We ran to the door marked 'STAFF ONLY'. It was locked. Figures. Darn doors fulfilling their purpose in life.

'We have to get in. Is there another entrance to the back?' I wondered aloud.

'I don't know. Let's try that hall,' said Fleassy, pointing to our right.

The two of us ran through the room we were in and into the next. It, too, was full of books. Not too surprising, for a library. Someone was just exiting through a second door that seemed to lead to the back. It swung open for a moment and then began to shut.

'Quick! Stop it from closing,' I said, running, even though I knew there was no way we could make it in time.

A book came flying from over my right shoulder. It narrowly missed my head and flew through the air toward the door. I watched in slow motion as the book sailed right into the crack between door and frame and stopped the door from closing.

'How did you even . . .?' I turned to Fleassy, only to see Jasmine standing there with a huge grin on her face. I should have guessed. 'Nice shot.'

'Thanks.'

'Quick! Marlie is in trouble back there. Let's go.'

The four of us burst through the now-book-jammed doorway into a back corridor. Turning in the direction of the scream from moments before, we ran down the hall, skidded around the corner, zoomed past the door that had defied us earlier and I thrust open a door opposite. It was just a storeroom. Another door on the left. An empty office. One more on the right. This door opened up into a long, dark, huge room filled with shelves and shelves of books. The library stacks. This was where all the books were stored that weren't out on the public shelves.

In these stacks, down the very end, was Marlie. The room was dimly lit, but it was definitely her. She was sitting on the floor, looking up at someone standing over her. Someone with a Hawaiian shirt and a ponytail. It was Denny, the Bellington High receptionist. *He must be an alien hybrid, too*, I thought.

I ran at him, unsure of what I would do, until I found myself leaping into the air, crash-tackling him to the floor, just as Marlie yelled, 'No, Andy, don't!'

Too late. I smashed into Denny with all my might, and down we both came with a crash and a tumble. A tangle of limbs, we smacked hard against the back wall of the big room.

'Nice tackle, McGee,' was all I heard from Nick behind me.

'What the hell did you do that for?!' groaned the receptionist.

'It's okay,' said Marlie quickly. 'He knows. He's one of us.'

'Then why were you screaming?'

'Because until a minute ago I thought that Denny was one of them, an alien. But he's no more alien than he is a . . . a potato.'

'I'm really not an alien, nor am I a potato,' grunted Denny as he went to get up.

'Prove it!' growled Fleassy.

'Prove I am not a potato?'

'Prove you aren't an alien.'

'How could I prove that? And why do I need to prove it to you little squirts, anyway?'

'Let's see if he bleeds,' snarled Fleassy, a smile on her face that would scare the bejesus out of anyone, alien or not.

'Wait,' I said, also trying to get up off the ground, and feeling a little foolish. I grabbed hold of Marlie's hand, and we helped each other up. 'Marlie, tell us what happened.'

'Okay. So, I was researching the school, which I'll tell you about in a bit. But I kept having the feeling that someone was watching me. I looked around quickly, and I didn't see him properly, but someone definitely ducked behind a bookshelf. As you can imagine, I panicked. So, I grabbed my stuff and started walking out of the library when Denny here jumped out from behind the bookshelf. He scared the crap out of me, so I ran as fast as I could through the nearest open door, which turned out to be into this back area, but Denny kept after me, and so I screamed. Then, right here is where Denny caught up to me. I thought he was going to attack me. But he was just trying to calm me down. Said he'd figured it out, too, what's happening at the school.'

'I have,' agreed Denny. 'I've figured it all out. And, I want to help. Maybe. Principal Jenkins hasn't been right for ages. Something has been way off. So I did some sleuthing of my own to find out what was happening. The workmen started pouring into the school yesterday, which was not scheduled at all. Principal Jenkins told me and the teachers to leave it alone. But I couldn't. I knew something was up. I just had no idea that I would stumble upon an actual alien invasion. I noticed you five were also scampering around the school during every period of class. So I followed you.'

'When?'

'After school yesterday. I followed at a distance in my car when I saw you chasing after the sedan.'

'You were the one in the blue buggy?' I asked.

'I was.'

'You're a really bad driver.'

'I had other things on my mind, okay? Anyway, yes, I followed you, parked in the empty yard next to that big house and was coming in from the side to see what was happening, when Henry Balooby jumped you. I was just behind the bush on the other side. And so I heard everything. And, finally, it all made sense.'

'So, how did you know Marlie would be here today?'

'I might have looked up where the Baloobys lived in the school database and thought I'd drive up there this morning. I got there just as you were all leaving, so I followed Marlie to see what she was up to. And the rest, you heard from her. I was just reaching down to help her up when you tackled me.'

'A likely story,' Fleassy huffed. 'Besides him obviously being a creep, following kids around the streets, how do we know we can trust him?'

'I swear I am not an alien,' pleaded Denny, desperately. 'I just want to do what I can.'

It was weird seeing him in this light. When he was sitting behind reception at school, he just seemed like a grumpy adult. But here, now, he seemed almost a kid himself, which I suppose he was, being only a few years out of school. He appeared to be just a particularly dweeby, sulky, nasally almost-adult desperate to not see humanity taken captive by aliens.

But we had to make sure.

Jasmine was holding a bag, which I assumed contained all the supplies she and Nick had been collecting throughout the day. I whispered to her to open the bag. Turning around so Denny couldn't see what I was doing, I reached in, past the walkie-talkies and under the rope, until my fingers found what I was looking for.

I quickly swung back around and, in the dark room

of the library stacks, I shone the torch straight into Denny's eyes.

'Oi,' he said, blinking and shaking his head. 'What are you doing? Would you get that torch out of my eyes? Come on, that's not funny, it's just annoying.'

'He's no alien,' I said. 'Remember, Henry said the aliens go berserk at sudden bright lights. Like, implosion-level berserk. But he's no more annoyed than any of us would be at someone shining a bright light in their face.'

'Nice work, McGee,' Nick said encouragingly.

'Yeah, nice.' Fleassy was almost being encouraging herself, before she caught herself again. 'So, we have a nerdy receptionist joining our team, do we? Whoopsie-doo. I mean, what would you even be . . . Wait! You are a nerd, aren't you?'

'*I* wouldn't say that. But, yeah, others might,' said the Hawaiian-shirt-wearing receptionist in his most nasally of voices.

'Like, even more so than nerdy Marlie and McGee, here.'

'Hey!' we both started protesting.

'No, don't you see? He's not just a nerd like you two. He's a tech nerd. You know, computers and all that.'

'Ah, yes. I am studying computer science part-time at university. Why?'

Four of us looked at each other, beaming. Marlie looked relieved. We had found our tech nerd. *The Clueless Checklist* was finally getting smaller. And, of all people, it was Denny the receptionist who was stepping in to save the day.

ONE DAY BEFORE THE HEIST

16

THE PLOT THICKENS (LIKE A RICH CHOCOLATE FONDUE)

SUNDAY MORNING

Sunday started early with some quality father-son time. I wish I could tell you it was because both Dad and I thought it would just be a nice thing to do. But no, I needed something.

Luckily, by this time, Dad's brain had justified what had occurred in our kitchen on the Thursday. (You know, when we seemingly boiled an alien alive.) He told me that he must have been SO tired that he'd been delirious. I agreed. Let him believe whatever he needed to. Though, it did make me wonder how many weird things we might see that our brain just rationalises away without our realising. It got me thinking about the magic tricks I had played with in primary school, which were now at the back of my cupboard. I wondered if that kind of magic relied on our brain's ability to trick itself, too. Interesting thoughts.

Anyway, I told him that I had another chocolate-based food-tech-science experiment for the same teacher and, after assuring him that my friends and I were all getting an A on the assignment because of his help the other day, he agreed once more to help. Or maybe he was just touched that I was suddenly taking an interest in his world. So I told him we needed to make something that would both destroy the chocolate and cause it to erupt at the same time. That's what the teacher was after. An instant chemical reaction. A food experiment like this was sure to get my dad excited.

What we came up with was some kind of concoction of various substances that all had acid or hydroxide in their names. I'm a smart kid, but I only understood about half of what he was saying. All I know is that it was some highly dangerous stuff you definitely should not combine at home. But, after years of study and working in his science-lab of a kitchen, my dad was an expert at this. And the saving of the world was at stake, too, not that he knew that. The mixture we made, Dad named Boom-shaka-laka. Which he said everyone used to say when they would slam dunk a ball back in the day. And this was the food explosion equivalent of a slam dunk. One drop. That's all it would need. Just add one drop to either a bar of chocolate or a vat full of melted chocolate, wait ten seconds and then stand back to watch the fun begin.

Later that morning, we five heisters sat in Marlie's lounge room and welcomed our newest member. Or, at least, our tag-along member. Fleassy refused to allow him to be seen as a full member. Not that we were like an incorporated entity or anything. We were all pretty protective of what we had become together. Strangely, Fleassy was the most protective of the lot of us.

Denny the receptionist was the oldest of us by seven years. He looked as out of place with our little group as he probably looked anywhere. Except, maybe, sci-fi and conspiracy theory conventions. Now *those* were his kind of people. So an alien invasion was right up his alley.

He sat there smiling, and I realised he was actually enjoying this whole thing. I mean, he looked terrified, too. If anyone knew what an alien invasion could do to the world, it was someone like Denny. He had played enough sci-fi games, watched enough alien movies, sipped enough conspiracy Kool-Aid to feel like he knew the ins and outs of the genre like the back of his hand. The problem was, this was no pop-culture genre, this was reality. Our reality.

Another problem was that Denny and Fleassy got on like a house on fire. And not in the good way. No, if there was a house burning to the ground with no chance of ever being made whole again, that was Fleassy and Denny. Instant animosity. Denny had tried to take over as soon as he arrived. With all the bravado of a late-blooming, Hawaiian-shirt-wearing, high-pitched-talking, incompetent receptionist, he strode in and started giving orders. It took all of two minutes for Fleassy to bring him to a huffing silence in a chair in the corner. Although in his twenties, he did sulking teenager like an expert. But, at least this took some of the edge off Fleassy's harshness to the others in the group. She was in a much better mood after getting to rip into Denny. At least, for a little while.

Nick and Jasmine cheerily reported that they had managed to get all the things on their list the day before, and then sighed heavily when we gave them a new list of things to round up today. Next, Marlie gave us the run-down on what she had discovered in her research at the library. None of us were ready for this.

She had gone straight to the librarian, a balding man with the name tag Horace Greenwood, and asked him for news clipping *12:135b.* Horace looked up where it was in their system and took her through the main library into the historical collection, where he took down a thick folder and opened it. It was filled with numerous clippings in plastic sleeves with little tags. But *12:135b* was not where it should be.

'Strange,' the librarian had said. 'It definitely should be here. Sometimes, these things do go missing, though. Look, this whole section here is all local history. There are books and folders of articles, and a box or two of old newspapers as well as a tonne of other stuff. If you're looking for something about Bellington, this is where it'll be.'

And so began Marlie's thorough search of Bellington history. She struggled to find anything. And, she told us, not because it hadn't been there, but because it was missing. A few times, she caught a phrase or two about some kind of supposed underground facility in Bellington, but then the next pages were either missing, or writing was blacked out. It seemed that someone had gone to great lengths to get rid of all mention of this conspiracy. But, she hoped, they wouldn't have been able to get rid of everything. So she scoured the rest of the history shelving. She had almost given up when she found a tiny article in the back of a newspaper from many years earlier. She easily could have missed it, but a surname caught her eye.

The launch of the eye-opening memoir by local Bellington author, Genevieve Jenkins, will be happening tomorrow night at the Town Hall. In her book, Hidden Underneath, *Genevieve tells of a family history caught up in a military scandal, criminal activity, missing ancestors and much more. Come and hear some of the tell-all tale before reading her surprising and sensational memoir. A must for any Bellington history buff.*

That was it. That was all it said. But it was enough to spark some curiosity. And nothing else had panned out so far. So she went to the library computers and looked up the author, Genevieve Jenkins. Sure enough, there was an entry. Not in the history section of the library, but in the biographical memoirs. Marlie had gone to the shelf, hoping against hope it hadn't disappeared, too.

But when she got to where it should be, it was not there. She had punched the surrounding books in frustration. And her punch, besides really, really hurting her hand, pushed a large hardcover book to the side. And there, squashed into the back of the shelf, was an old, small paperback titled *Hidden Underneath.*

Marlie pulled the book out of her bag and showed us.

'Nice,' I said, impressed.

'Pfft,' said Fleassy. 'Anything interesting in there?'

'Actually, yes,' said a beaming Marlie. 'A whole lot. Andy was right. It was a prison. But not what you might think. So, Genevieve Jenkins, who I'm pretty certain was the grandmother of Principal Jenkins, writes all about the story of her grandpa, Isaiah Jenkins. He was a soldier in one of the wars way back then. But, one night, when he was at home here in Bellington, he suddenly disappeared. No one knows what happened to him. Genevieve grew up not knowing anything at all. But then she started to ask questions. Questions that led to years of research and . . .'

'Oh, geez, just get to the point,' Fleassy cut in.

'All right, well, she interviewed a number of Isaiah's old army buddies, who were all old men by then. None of them gave her much. They all closed up as though they were hiding something. But then, there was one old man, who was Isaiah's best friend. Sadly, he had started to lose his memory, but he told her that one night Isaiah had gone off from his platoon with another soldier. This other soldier never returned. Isaiah did, but he was different. He'd seen something that had shaken him to the core. Something that he said he had to tell the world about when he got back home. So when Genevieve asked him what he'd seen, the old man just pointed up to the sky and slowly shook his head.'

'Flip!' said Nick. 'What happened?'

We all had our mouths open by this point. Even Fleassy.

'Well, he came back home to Bellington, and that was when he disappeared. The old army buddy said that he didn't see him again, except just once, years later. He woke up in the middle of the night, and there he was, Isaiah Jenkins, just standing there in his room, looking really beaten up and haggard. He was raving, shaking, scratching at his skin and pointing upwards. Isaiah gurgled and spluttered before managing to say that he'd been taken by a secret government organisation and locked up underground for years.'

'I knew it! I knew it!' shouted Denny, looking as giddy as a long-haired hippy cat at a mouse convention. All his conspiracy dreams were coming true.

'Shhhhh!' We all shushed him.

'Fine!' He resigned himself back to listening. Marlie continued.

'Okay. I'm almost finished. So he told his old army buddy he'd been grabbed in the night, taken by a truck through an underground tunnel, then through a massive impenetrable blast door, or something like that. Then he was held in a cell. And, he told him that he had just escaped that night, said he'd gotten out through a passageway somehow and realised he was still in Bellington when he saw he was right near the large fig tree. Then he ran all the way to his friend's house. The old man said he went to get up out of bed, but Isaiah started scratching at his skin again and ran from the room, down the stairs and out into the night . . . and he never saw him again.'

Silence. We all sat in silence. None of us quite knew how to comprehend what we had just heard. It seemed that, not only were aliens about to take over the world, but they had perhaps been here for a few generations or even longer. And some secret group of humans knew all this already. There were A LOT more unanswered questions now than there had ever been. But what was most important was that the book did confirm there was a secret underground prison facility in Bellington, which a truck would deliver people into through an underground tunnel. And that there had been a large fig tree on top of it, which must be the fig-tree stump in the main quadrangle of Bellington High.

'All right.' I broke the silence. 'That explains a lot. The truck entrance and exit to the underground must be where the mechanics' is. We know we can't get in that way, that blast-door part of the story confirms that. But that will be our exit. It'll have to be. Nick, you sure you're good to drive that truck outta there? It seemed pretty big.'

'Yeah, totally fine. I've been driving motorbikes and four-wheelers and pick-up trucks and whole massive sheep trucks on my uncle's farm for years. I can drive anything. Trust me.'

'Well, there's no other option. So we *are* trusting you. Now, come on. Let's stay focused and get back into what we need to do.'

For the rest of the day, we cracked into gear. A rope was hung up to the roof of Marlie's house so we could run through Jasmine's entry into the school over and over and over, trying to get her time down. By the end of an hour she was exhausted, but she'd knocked a good twenty seconds off her initial time. The rest of us had a lot of stuff to practise, too. Like walking quietly. We practised throwing anchors. We set off sparklers. We tried out the distance of our water guns. You know, all the normal, extremely professional heist-type things.

At some point during the day, Denny then went and pulled a drone out of his backpack, wondering if it would be of any use. We just stared at him.

'Are you kidding me, DENNY?!' Fleassy went off at him. 'Of course we need that. We needed that, like, yesterday. Sheesh.'

It was true. His drone was going to make things a lot easier. So, down we went that afternoon to where Fleassy and I had scoped out the school the day before. We flew the drone around, taking as many notes as we could about the movements of those inside the walls, and being careful the aliens didn't see or hear it flying around. Denny was, thankfully, a good drone pilot, and so we were able to get the information we needed as well as snap a crucial photo that was important for our plan the following day.

17

FIREWORKS

SUNDAY EVENING

We all knew what we had to do. We each had our instructions given to us by our heist planner, Fleassy. We'd rehearsed our roles. Denny had gone off to wherever he lived to print the photo we needed. The gear was stowed in our backpacks ready for the following day, and we were sitting on the back verandah finishing off the pizza Nick had somehow manipulated Denny into buying us before he left.

We were also doing a final run-through of plans A through to X, or whichever it was we were up to now. The heist itself had been divided up into seven stages, each crucial to moving on to the next stage. Precision would be critical. Teamwork, essential. Clarity, vital.

But, as with any plan, things can go . . . slightly awry. And, oh boy, things were about to take a nosedive. Like a penguin thinking it can fly and leaping from a cliff in the middle of a cyclone kinda nosedive.

I was sitting back, belly full, enjoying the moment, thinking about all the great work we had done and admiring the heist squad. Fleassy was looking something up on the computer and had written down 636 on the back of her hand. I wasn't sure why. At the moment I didn't care. All I knew was that we were a well-oiled . . .

'Get the heck away from me!'

. . . machine.

'I'm not near you.'

'Yes you are! You're breathing all over me.'

'I am not, Fleassy! You're just –'

'Just what, Nick?'

I sighed. Everyone had been laughing over dinner at a joke Nick made, and the laughter, in the midst of the dread over what we were about to do, felt good. But Fleassy caught herself laughing and instantly turned grump once more. It was as though the more we were coming together as a team, the more she pulled away. But, I couldn't really be mad at her. She had completely stepped up with regard to planning out this chocolate heist.

'Come on, you two.'

'Shut up, McGee,' spat back Fleassy. 'You're not the boss of me.'

'Yeah, McGee,' copied Nick. 'You're not the boss of me,' he quipped, and then started a chant. 'McGee, McGee, he's not the boss of me. McGee, McGee, he's not the boss of me.'

I rolled my eyes. Fleassy joined in with him. At least they had a common enemy now. Me.

'McGee, McGee, he's not the boss of me. McGee, McGee, he's not the boss of me.'

Sometimes, it honestly felt like I was herding a crew of hyperactive ferrets, all jacked up on energy drinks.

Marlie interrupted. 'If you two don't –'

'Oh, and once again, McGee's lover girl steps in for him 'cause he can't fight his own battles,' Fleassy spat back at her.

'What is your problem?' Marlie arced up. 'I am so sick of your –'

'Of my what?'

'Of your small-minded –'

'I'm not the small one, Marlie,' Fleassy joked, but then I saw her narrow her eyes. Her expression changed. I suppose aliens are not the only things that can possess us humans. This was not going to be good.

'We've had to carry you and your limping leg the whole way through this, and it's *your* brother that went and got himself infected by aliens. You're too busy making eyes at McGee to even see the fact – We. Don't. Need. You.'

To her credit, Marlie didn't punch Fleassy, though she really deserved it. Instead, Marlie turned around and stormed off inside. I was about to speak in her defence and tell Fleassy how out of line she was, when . . .

'Not cool, Fleassy,' Jasmine said softly as we watched Marlie go.

'Shut up, Quinn.'

'It really wasn't, Fleassy.' I was surprised to hear Nick speak to her like that.

'What do you know, Nick? You and Quinn are NO better. Making eyes at each other.'

This is when I spoke up. 'So that's what this is about? You're picking fights because, what? You're jealous?'

'No! No, I'm not jealous. Why would I be?'

'Nah, its 'cause she's scared of being left alone,' said Nick. 'It's just what she does. Whenever she starts to have friends, she pushes them away.'

Fleassy stopped raging. Her face lost its anger. She just stared at Nick, who stared back at her. I gotta admit, I kinda peed my pants a little in that moment. An angry and irate Fleassy, this I can handle. A silenced Fleassy . . . It was just plain scary.

But, like Marlie, all she did was turn around and walk away. She went straight to her bike. She was leaving.

'Fleassy, you have to be there tomorrow,' I called out. 'You have to be ready. You can't –'

'I will be, McGee,' she seethed, not turning around. She went around the corner of the Balooby house and was gone. I turned to Nick.

'She has to be there tomorrow, Nick. Like, the fate of the entire world is riding on her being there tomorrow.'

'I know. She will be. She . . . I'll make sure of it.' And with that, Nick got to his feet. He looked at me and said with a kind of genuine, heartfelt something that I had never heard Nick speak in before, 'You're doing a great job, mate. Don't worry about this. We'll make it work.'

He then looked at Jasmine. 'Sorry,' was all he managed to say to her as he, too, grabbed his bike and went off around the front of the house. He had changed a lot these last few days. I suppose we all had.

'I had better go see if Marlie is okay,' I said to Jasmine.

'Yeah, that'd be a good idea. I'll head home and go see my parents for what might be the final time, hey?'

The thought struck me cold. It was one of those moments when the reality of what we were about to do caught up to me.

'Yeah, yeah . . . I had better do that, too.'

Jasmine grabbed her bike as I turned to walk inside.

'Oh, and Andy,' I heard her call out. I turned back around at the door. 'Nick's right. You're actually a really great leader. We're all going to get through tomorrow. You know why?'

'Ah . . . no.'

'Because we trust in you. Obviously, Fleassy will never tell you that. But, without you, this team would have all fallen apart before it even got started. It's only because of you we are all still here. So . . . thanks.'

'Ah . . . don't mention it,' I joked, trying to bluff off her encouragement. But some of it got through, and it made my heart swell. 'Thanks, Jaz. Truly. I'll . . . I'll see you tomorrow.'

'You're on,' she said, giving me her dorky double thumbs up. 'See you at six.'

'See you then. And hopefully Fleassy, too.'

It was time to find Marlie.

When I found her in her bedroom, Marlie was fuming. Ignoring me and fuming. She was storming around her bedroom. Or maybe creating a storm *in* her bedroom. A circle-turning hurricane. Shoulders hunched. An angry face. Clenched fists. Her whole body was clenched. Around and around she drew the winds of anger. Until suddenly she seemed to enter the centre of the hurricane, the eye of the storm, without warning. I saw her glimpse a photo on her desk of her family. Of Henry. The anger dropped and, in that moment, she seemed to be able to do nothing more than sit down on her bed.

I came and sat next to her. We didn't say anything to start with. Truthfully, I didn't know what to say. I just looked around her room. It was massive, though still a typical young teenage girl's room, I guessed. A mix of the girl she was and the teenager she was becoming. Posters of bands. Teddy bears. Make-up. Old toys. I spotted the walking stick she used to use at primary school, and wondered whether she still needed it sometimes. There were some of those elastic leg-stretching bands on the floor next to it, which I realised she must use to help keep her leg strong. She had a rich family, so there was also a TV in her room, a desk full of all the computer and tech stuff she was into and an exercise bike. Lastly, if you can believe it, there was a piano. An actual mini-grand piano. In her room. I told you it was massive!

'Nice piano.' It was the first thing that came out of my mouth.

'Yeah. I hate it. Well, I don't mind the piano, but piano practice . . . now *that* I hate. Andy . . .?'

'Yes?'

She looked at me. 'You know when you rejected me in science class the other day?' She said it softly, and my guts instantly tied themselves in a knot.

'Marlie, I am so sorry about that.'

'No, I am not bringing it up 'cause I want another apology. I know you're sorry, Andy. I'm just realising that, well, whether it was you that day, or Fleassy today, it's never . . . ah, how do I say this? What Fleassy said to me today was NOT okay. I mean, I know Fleassy was just being Fleassy, but that doesn't excuse what she said. It *can't* excuse what she said. I know she's got her own issues, but what she said just now, about my limp, about the group not needing me, as if I have nothing useful to contribute, it didn't just hurt my feelings, Andy. It was so much more than that. It was what I feel like the world has told me about myself every day since I was born. That I need to be grateful for everything others have done to *carry* me. I don't need carrying! Yes, I might move a bit slower and differently to other people, but why does that mean I should be treated as less? Why does that mean that I should expect less? Why does that mean what I can contribute is less? But that is what the world tells me, in some way, every single day. Can you even imagine what that feels like?'

'I . . . no. I can't. I don't know, Marlie.'

'Well, it sucks. It REALLY sucks. And what I am saying is that it's not just when someone like Fleassy says something mean. Of course, I am angry about that. But it's all the other ways, all the other things that are not so easily seen, that make me feel less. That make me feel small. I'm angry because Fleassy treating me small today is how the world treats me *every* day, and it is also how I treat myself. Small. That's how I felt in science class the other day, too.'

'I'm sorry.'

'Stop apologising! It's not about you. It's about me. And what I am saying is . . . I've had enough. I am not going to do that any more. I am not going to let others make me feel small, and I am not going to let *myself* make *me* small.'

It was then that Marlie burst into sobs.

I didn't have an answer, or anything to help. I had no idea about any of this. I knew I often felt like I was different, like I didn't always fit in, but this was more than that. This was bigger than anything I'd ever felt. My mind was whirring, trying to think of something to say to reassure her. But I had nothing. So I just put my arm around her and held her. Perhaps that was the best thing to do, anyway.

After a few minutes, the shaking sobs turned into quiet sniffles and, after a few minutes more, the sniffles turned into silence. Still, we sat on her bed. Her head on my shoulder. My arm around her. The silence between us felt . . . nice. Safe. I liked it. I liked her. I really liked her.

'Andy?'

'Yeah?'

'What I'm about to tell you, I haven't told anyone outside my family before. But, I want to tell you.'

'Umm, okay . . .'

'It's why I have this limp.'

'Right.'

'It's . . . It's C-P.'

'C-P? What's that?'

'It's what I have, after I was born early. Cerebral palsy. Mine's considered mild, and I have good days and bad days, but it affects the muscles in my legs and is why I limp. I . . . I just wanted you to know.' She looked down at her hands in her lap, and we sat like that for a moment.

I moved my arm from around her shoulder and placed it over her hands. She looked into my eyes then.

'Does it hurt?' I asked.

'Sometimes. Like I said, I have good days and bad days. It mainly affects my leg muscles, but when they start spasming the pain can go all the way up to my hips. And then, ya know, when I have to chase after aliens on bikes . . . it can really bloody hurt.'

'Um . . . can I . . . I mean, is there anything I can do? You know, to help?'

'Not really. Just, please don't tell anyone else. I'm not ashamed, I just want to be able to choose who I share this with and who I don't.'

'I won't tell anyone, Marlie. I promise. Is it okay if . . . um . . . if I ask you how you are, sometimes, with this?'

'That would be nice. It's actually helping me, to talk to you like this, as if it's normal. It is normal for me. But it's not for the others out there. I don't really know how to talk about it. But I'd like to. I'm pretty strong, Andy. I can manage it all myself. I've seen so many therapists who have taught me so much about how to look after myself and how to adapt my movements to help my body, and I have so much fancy exercise gear, thanks to my parents throwing money at it, that helps me to stay strong, and so I'm lucky. As long as I look after myself, I'm fine.'

We sat like that, holding hands, a little longer.

'You know, we were meant to have a date tomorrow,' she said quietly.

'Oh yeah,' I chuckled. 'I kinda forgot about that.'

'Ha! I had, too. You know, some other stuff has come up that might be a bit more important.'

'Ha-ha, you can say that again.'

'Some other stuff has come up that might be a bit more imp–'

'Oh my goodness, you are as bad as my dad.'

'Well,' she looked up at me. Like, really looked at me. I stared into those eyes, magnified by her glasses. This close, I could see the patterns in them, like little green fireworks exploding. My heart didn't just do the weird skip-rope thing, it literally stopped. 'How about, when this is all over, if we survive, then . . . we . . .'

'Go on a date?' I offered in a strained, breathless squeak of a voice.

'Only . . . I mean, only if you want to.'

'I'd . . . well . . . I'd love to, Marlie.'

And with that, Marlie Balooby, the annoying girl from my primary school, the one I wanted nothing to do with, she reached up and she kissed me. Right on the lips.

The fireworks that were in her eyes, they exploded in my brain.

Not much later, I arrived home. My parents were reading books in the lounge room.

'How you going, mate?' asked Dad as I walked through the front door. 'You've spent a lot of time with Marlie this weekend, hey?' he added with a cheeky grin.

'Yeah. It was nice. I mean, she's nice.'

'Glad you don't think she's annoying anymore.'

'Nah, there are MUCH more annoying people than her in my life these days.'

'Yeah, I think she's great, Andy. What a keeper,' Mum chimed in with her over-enthusiasm.

'Mum. We are just friends.'

'And they're only in Year Seven,' Dad added. 'No keepers in Year Seven.'

'I know. I know. But you and I met when we were in Year Seven, love. Now look at us.'

'Muuuummmmmm!' I said, plonking myself down on the beanbag in the lounge room.

'Sorry. Is she doing okay, though? After her frantic call the other night, I mean?'

'Yeah, she's . . . well. She's learning a lot from all she's going through at the moment. I think she's learning how to be herself. You know.'

'Well, you can't get much better than that,' said Mum with a smile.

'Yes you can,' interrupted Dad. 'You can become a master IKEA furniture assembler, thus saving the masses from the migraines caused by such things.'

I shook my head, but chuckled. 'A Swedish furniture sensei, hey?'

'That's the spirit, son,' Dad said with pride. 'Look at you, already telling better dad jokes than me.'

'Well, honey, your jokes did win me over . . . somehow.' Mum smiled at Dad.

'Yeah. They won you a lifetime supply of eye rolls,' I quipped.

'Ha-ha. There you go again,' Dad beamed. 'Like father, like son.'

It had been a while since I'd sat with Mum and Dad like this. This quirky, loving family of mine. I really didn't want to spoil it by telling them that the next day I was going on a highly dangerous, world-saving mission, so I didn't. We just sat around telling bad jokes and laughing at each other. Finally, I gave them each a hug and walked to my bed as though it were just any other night.

THE DAY OF THE HEIST

LET THE HEISTING BEGIN

MONDAY MORNING
6:01AM

On Jamieson Street, around the corner from Bellington High School, sat a small blue buggy car, stationary and somewhat inconspicuous, despite there being six orange-clad CVW building-site workers all squished into its tiny interior – like paprika sardines that had been packed tightly into a blue tin can. I was one of them, the sardines, and I'm sure you can guess the other five.

Denny the receptionist had picked us up from our houses that morning. Four of us squashed into the back together whilst Fleassy had all the room she needed in the front seat. Still, she sat scowling and making the occasional grunting comment about the people in the back seat. But at least she was there. We were all there. The whole team. Granted, Marlie and Fleassy hadn't looked at each other once, nor had Fleassy and Nick. The tension in the team was so thick you could butter a loaf of bread with it and still have enough for seconds. Nevertheless, a team.

'Distinguished guests and stylish visionaries,' Nick began, speaking like an announcer, trying to break some of the tension. 'Our attire for this particular heist is brought to you courtesy of the C-V-W construction company. A fashionable masterpiece showcasing the emblematic C-V-W logo emblazoned upon their iconic orange. Feast your eyes on that electrifying colour, on that comfortable yet sturdy fabric. The blending of utility and style. Durability and comfort. Work and play. Picture yourself striding confidently through your own alien-infested high school on a mission to save the world, adorned in this glamorous extension of your unique self.'

Nick was certainly something when he got going. Even Fleassy cracked a tiny smile before quickly smothering it in another scowl.

'Not funny, Nick,' she groaned.

So, there we all sat on Monday morning, dressed in our less-than-crisp CVW overalls. We knew they would not pass if we came face-to-face with one of the aliens. But they did give us an extra chance of the aliens not noticing we were just kids if they saw us from far away.

The dawn sky was just coming grey as we smudged our faces and attempted to make ourselves look older. Henry had told us that the aliens could see way better in the dark, so we waited until just before sunrise for our infiltration.

We couldn't work out a way to get through the underground tunnel, complete with blast door, and the only other way into Bellington High School was through the big, black iron gates at the front of the school. And the only way to open those gates was with the key that was *always* hanging around Principal Jenkins' neck. Or so we thought.

Our new friend, Denny the receptionist, was able to confirm what I had suspected. A second gate key lived in the key cupboard under his desk in reception, which is what I had glimpsed the other day. If we were going to get all of us inside the school to pull off the heist, we needed to get to that key.

But how do you get a key from inside the very place you are trying to break into? What you need is someone who can go where no one else can go. Someone who can scale walls that are way too high for the rest of us. Someone who can disappear into the shadows.

You guessed it! Jasmine.

Jamieson Street was a jacaranda tree-lined cul-de-sac running down the side of Bellington High. The houses on one side backed onto the looming side-wall of the school, which, to the house owners' annoyance, forever cast a gloom over their backyards. At the very end of these houses was an empty block. It was here that the high school's perimeter wall doubled as the gymnasium wall, and this was to be our way in . . . at least, for Jasmine. There was no way the rest of us could scale such a thing.

Three of us got out of the car and headed down the path into the vacant lot. Jasmine, Denny and me.

'Good luck, Jasmine!' Nick called from the car.

Fleassy scoffed.

Jasmine looked back and gave one of her dorky double-thumbs-up-with-one-eyebrow-raised grins. As she turned from the car, her grin faded into focused concentration. This would not be easy. We walked down the path as the others grumpily sat in the car. They weren't happy. But three people standing in a vacant lot was less noticeable than six. I just hoped that when we got back, Marlie and Nick would still be alive.

'You feeling good about this?' I asked Jasmine as we walked.

'Yep. It'll be fine.' She looked at me seriously for a moment. 'I was born for this, McGee,' she said with a wink.

We moved quickly to the bottom of the wall. The bushes and trees of the spare block gave us cover from prying eyes, just as they had for all the graffiti artists that had tagged this wall over the years.

I lowered the pack on my back and took out the grappling hook. Well, the boat anchor tied to the end of a rope, which mildly passed for a grappling hook. It was from Marlie's parents' boat in their garage. Jasmine wrapped the rope around her body like a sash as I handed her one more rope without an anchor. Two ropes. She'd need them both.

All three of us looked up.

'Geez, it looks a lot higher than the practice wall at Marlie's,' I said, biting my lip.

'Yeah, yeah it does,' Jasmine whispered.

Denny set his drone down on the ground. I took a ball of twine from out of the pack. According to Denny, he was the only one who was allowed to touch his drone, he didn't care if it was the end of the world or not. It was *his*. Fleassy might have threatened him enough that he'd let her, solely out of fear, but definitely not the rest of us. So, Denny leaned down and tied one end of the twine to the leg of the drone. It was the only thing that was light enough *and* strong enough for what we needed to do.

He turned it on. The buzzing sounded like loud bees in the morning air, but we had flown it around yesterday and made sure the aliens couldn't hear the sound from a distance away.

Jasmine and I crowded around the screen that Denny held to see what the camera was showing. Up it flew. Up and up until it rose above the wall and peeked above the roof of the gymnasium. Denny flew it a little higher and we could see the two pairs of alien guards making their rounds, just as they had the day before.

'Wait! Oh no,' said Jasmine. 'Look, it's now three pairs. Not two.'

'Ah crap,' I moaned. She was right. Three evenly spaced pairs walking around the roof of the high school. One of those pairs was getting close. 'Quick, duck the drone back down.'

Denny flew it below the roof line again. 'Will the plan still work?' he asked, looking at Jasmine and me. 'Can we do it?'

'Depends how much time I now have,' said Jasmine. 'I'm no miracle worker.'

'Denny, how much time? Can you figure it out?' I asked.

'Not in my head, computers do all the maths equations for me.'

'Well, I can't, either,' I said. 'But wait, I think I know who can.'

I pulled one of our walkie-talkies out of my pocket.

'Team A to Team M, you there? Over,' I asked, pressing down the button on the walkie-talkie.

'Course we're bloody here, Andy. You only just left us,' barked Fleassy.

'Team F, please don't use my name, and when you finish, say over. Over.'

'Oh for goodness sake. What do you want? You are, like, twenty metres away. You could just come and talk to us.'

'I need to talk to Marlie. Oops. I mean, Team M. Over.'

'Of course you do.'

'Hey, it's me.' Marlie's voice came down the line.

'Right. Thanks. We need your mathematical brain right now,' I told her, and then shared the problem we faced.

'Okay. Well . . .'

I could almost hear her brain kicking into gear.

'Let me see. If there were two groups yesterday and each group did a loop in ten minutes and we worked out Jasmine had, what, a hundred and twenty seconds of time she wouldn't be seen for? That means she now has less, obviously. Ummm . . . and they're evenly spaced, the three of them, yes? Yes?'

'You're meant to say over. But yes. They are. Over.'

'Okay. So that means instead of halving the roof into

two sections of five minutes for two pairs, we now have three sections of three minutes with thirty-three seconds between the three pairs. So then one-hundred-and-twenty seconds out of three-hundred-and-twenty seconds is about thirty-seven per cent of that time. Which means thirty-seven per cent of three minutes and thirty-three seconds is approximately eighty seconds. So, you should now have eighty seconds instead of one-hundred-and-twenty. Over.'

'Gosh, you're amazing. Over.'

'Um, thanks. Over.'

'Right. Great. Thanks. Ah . . . over and out.' I turned to Jasmine. 'So, what do you think?'

'I don't know. I haven't done it in that time in any of the practices. Nowhere near.'

'Jaz. If anyone can do this, it's you. Trust yourself. For this part, we have no other plans, it's our only way in and so it's gotta work.'

'Okay. I'll make it work.'

'All right. Let's do this, Denny.'

Denny looked at his controller screen and manoeuvered the little drone high up on the wall, right up to the edge of the roof, one more time. There was a row of windows up there just beneath the roof line, with thick frosted glass covered by vertical metal bars on the outside. From our reconnaissance with the drone the day before, we knew the small drone fitted perfectly between the bars and the glass. So, Denny, with the kind of finger-and-thumb dexterity that only comes through countless years of computer gaming, was able to fly that drone through the small gap and back out again, looping the twine around the bars. It was really quite impressive. There must have been less than half a centimetre either side of the drone blades to spare. But he did it. Back down the drone came, the twine spooling out behind it.

Once we had the end of the twine back in our hands, we tied a slightly larger rope to the end and pulled. Up the thicker rope went, around the bar and back down to us. We then tied a climbing rope to that one and did the same thing. We pulled down on the other end, and the climbing rope went flying up, up, up . . . until it got jammed, right in the gap at the metal bar. I pulled at the end. Nothing. I tried again. Nothing.

'Denny, can you look with the drone? What's stopping it?'

Denny set the drone off again and flew it back up to the barred window.

'Nothing I can see. Oh, it's just caught a little bit. You should just be able to pull it.'

'Well, I can't, it's stuck on something.'

'Oh, yes. Yep. Now I see. It's a little nail or screw or something. Ah. It does look like it's really jammed on it.'

'Damn.'

Our heist was not going well so far. If we had little snags like this all the time, we were never going to make it inside and down into the basement. I was getting agitated.

'Far out. This is ridiculous.'

Yank.

The rope was wrenched from my hand. I turned in shock to see Fleassy tugging on it with all her might.

'Fleassy! Don't! It might snap!'

But suddenly it was free. The nail gave. The rope pulled free. Down it came.

'Bloody McGee, sometimes you just gotta give it some muscle,' Fleassy said with a grin.

'You're meant to be in the car.'

'Well, aren't you glad I'm not? Or you drongos would still be looking up at the rope trying to work out what to do.'

She was right. But it was still annoying.

'Besides, I want to make sure of something.'

'Make sure of what?'

'We couldn't stop her,' interrupted Nick, running down the path.

'So you decided you'd just come, too, did you?'

'They wouldn't listen to me!' Marlie said, coming along behind them.

I shook my head. 'You guys are unbelievable.'

'Ah, get over it, McGee,' Fleassy sneered.

'Fine. All right, Jasmine,' I turned back toward her. She wasn't there. She was already scaling the wall. 'My goodness. She's –'

'A ruddy lizard!' Fleassy said in shock.

'Unbelievable,' said Nick, gaping at Jasmine.

Fleassy's jaw twitched.

'Jasmine, you ripper,' said Marlie.

'More than impressive,' said Denny.

'Be quiet, Denny, no one asked you,' barked Fleassy.

Jasmine had told us earlier in the week that she'd been

doing gymnastics since she was, like, three. A gymnast extraordinaire is what she was now. Twenty seconds later and she'd made it to the metal barred windows above. She fumbled with something in her pocket. Our walkie-talkie squawked.

'All right. I'm up. Over.'

'Quick, Denny,' I urged. 'Get the drone up higher so we can let her know when to go for it.'

'All right, Team J,' I spoke into the walkie-talkie. 'Team D is just flying the drone up. Wait for our signal. Remember. Eighty seconds. That's all you've got. Then we will see you at the main gate. Over.'

'Got it. Over.'

Denny looked intently at his controller. We all looked intently at Denny.

'Well, Denny?' asked Fleassy impatiently.

'Wait. Just wait. Here . . . they're about to pass . . . and three . . . two . . . one . . . NOW!'

'Go! Go! Go!' I said into the walkie-talkie, and at the same time pressed the stopwatch on my wristwatch. We stared in awe as Jasmine used her leverage from the metal-barred window to swing herself up and over the gutter, and onto the roof. She disappeared from view. The five of us crowded around Denny's controller screen as he took the drone high up over the roof. We could see the three pairs of alien-infected human guards walking around. And we could see what looked like a blur streaking across the rooftop.

'Look at her go,' cheered on Nick.

'Come on, Jasmine,' joined in Marlie.

‘She better darn well do it,’ said Fleassy.

‘Fleassy, maybe some encouragement,’ Marlie said.

‘Encourage who? She can’t hear me.’

‘That’s twenty seconds,’ I said, looking down at my watch. ‘She’s already at the gutter in the roof, she’s flying. Go. Go. Go.’

The gymnasium roof gently sloped upward from both sides, meeting at a central ridge, where it vertically dropped down about a metre. This drop formed a long, horizontal drainage gutter that ran the entire length of the roof. The trough ensured water was channelled along it, and also made a fantastic hidden pathway for Jasmine to crouch and run down.

On Friday, during PE in the gym, in Dante’s Dungeon, we’d noticed the smallest chink in the armour of Bellington High School’s defences. A fault in the impenetrable prison. A piece of plywood.

‘She’s at the window. Ducked behind it. She’s getting the screwdriver out now. Come on, Jasmine.’ I kept commentating, to the annoyance of the others.

The sides of the wide roof gutter were all thickly frosted windows, just like the outer wall windows but with no metal bars, and someone in the past must have smashed one of the windows because in its place was a piece of plywood, kept in position with four screws. Screws that were now being screwed out with a mini-drill from Marlie’s house.

‘That’s two screws done. Two more. Come on.’

‘Enough, we can see it ourselves, McGee. You don’t have to give us a blow-by-blow,’ quipped Fleassy.

'Sorry. I can't help it . . . that's three. Come on. Forty seconds left. Halfway. Another screw done.'

Fleassy shook her head at me as we all watched on. Jasmine slid the wood to the side, about halfway along the window, which was just enough space for her to climb through.

'Thirty seconds.'

'It's okay, it's six thirty-five a.m.,' said Fleassy, pointing at the time in the top corner of the screen.

'What's that got to do with anything?' I asked.

'You'll see.'

Jasmine unhooked the anchor and spool of rope that was wrapped around her, and jammed the hook onto a metal pole that ran below the window.

'Twenty seconds.'

'She's not going to make it,' Denny said.

'She will,' Nick argued.

'She must,' said Marlie.

'Just watch, I planned for this,' said Fleassy with her annoying smugness. 'Even with the change in guard patrols, it'll work perfectly. It'll be just in time.'

We watched the tiny screen as Jasmine checked inside the gymnasium and threw down the rope.

'Ten seconds,' I said.

'Ah, I can't look,' said Nick.

'YES! Six thirty-six exactly,' said Fleassy in triumph.

Jasmine crouched for a moment more.

'No. Don't stop,' gasped Marlie.

'Five seconds,' I counted. 'They're about to –'

In that moment, two important things happened

at the same time. The first was that Jasmine leapt through the window and into darkness just as two alien guards walked around the corner on the gymnasium roof, looking straight down the gutter as she leapt. They would have seen her. They should have seen her. Except for the other thing that happened. For, at that exact moment, at precisely 6:36am, the early morning sun rose above the horizon line of the roof and the first rays of the day pierced straight down the large drainage gutter Jasmine was in, striking the alien guards when they turned that corner. They both shielded their eyes which, luckily for them, were protected by their dark sunglasses so their brains didn't implode, but they certainly couldn't see.

We watched on the drone screen as Jasmine's hand reached back outside from where she must have been perched on the grappling rope inside. She pulled the piece of plywood back over the gap right as the alien guards on the roof recovered and let down their hands. They were now looking straight down the gutter, and it looked just as it always had.

We all breathed out.

'Told you I'd planned it,' boasted Fleassy.

'You did not plan that sunrise. No way. What are you talking about?'

'Yes way, McGee. Six thirty-six precisely.' She held up her hand, and I blinked in disbelief. There, scribbled in ink, was 636. She had written it on the back of her hand the night before.

'What? You think I wouldn't take into account the time and angle the sun was going to rise over the school building this morning just in case we needed some extra rays? I know what I'm doing, McGee.'

'Genius! You are a genius. But you didn't think to tell us about this part of the plan?' I asked.

'Gotta keep us all on our toes a little,' she said with a smile. Her first smile of the day.

'That was . . . that was amazing, Fleassy,' Marlie said, staring at Fleassy.

'Yeah, Jasmine was incredible,' said Nick, still looking down at the screen, not hearing what we had been saying to Fleassy.

Fleassy huffed at Nick and walked back up the path, the rest of us staring after her. She truly was infuriating and yet, so very brilliant.

'Come on,' she called back. 'The aliens aren't going to wait for a bunch of dweezle-faced dung-rats to get their brains together.'

MALTESERS AND MARS BARS

6:50AM

Once Jasmine was in the school, her job was to make her way to the reception area, retrieve the key to the massive front gates and then open them to let the rest of us inside. The rest of us, who were now impatiently waiting in the bus stop out the front of the school. Nick was pacing, worried about Jasmine. Fleassy was pacing behind him, perhaps just to annoy Nick.

Cool-boy Nick seemed to have lost some of his smooth edge when it came to Jasmine. And the closer they'd gotten during the week, the more snarky Fleassy had become.

'Something must have happened,' Nick said.

'Lizard Girl will be fine,' snapped Fleassy.

The walkie-talkie crackled in my hand. We all stared, but it didn't make another sound. Just some static.

'Andy . . .' Marlie whispered beside me. 'What if we're too late?'

I looked down and took her hand in mine. 'We won't be. We can't be.'

'But, what if it's too late for Henry already? Even if we get the rest of the chocolate?'

'I think –' I began, not knowing how to answer.

'DENNY! Would you stop it with that whistle?!' Fleassy demanded, cutting me off.

'What whistle?'

'Every time you breathe you whistle through your teeth.'

'I do not.'

'Oh, you really do. It's like a teapot attempting an opera. I'm gonna punch those teeth out in a second.'

'Fleassy, I am not one of your little friends here. I'm almost a teacher at the school. You need to show me some respect. I'm your elder.'

'Oh for goodness sake, you are nothing but a –'

Another crackle on the radio. This time followed by a word. Just one word.

'Maltesers.'

We had argued for quite some time about what words to use for the start of each stage of the mission when we had to communicate over the walkie-talkies. We decided to use chocolate names. So phase two was to begin with the word *Maltesers*. We were on.

'Go, Denny,' I said.

Denny immediately sent the drone up into the air again, a photo stuck onto its front. We watched it fly up, then we put our packs on our backs and walked quickly toward the front gate, all the while trying to look like we were workers who were meant to be there. The five of us came to where the wall that surrounded the school led into the front gates. We gathered at the wall and I peeked around the corner at the gates. We knew that as soon as we walked around it, a camera pointing directly at the front gate from inside the school would pick us up in its sight. But we'd planned for this.

The drone soared high into the air. Denny flew it down right on top of the camera and hovered for a moment, in the same place we had taken a picture with the drone the day before. The photo that was now stuck to the front of the drone.

'Good to go,' he said, looking at me. They were all looking at me, waiting for me to give the go ahead. Even Fleassy. Whether I wanted it or not, I was indeed leading this team. I am not sure quite how or when it happened, but I was. This was the first time in my life that I had ever considered I might be the kind of person that others could trust enough to follow. Such a strange thought. Now, I just had to not get them all killed.

'All right, Jasmine should be in position,' I said. 'Let's go.'

With that, Denny piloted the drone in one fast soaring movement down in front of the security camera. There was a risk in this, that the movement would be seen through the camera and investigated. But, it was the best chance we had. The drone now hovering there, with the static scene blocking the camera's view of what was actually happening, meant they would not see us.

The camera would just show the image of the empty walkway with closed iron gates.

I pressed the walkie-talkie button once. It was the signal for Jasmine. A shot of static came through from the other end telling us the coast was clear.

'Go. Go. Go,' I whispered. 'Oh, wait. Sunglasses on, everyone. We must look the part in case they see us.'

We quickly slipped on our sunglasses before moving down the entryway into the school. The great gates were before us. Impassable. Unless you had a key.

And there was Jasmine with the key. She came forward from the other side of the gate. I glanced up to check on the drone, which was hovering exactly where it should be, blocking the view of what we were doing. Jasmine put the large key into the lock. I held my breath. The key turned. Clunk. The impenetrable gates of Bellington High were unlocked. We pushed them open, just enough for us all to squeeze through, then turned around and pulled them shut again.

We were in.

When we were safely out of the camera's view, Denny piloted the drone straight up out of the shot of the camera and over to where we now were.

The five of us quietly followed Jasmine back to where she had been hiding – a cleaner's cupboard in a little alcove near the entrance of the school.

'Get your elbow out of my gut, would you, Denny?' Fleassy spat as we squashed into the small room. Thankfully, Denny didn't argue and plastered himself back against the wall.

'That's phase two complete,' I whispered. 'Everything went okay, Jaz?'

'Yep. All good. It just took me a little longer to plot out the route to avoid all the cameras. They've certainly put up more of them. But I did everything we'd planned. I cut a gap through the construction fence around the admin block with Fleassy's wire-cutters, and then got to the reception area. I unlocked the window of sick bay, ducked out into the hall, threw a rock into the sick-bay room to distract the guards. When they went to investigate, I jumped the desk, opened the key cupboard, grabbed the key and was out of there.'

'Bloody brilliant,' Nick said, clapping.

'Without a hitch then?' I asked.

'Without a hitch.'

'Phew,' said Nick with a smile. 'Good stuff.'

'Fawning dipstick,' said Fleassy with a frown.

'Okay. You need to get going,' said Marlie.

'You know what to do for phase three then, everyone. Mars bar phase. Let's take care of those security cameras.'

Jasmine, followed by Denny and myself, took off out of the cupboard whilst Nick, Marlie and Fleassy remained there, waiting until they heard from us.

We made our way down the side of A-block through the quadrangle, heading back to main reception where Jasmine had stolen the key from. This was where the aliens had set up their security camera screens.

Thirty seconds into our crouching run and we came to the CVW construction fence around A-block. The entrance through the fence had a security camera pointed right at it, so Jasmine had cut another little entrance further along, in the shadows. We slipped through the hole in the fence and scurried down through the courtyard alongside A-block. Ten metres through and Jasmine held up her hand. We halted. Right in front of us, one of the doors into A-block was starting to open. I looked for somewhere to hide. On one side of us was the length of construction fence. On the other side were the cubicle seats of the quadrangle that ran along the wall of A-block, each separated by brick pillars. It was the only place that would shield us from view.

I easily ducked and slid under one of the bench seats. Jasmine did the same in the cubicle next to me. I heard grunting from Denny as he attempted to squeeze his much larger frame under another of the bench seats. All went quiet, and so he must have just fit. The only sound now was that of feet getting closer with murmured talking. Heart pounding, body shaking, I desperately wished I was invisible. All it would take was one glance at the cubicles and we'd be done for.

The voices got closer. Closer. Closer . . .

And then they had passed. They hadn't seen us. I breathed out, gasping, and realised I'd been holding my breath the entire time.

Okay. I willed myself. *Now, Andy. Get up NOW.*

Up I got. And so did Jasmine. Denny, on the other hand, was stuck. Well and truly stuck. It would have been quite hilarious had it not been for the fact that if we got caught we'd be dead. Jasmine grabbed one of his arms. I grabbed a leg. We both heaved as hard as we could. With a scrape and a groan, Denny finally popped out from under the bench seat like the cork of a shaken champagne bottle.

'You both okay?' Jasmine whispered.

Denny nodded, but did not look okay at all. I gave her the two thumbs up with an eyebrow raise and goofy smile that she was famous for. She rolled her eyes.

'Let's go,' I said.

We crouch-ran along the building's wall to the window at the end of the block. The now-unlocked sick-bay window. Jasmine reached up and, without a sound, slid it open before leaping through, sly and nimble as ever.

I climbed in myself. Nowhere near as agile as Jasmine, but I was inside without a sound. Denny, we had known, would not make it through that window without a struggle. We had to take care of the guards first. So, Denny would be our bait on the outside. Whilst Jasmine peeked around the corner, I quietly opened my backpack. There it was. The gun. No, no, not a real gun, not a gun with bullets. This was the tranquilliser gun my mum kept in the lock box out the back of our house for any renegade large animals that she brought home from the zoo. The gun held two vials of a heavy-duty tranquilliser. Two vials. Two guards. We had to get this right.

Jasmine and I pulled the privacy curtain – like those you find in hospitals – around the sick-bay bed and hid there. We looked out the window at Denny and gave him a thumbs up. He responded in the same way and then grabbed a hold of the window as though he were climbing in.

'Here we go,' I whispered. And with that, Jasmine kicked her foot against the metal bed.

Clang. Clang.

We heard shuffling from the other room.

'Who's that? Who is there?' Voices called out, and then two guards charged into the room just as Denny was climbing in. They ran at him to seize him.

I kinda felt bad that Denny was the bait for this part of the heist, but not bad enough that I stopped it from happening. And, thankfully, it worked. The two guards ran over to the window to grab a hold of Denny without even a glance at the curtain Jasmine and I were hiding behind.

This was it, my moment. I pointed the barrel of the gun out from the curtain. I don't know if you've heard the phrase *sweatin' bullets* before, but it feels like an apt description. I was sweatin' those bullets pretty darn profusely. Sure, I had practised a few times with some empty vials over the weekend. But this, I was actually shooting a human. Well, tranquillising them, but still. I pointed the gun with my sweating, slightly shaking hands and squeezed the trigger.

Peuw. Peuw.

Maybe not as satisfying as a bang, but those guards didn't know what hit them. One moment they were running forward, then they would have felt a sting in their backsides, a bite in the buttocks. They turned, only to see a closed curtain and then . . . they were out cold. Slumped on the floor. Knocked out completely. It had worked. Phew.

Jasmine and I came out from our hiding place and hauled Denny in as quickly as we could. We shut the window and drew the blinds.

'How long do you think they'll be out for?' Jasmine asked.

'Well, I asked Mum the other day, just hypothetically, if a human got shot with one of them how long they'd be unconscious for. And she told me, hypothetically, it would be, like, three hours. So, we've not-so-hypothetically got three hours from now to save the world.'

'Easy.'

'Yep. Easy-peasy.'

'All right, Denny. Now it's your turn,' I said, taking out the walkie-talkie. I spoke into it. 'The Mars bars have been eaten. Repeat. Two Mars bars have been eaten. Get prepared for M and Ms. Will advise when it is good to eat the M and Ms. Over.'

M&M's

7:25AM

In the now-empty reception, Denny bee-lined to his computer. He wiggled the mouse and all the screens flashed on, but only to reveal a small box requesting a password.

'Damn it,' said Denny.

'But you know the password, right?' I asked.

'Not through this system. Someone's been messing with it. I'll need to hack into it, but that could take hours.'

'We don't have hours,' I said.

'What about the password?' offered Jasmine.

'Any guesses?' Denny replied.

'Ummm . . . Try . . . ah . . . Bellington High?' I suggested.

Click. Click. Click.

'Nah. Didn't work.'

'Chocolate?' said Jasmine. 'Try chocolate.'

'Nope. Not it.'

'Darn, how are we ever going to –'

Kssshhhhhhh.

There was a squawk of static coming from what was obviously a two-way radio system on the desk by the computers.

'This must be the their comms base, too,' I said.

Through the radio came a series of check-ins by the guards around the school. Each followed by a spurt of static.

'Team Athena reporting. Section three clear. Over.'

'Team Heracles reporting. Section two clear. Over.'

'Team Apollo reporting. Roof is all clear. Over.'

'Team Persephone reporting. Lower levels all clear. Over.'

Next came check-ins from Team Artemis, Team Hades, Team Hephaestus, Team Ares, Team Dionysis, Team Chronos and, finally, Team Aphrodite. We looked up at one another. All of us wondering the same thing . . . did we need to respond?

'It's okay,' I began to say. 'Maybe we don't need to –'

'One more team to report in,' came the voice over the radio.

'Crap. Crap. Crap. That must be us,' said Denny.

'But what do we say?' asked Jasmine.

'Well, each team was a Greek god, right?' I posited.

'As far as I could tell, yes,' said Jasmine.

'I have no idea,' said Denny.

'Okay. So Apollo was the god of the sun. Hence the team on the roof,' I said, looking for the logic to figure this riddle out.

'And Persephone . . . I know that one,' said Jasmine

excitedly. 'The god of the underworld. So the aliens underground.'

'So who would this team be then? The main security base. Was there a god of security?' asked Denny.

'Ah, I don't know,' I said.

'TEAM ZEUS CHECKING IN ON THE TEAM STILL TO REPORT IN . . . ARE YOU THERE? SECURITY AND COMMUNICATIONS TEAM?'

'That's Jenkins. Okay. Team . . . Wait! I think, maybe . . . let's try . . .' I reached down to the microphone.

'Are you sure?' Jasmine asked.

'Nope.' I pressed the button and tried to speak with a deeper voice than normal. 'Yep. We are here. Team . . . Hermes reporting. All clear here.'

There was a pause. My heart was officially stuck in my throat like a gobstopper that I was choking on.

'THANKS, HERMES. ALL TEAMS CLEAR. NINETY MINUTES UNTIL NEXT REPORT AND CHANGE OF GUARD. OVER.'

'YES!' Denny whisper-cheered. 'You did it!'

'But how did you know which Greek god to say?' Jasmine asked.

'Hermes – god of communication. The messenger. The herald. You can thank Mrs McGuire's history class for that one. If this is the comms centre where all the communications run through, then I just guessed . . . Hermes.'

'Fantastic, Andy!' Jasmine beamed.

'Nah, lucky more like it. But did you hear Jenkins? Ninety minutes. We gotta get this heist done in that time now, otherwise they will know. Our not-so-hypothetical three hours just became ninety minutes.'

'And we don't even know the password to the computers yet,' added Denny.

'Actually, I think we might,' said Jasmine. 'Try H-E-R-M-E-S.'

Denny typed it in. The computer whirred to life and all the screens came on. We grinned.

It didn't take long for Denny to find what we needed from there. On the screens, he pulled up the view from every single camera. Aside from the camera at the school gate, there were at least ten more cameras set up throughout the school that covered the entrances from every angle into the admin building, the science block and around the bell tower. We could see the guards constantly patrolling the areas around the bell tower, in particular. For a moment, I thought I saw Henry Balooby walk past a camera, but I couldn't be sure it was him.

There was one camera that was located inside an office, and closer inspection showed it to be in the principal's office next door to us. Thankfully, the camera showed it to be empty. And then there were a number of cameras in the underground tunnels themselves. We could see patrols moving back and forth within them. I recognised the tunnel we had been in the other day – it now had at least six guards wandering up and down it, and the science storeroom area seemed to have just as many. It looked like the tunnels inside the bell tower, though, only had two.

According to Henry Balooby when he was in his lucid state, the bell tower was our best way to get down to the underground level, and it certainly looked that way from the cameras we had now commandeered.

'That is a lot of cameras. You did so well to not be seen this morning,' I told Jasmine.

'Ah, thanks. Just took a bit of sneaky sneaking, is all.'

'Well, with Denny at the helm, it shouldn't matter now whether we're captured on camera. So, let's eat some M and Ms, Denny. Metaphorically, of course.'

We knew we had to implement phase four quickly, to deal with the guards on ground level before we were discovered.

I spoke into our walkie-talkie. 'It's time to eat M and Ms. We will let you know if we see any while you set up. Get to the gym. Over.'

We watched the screens. Now that phase three was done, the others could walk through the school and not worry about the cameras, but they still had to avoid the patrols. And that's what we needed to deal with now. Neutralise the guards wandering through the quadrangles. We couldn't get into the bell tower unless they were dealt with.

'There they are. Look!' Jasmine pointed at a screen where Fleassy, Nick and Marlie scampered through a quadrangle toward the gymnasium. But then, out of the corner of my eye, on another screen, I clocked three alien humans in sunglasses fast approaching them.

I quickly spoke into the walkie-talkie, 'Turn around. Back where you came from. M and Ms approaching. I repeat. M and Ms approaching. Turn back. Over.'

The three of them turned and ran back to where they had just come from.

'It's going to be too late,' cried Jasmine. 'They'll be seen.'

Jaz was right. The guards were walking much quicker than I had realised. They would turn around the corner in a moment and the others would still be in the quadrangle in plain sight. I pressed the button on the walkie-talkie.

'Stop. Don't run. Walk. Just walk. They will see you. But from behind. You need to pretend you're meant to be there. Over.'

Fleassy, Marlie and Nick slowed to a walk as the alien guards turned the corner. One of the aliens pointed ahead at our crew as they came to another corner and turned sharply into it. Thankfully, though, the guard patrol turned in a different direction to continue their patrol. The disguises had worked.

'Phew.'

'Okay. You can turn back now. Continue with phase M and Ms,' I spoke into the walkie-talkie.

The three of them slowly turned around and ran as quickly as they could back toward the gymnasium. Fleassy was obviously annoyed at both of the others about something. Nick made some kind of annoyed 'go away' gesture. Fleassy raised her middle finger.

'Oh boy,' I whispered, shaking my head.

'Okay. They're there. They're in the gym.' Now that they were in the gym, we wouldn't be able to see them. It would be a few minutes of going blind before finding out if our plan had worked.

'We wait for their signal and then we make the announcement,' I reminded the others.

'Gosh, I hope this works,' Jasmine said.

'It should, we just gotta short-circuit their little alien brains.'

We waited in silence. Two minutes. Three. I looked at my watch.

'Come on.'

Thirty more seconds.

'If they –'

Squawk came the static on our walkie-talkie.

'The package has been delivered. We are in position. Over,' said Marlie.

'Okay. They're in the change rooms. Let's do this,' I said.

'Put on the same voice you did before,' Jasmine said quickly.

'Right. Good idea.'

I leaned down, held my breath for a moment, pressed the microphone button and spoke. 'Team Hermes here. All teams above ground, report to the gymnasium. Possible disturbance. Repeat, *all* ground teams, report to the gymnasium.'

'Check, Hermes. Heading there now. Over,' came the response through the radio.

But then Principal Jenkins' voice boomed out from the system. 'TEAM ASCLEPIUS! YOU STAY PUT. AND YOU, TOO, TEAM CHRONOS AND TEAM APOLLO AND HERMES. EVERYONE ELSE, CHECK IT OUT. OVER.'

'Check that, Team Zeus. Staying put. Over.' Three teams responded the same way.

'What teams are those?' asked Denny.

It was a good question. I desperately thought back to history class, trying to figure it out.

'Um, so Apollo is the roof patrols. And Chronos was the Greek god of time, so that must be the bell-tower team. And Asclepius . . . I guess, maybe the science lab entrance? He or she was god of science or something?' I answered.

'Okay. So, if the bell-tower patrol is staying where they are, we will have to go with plan B for phase five,' Jasmine said.

'Yep. Sorry, Jasmine, that's not a fun one.'

'I'll be fine. I've got my clothes peg.'

Through the screens we could see patrols from all over the school descend on the gymnasium. This was it. One of the biggest risks of the whole heist. A plan we had tossed out and then come back to as the best way for this to work. We were going to take out all the guards in one strike. Well, as many of them as we could.

'I count twenty,' said Jasmine. 'That is A LOT!'

'Twenty M and Ms en route. Over,' I said into the walkie-talkie.

'Flopsticks. Over,' was all Nick said back.

'Flopsticks indeed. Over.'

'I hope they don't crack the change-room door open too much to look in!' I spoke anxiously to the others, all three of us now on office chairs staring at the screen that showed the last of the aliens walking into the gymnasium.

I couldn't see them but I could imagine the others as they peeped through the change-room doors into the gym and watched as twenty different human-aliens came into the hall to see the bag that Nick had carefully placed at the centre of the court. The room would still be dark enough for what we wanted, being that it was still early morning and the lights in the gymnasium took about five minutes to warm up if the aliens turned them on.

'Come on,' I said out loud. 'Come on!' I hated waiting. It's far more stressful than when you are in control yourself. My fingers were drumming the desk as, in my mind, I could see the tiny cord coming out of the bottom of Nick's bag. It would lead straight under the strip of blue painters' tape we had also brought along. The tape that would run all the way along the blue line of the basketball court, indistinguishable in the dark of the room. The cord it was hiding running to the button in Nick's hand behind the change-room door.

If all was going to plan, the aliens would be gathering around the bag now. A noise drawing them in. The noise was a toy dog we had borrowed from Jasmine's little sister, which, when switched on, yapped and moved its legs.

There was static from the aliens' radio on the desk. Jasmine, Denny and I startled on the edges of our seats, even though we'd been waiting for this.

'Teams all here,' spoke one of the aliens. 'We have found a bag on the floor of the gym, which seems to have a small dog inside it. We can hear it barking, and there is movement in the bag. Over.'

I quickly pressed the microphone button and spoke in the voice I'd used before. 'All teams in the gymnasium, approach the bag. I repeat. All eyes on that bag, don't let that dog or whatever it is slip past you. Over.'

'Copy, Hermes. All teams moving toward the bag. Over.'

I locked eyes with Jasmine. She looked as stressed as I'm sure I did. We waited, and we waited some more. Talk about a tense few moments. It was like waiting for the toast to pop, but with a side of existential, extra-terrestrial dread. (Try to say that three times.)

Then it happened. On the screen, we saw the sudden blaze of white coming out of one of the entrance doors. The whole gymnasium was ablaze with the whitest of white lights from the massive jar of magnesium that was in the doggy bag.

Turns out Nick had been 'borrowing' a whole lot more magnesium from the science labs than just the little bit I saw him pocket a week ago. A whole jar of it, in fact. And it had been set off by the spark from the igniter in his hand, which came from Fleassy's old gas hot-water system. This was another of her genius ideas, to use the igniter, which she had taken to use for some other mischievous thing, to spark the magnesium's reaction. All we needed was the extender cord to go between the two, which was easily purchased from the hardware store for just a few dollars. And it worked. It had worked during our tests. And now . . . now it had worked for real.

The blazing white finally ended after about a minute. We just had to hope it had been bright enough to short-circuit the brains of all the aliens in the gymnasium. Henry Balooby had told us the other day that really bright light would knock them out for hours. We hoped it was true.

Kssshhhh.

'That's it!' Fleassy's voice came from our walkie-talkie. 'It got all the little buggers. Creepy as, but they're all frozen to the spot where they stood.'

We three in the security room high-fived.

'YES! Copy that,' I responded. 'We will pretend to be one of the teams on the alien comms and say it was a false alarm. Good work. Phase M and Ms is complete. It's time for a Snickers.'

SNICKERS

7:40AM

There we were, the five of us kids, in the main quadrangle. We'd left Denny stationed at the security screens with a walkie-talkie. He was our eyes to see around any corner. It was time to infiltrate the belly of the beast through the gullet of the bell tower. Even though we knew that the guards who patrolled around the tower were now frozen in the gymnasium, we still hid behind the construction fence that circled its imposing form – a plain, four-walled brick tower that rose two storeys into the air.

A spiralling staircase ran up the inside of the tower to the large bell that hung there. The school now had an electronic bell, but they'd kept the old bronze one at the top of the bell tower. Principal Jenkins had wanted to keep some of the history in place.

Looking through the fence, we could see the door that led inside to the bottom of the tower's stairs. This was where, according to the blueprint plans on Jenkins' desk the other day, there was a door of some type leading downward to the lower levels of the school. Our way into the underworld.

But first, we needed to get past team Chronos, which consisted of two alien guards just inside that door, who were still there thanks to Jenkins' order that stopped them from going to the gymnasium. And so the only way to succeed was to launch a sneak attack from on top. Which, of course, meant Jasmine. Snickers. Stage five. Plan B.

'I still can't believe Denny is actually allowing you to fly that thing,' Nick said to Fleassy as she set down the drone to start it up.

'It's 'cause he knows he can trust me not to get distracted and break it like SOMEBODY would, Nick.'

'You sure it isn't because you threatened to go to his house and destroy every one of his computers if he didn't let you?'

'Okay. Maybe that, too,' Fleassy replied with a grin.

Fleassy flew the drone up into the air. Maybe not with the same skill as Denny, but she managed it. As it soared high into the sky, the screen showed the roof of the school once more.

'All right, there are those three patrols,' I said. 'Looks like one is up on the roof above us. So we've just gotta wait for it to move on and then we go.'

'You better have remembered that grappling rope, Jasmine,' Fleassy shot at her.

'Of course I did. Don't you think you would have seen it hanging down in the gym if I had left it?'

'I suppose.'

Jasmine took the rope with the anchor grappling hook out of the bag on her back. She was ready. But first, we had to set her up.

'Okay. The aliens above us have moved to the other building,' Fleassy told us. 'We have three minutes. Go.'

We all quietly squeezed through the gate of the construction fence that surrounded the bell tower, making sure to shut it again behind us.

We knew none of us would be strong enough to throw the hook and rope the whole way up the bell tower. And there were no bars up there for the drone string trick again. What we needed was some height. The large, wooden picnic table was exactly where it had been the past few days. Right near the bell tower, within the construction zone. Nick, Fleassy, Jasmine and I attempted to move it while Marlie kept look-out for any alien guards.

'Come on, weaklings,' taunted Fleassy. She was harsh, but it worked. No one wanted to be the weakling that Fleassy was speaking of. So we shuffled along, carrying it closer to the back wall of the bell tower.

'That'll do,' Marlie told us. 'That looks like the right distance for Nick.'

Nick then jumped up, took the rope from Jasmine and grabbed the hook in his hand. He had been practising this over the weekend. Nick was by far the strongest of us, and so this was his job, to get the anchor up and over the top of the bell tower. From this elevated height on top of the table, we knew he could do it.

'Here we go.'

Nick started swinging the hook around in circles. Once. Twice. Thrice. He sent the makeshift grappling hook up and up . . . but it struck the wall, just short. It fell to the ground with a loud clang.

'Damn!' Nick chastised himself.

We all ran and pressed against the wall, just in case the guards inside had heard and were coming out. Thankfully, there was no sound of the door opening.

'You flipping weakling, Nick. Let me have a go.'

'Shut up, Fleassy. I can do it.'

'All right. Come on, Nick,' I urged. 'We know you can do it.'

'Wait,' Fleassy said, looking at the screen for the drone again. She had left it hovering up there. 'We need to wait. There's another roof patrol on the nearby building that will see us from where they are. Quick, against the fence.'

Two minutes later and the roof patrol had passed, and Nick stood once more on top of the table in the quad below the bell tower. One swing. Another. Another. He grunted like he was an athlete going for a world record and tossed it with all his might. It worked. Though I'm not sure the grunting was the thing that made the difference. But the grappling hook did make it over the outside wall of the bell tower. Now, it just had to hold.

Nick gave the rope a shake to make sure the hook ends were open, and then pulled slowly. It caught. He pulled tighter. It held. Jasmine took the rope from him.

'You good?' I asked Jasmine.

She put her hand into her pocket and pulled out a peg. 'All good now.'

'I don't envy you.'

She gripped the rope, put one foot up on the wall and pulled herself skyward.

'Go, Jaz,' Nick whispered.

Fleassy shot him another dirty.

A moment later, Jasmine was up and over the edge. She pulled the rope up after her so it couldn't be seen hanging down the wall. Now came the stinky part.

I was thankful that it was not me having to do this. It was gross enough having to collect it from Mum's zoo the day before. Startling a skunk is *never* a good move. But it was exactly what we needed. I'd crept into Stinkerbell's enclosure, blanket held in front of me. I snuck right up to her . . . and then gagged when I'd succeeded. Stinkerbell sprayed the blanket. The blanket that went straight inside a bag that was now inside another, that was inside another, that was inside yet another plastic and sealed bag. This stink bomb is what Jasmine had just carried up the bell tower in her backpack, along with the three battery-powered little fans we had purchased for this part of the operation. It shouldn't take more than a minute, and then, *Hey presto.* Or, *Hey stinko,* as the case may be.

I could smell it already from where we four pressed ourselves against the back wall of the bell tower. Jasmine must have worked quickly to open the bags and get the fans cranking. Even from outside the brick building there was suddenly a definite taint in the air. A putridness. I hated to think what it must be like in there. According to Henry, the aliens HATED stink. They could not handle it. So any moment now . . .

BANG!

That didn't take long. The door of the bell tower swung open and the two guards came tumbling out, pushing each other as they fell. The sounds of wretching echoed through the quadrangle.

'Ugh. What the hell . . . *cough* . . . is that?'

'I don't know.'

'It's the most disgusting stink I've ever encountered on this repulsive planet.'

'Ugh. It's still strong out here. It's like it's stuck on me.'

'I'm going to the bathroom to wash it off. Let's not call it in, though. Jenkins would not be happy with us leaving our post. Although it looks like the patrol out here already have.'

'Well, he can come and put up with that stench if he wants to. Ugh!'

We heard the clanging of the building zone fence as the two opened up the gate and scampered away. Stage five of the plan was going smoothly. We basked in the sweet smell of success, or the not-so-sweet smell of Stinkerbell.

As quickly as we could, we all moved around to the front of the building. The door opened again and a peg-nosed Jasmine stuck her face out and beckoned us in. We each took a peg from our pockets and clamped our noses shut with it. I don't know if it made any difference. That little room was like the personal sauna of a family of skunks. Fleassy and Marlie were gagging. Nick was very unsuccessfully trying to hold his breath and ended up splurting out a coughing fit, and I felt like I was about to faint, it was so bad. Jasmine, who had been in there the longest, looked surprisingly okay. She held up a little bottle of eucalyptus oil.

'Try this,' she said with a nasally voice. We rubbed it under our noses. It definitely helped.

'So, where is this door then?' asked Marlie.

'Well, it has to be under us, doesn't it?' I said.

We all looked under our feet for the trapdoor that must be there. There was nothing. Not a mark. Not a scratch in the ground. The staircase came downwards from the levels above and then finished at the concrete floor.

'Hmmmm. Are we sure it's really here?' asked Nick.

'Why would they have guards in here if it wasn't?' asked Marlie.

'Good point.'

'Quick,' I urged. 'We gotta find it before those two get back. Get down on your knees. Look around the walls. Walk up the stairs. Anything.'

'I'm not going any closer to that stench than I have to,' complained Fleassy. 'Not even for the sake of the world. Nothing is worth that.'

Nick and Marlie ran their fingers along the walls. I was on my knees, checking every part of the stone floor. Jasmine checked up and down the stairs. Nothing. But then, as she neared the bottom, there was a definite clunk.

'What was that?' Fleassy asked. We all turned toward Jasmine.

'Just a clunk. But I didn't hear that when I came down before.'

'It was definitely something,' I urged. 'Keep moving, Jasmine.'

The next step down also made a sound, but it was more like a tic. Then the bottom step . . . nothing. Jasmine stepped back onto the third step. It made the same clunk of a sound, like something falling into place. She moved up to the fourth step, and the same tic happened that had sounded on the second step. Jasmine frowned.

'Try the third again,' said Marlie.

Jasmine did so. Clunk.

'Now, skip the fourth and step on the fifth instead.'

'Ummmmm, okay.'

Clunk.

'Oh, that's something,' said Jasmine. 'It made a sound, too. Now where, Marlie?'

I was still on my knees watching all this unfold, wondering what the heck Marlie was getting at. She stared at the steps, her fingers twitching by her side, as if they were restless. She started humming a tune. If I hadn't seen a lot of strange things over the days before, this would seem rather an odd thing to be happening. But right now the rest of just watched, unsure as to what exactly we were watching. Marlie started directing as she hummed.

'Step seven. Now, step five. Leap to step two. Step four. Step six. Step seven. And finally step five. '

CLUNK. CLUNK. CLUNK. KSHHHHHHHH!

'What the . . .?' Nick said in shock. We all took a step back as the bottom two steps of the spiral staircase swung down and opened.

'What the heck was that, Balooby? How did you know?' asked Fleassy.

'It was that weird tune that Principal Jenkins is always humming. Remember the musical note that marked the bell tower on the plans in his office? When I first saw it I just thought it meant, you know, the music of the bell. But, I don't know, when Jasmine started moving on the steps I could just see it. Or hear it. The stairs became a piano in my head, and I could direct Jasmine which notes to step on. I guess I do need to thank my parents for those piano lessons I hated.'

I think my heart might have exploded a little in that moment. This was Marlie at her nerdy best. I loved it. But before I could say anything, Fleassy stepped forward.

'Marlie, that was . . . that was pretty damn genius.'

A compliment like that from Fleassy Davies to Marlie Balooby. It was the equivalent of wrapping someone in a hug and squeezing them. I half expected confetti to drop from the ceiling and a victory song to start. Marlie just smiled.

'Now, let's get the hell out of this stink hole,' said Fleassy. 'It smells as bad as Nick's bedroom.'

There was a ladder going down to the underground through the now-open trapdoor. We each climbed down through the opening, glad to be rid of the stench of the bell tower. A button on the wall shut the trapdoor above us as we made our way into the underworld.

22

THE UNDERWORLD REVISITED

8:05AM

The thing about the underworld of Greek mythology, according to Mrs McGuire, is that should such a thing exist, no one really knows what it's like. People can guess, and many have. That is what the stories are all about. The important thing is not *if* it exists, but *what* it has to teach us. So, as we made our way into the underworld of Bellington High School, I wondered what lesson we would learn down there, and if it would be a hard one to learn.

We'd had detailed information to be able to plan out the stages above ground: Maltesers. Mars bars. M&M's. Snickers. But the next stages were about as detailed as . . .

Phase Oreo: Get to the chocolates.

Phase TimTams: Destroy the chocolates.

Phase Cherry Ripe: Run like hell.

Turns out, Fleassy hates Cherry Ripes. I cannot tell you the arguments that occurred about the naming of that last phase. My goodness. These are the people I have to work with.

Though, perhaps I am being too negative about all the things we did not know, 'cause we did know some things. We had even prepared for some of the things Henry Balooby had mentioned might be down there. But, it still felt like so much was a mystery from here on in.

The tunnel we were in looked very similar to the one we had descended into the other day. Secret government prison decor. Probably not gonna find it on *Grand Designs*. Marlie pulled out the map she'd scribbled down in Jenkins' office, and we set off. We walked down the hall as quietly as we could, just in case there were any patrols coming the other way.

KSSHHHHHHH!

We all jumped. In this stark hall, the static from my walkie-talkie echoed loudly.

'Bugger. Sorry,' I said.

'I see you guys on the screen. You're underground. I can see you. Over.'

'That's great, Denny. Really great. Now, PLEASE don't do that again unless it's something of VITAL importance, like, we're about to walk straight into some aliens. Over.'

'Gotcha. Over.'

'Who invited that guy?' moaned Fleassy.

We cautiously continued down the tunnel. Henry's intel was right – this part of the tunnels seemed pretty much deserted. A labyrinth, but deserted. We turned right. Turned left. Right again. Walked past two corridors leading off down to the left. Two more on the right. Turned into the next one on the left.

'Geez, I hope you know where you are going, Marlie,' quipped Fleassy. But it was with considerably less venom than she had been using all morning. Marlie's efforts in the bell tower had garnered some respect from Fleassy.

'Yes. I do. The map has been right so far. We'll turn to the left here, and then there'll be a room on our right and one on our left. We take the tunnel on our right.'

We turned the corner.

We were facing a wall.

'Oh dear,' said Marlie.

'Flip,' said Jasmine.

'Darn,' said Nick.

'Well, screw everything and everyone.' I am sure you can guess who said that.

'What are we going to do?' I asked.

'Not trust Marlie anymore?' queried Fleassy.

'All right. All right.' I interjected before a fight could start up again. 'Or we could –'

A sniffle echoed in the corridor. A sniffle that quickly turned into a sob. It was Marlie. She was staring at the dead end. Her shoulders were shaking.

'We . . . I . . . it should be here,' she cried. 'We have to save Henry. I messed up. I must have, and now we don't know where to go. Oh, Henry.'

'Marlie, it's okay,' I consoled. 'Don't worry. We've got this far. We can't let a little –'

'It is NOT a little anything!' Marlie's despair was fast turning to anger. Loud anger. We needed her to stop.

'I hate these aliens!' she hissed. 'I hate them! And you know what . . .?' She'd turned to face Fleassy now with a look that could murder. '. . . I hate you, too, Fleassy Davies! How *dare* you make me feel small just because I have a limp.'

I truly thought Marlie might actually deck Fleassy there and then. I'd certainly never seen Fleassy's face quite so shocked as when Marlie gripped her hand into a fist, as if a pounding were about to take place. But rather than pounding Fleassy, she turned and pounded on the dead-end wall in front of her. And instantly disappeared.

It was like finding platform nine-and-three-quarters, yet we were definitely not at London's King's Cross station. I highly doubted that Marlie had just fallen into the wizarding world. That would put a slight complexity into the heist. Unless, of course, Dumbledore walked back through that wall. We could certainly give the aliens a good time if we had a magician as part of our crew. I shook my head to clear the random wizarding-world daydream my brain had immediately escaped to in the fright of the moment, and moved to where Marlie had been standing.

'What the hell just happened?' asked Nick.

'It's okay. It's okay. I'm okay.'

We could hear Marlie but we couldn't see her. Until her head stuck back through the wall. Yes, you read that right. Her head stuck *through* the wall.

'Come and look,' she beckoned, wiping the tears from her eyes.

We walked hesitantly up to the wall, with our hands out before us. And, sure enough, we each passed through to the other side. Next to where Marlie stood was some kind of high-tech projector machine. More high-tech than I had seen before. It was projecting the most realistic and solid-looking image of a wall onto . . . nothing. A projection we had just walked through.

'Ha! Neat trick,' Fleassy said, looking undoubtedly sheepish and definitely avoiding looking at Marlie.

We carried on down the tunnel, past the projector, and found exactly what Marlie had said we would find. A room on our right. Another on the left. We took the tunnel past it on the right, as per Marlie's instructions. I took hold of her hand as we walked behind the others. She looked at me and smiled. A worried smile. But still . . . a smile. Better than angry sobbing.

'Sorry,' she said. 'I just lost it for a bit there.'

'Don't ever apologise for that,' I replied, squeezing her hand.

'Thanks, Andy.'

'Hey, this is what friends do.'

We walked around the corner. Then the next. A turn. An intersection. A hesitation from Jasmine up front. She stopped.

'Wrong way?' I asked.

'No. No. But this hall is wider than the others, and I just thought I felt the temperature change. And now, actually, I can see . . . Look. Just ahead, there are definitely some sensors on the walls there. With yellow lights. But some further on with green. Nobody move.'

'What kind of sensors?' Nick asked.

'Well, they're not sound sensors, or they'd be going off by now,' Marlie answered.

'True. I'm just going to slowly back out again,' Jasmine said, edging backwards toward us.

'Oh, the sensors just went green again.'

'Well, my guess is you don't want them to turn red,' said Nick.

'Ruddy genius you are, mate,' Fleassy sniggered.

'It must be one of the sensor rooms Henry told us about,' said Marlie. 'Audio, motion or temperature.'

'Well, if it's not audio, my guess would be it isn't motion, either,' I offered.

'Yeah, I had taken, like, one step into the hallway when I stopped and then backed out,' Jasmine said. 'So it must be temperature. It triggered some kind of heat change when we came close to the hall, but not enough to set it off. So when I backed out, it went back to green.'

'Sounds like you might be right,' said Marlie. 'What plan did we have for that again?'

I motioned for us to move back down the hall, away from the room, then put my bag on the ground and opened it up.

'Don't worry,' said Fleassy. 'I thought of everything. McGee has the goods in his bag. But remember, it was my idea. If it works, that is. If it doesn't, it was McGee's.'

From the bag I pulled five silver blankets. *Thermal emergency blankets*, their labels said. We'd found them on the Baloobys' boat – for if someone fell into cold water and got hypothermia or something, we figured.

'Everyone, wrap these tightly around yourselves so that your warmth stays inside them,' I said.

'Ah. And, now what?' asked Nick.

'Did you listen to any of the plans, Nick?' Fleassy shot at him.

'There were a lot of them, Fleassy.'

'Get in the game, mate, and stop fawning over Quinn there, would ya?'

'Shut up, Fleassy.'

'Now we use these, Nick,' I said as I tipped my bag and ten little plastic pouches fell out. 'My mum had them in her vet supplies. They are instant freeze pouches. So you squeeze the thing inside and . . .' I squeezed and showed them the pouch as whatever chemical reaction inside turned it instantly freezing.

'Everyone, grab two, and squeeze. Quickly, put them underneath your blanket and then wait a minute to let it get chill under there. Then we cross. One at a time. We need the least temperature-change in the room as possible.'

Two minutes later and Jasmine hesitantly stepped out into the hallway. Her blanket fully cloaked her – she could only just peep out the front where the blanket join was. Honestly, she looked like an upright disco worm shuffling across the hall. But, whatever she looked like, the sensor stayed green. One more step. Green.

'It's working!' I exclaimed.

'Of course it is, McGee,' said Fleassy with an eye roll. 'It was my idea, after all.'

Jasmine was halfway across the room when one of the sensors turned yellow. Another shuffle, then it turned orange. She froze.

'Just keep going,' I urged her. 'Get through, as quickly as you can. It's not motion- or sound-sensitive, so the quicker the better.'

Jasmine ran the rest of the way. She was through, and the sensors went back to green in a moment.

'Okay. Let's all go quickly. One after the other. Come on.'

Fleassy went next. She shuffled as fast as she could inside the foil blanket. Green. Yellow. Orange. But she was through.

Next was Marlie. It didn't even get up to orange for her.

'Cold-blooded,' joked Fleassy with a grin as Marlie reached the other side. Marlie turned away from her but grinned back at us.

Nick stepped into the room now. Two steps forward, and the blanket somehow slipped out of his hands. He reached out and grabbed it as it fell, quickly pulling it back around himself. The sensor instantly turned orange while we all held our breath. My throat tightened. But Nick played it cool and scurried quickly through. He'd made it, although only just.

'Nick Delancey,' was all Fleassy said as she slowly shook her head.

I was last. Green, yellow, orange . . . and we were all through. No sensors triggered. No alarms sounding off.

'Hopefully, that's the last heat sensor thing. 'Cause these are starting to lose their coldness,' said Jasmine.

We stashed the blankets and the ice packs back in my bag and continued down the hall. The team was walking slower than we had previously, conscious of the fact that we were getting closer to the main event and didn't know what might be round a corner, or down another hall. We moved silently, which was lucky because the next hall we came to had a sound sensor.

We knew it was a sound sensor, because it was the exact same brand that had come up on Google search when we looked up 'sound sensors' over the weekend. Jasmine was the first to clock the device on the wall of the tunnel far ahead. The logo of the company, ShhhProtect, was proudly displayed on their sensor system.

The product description said these things could pick up the slightest of sounds. So even from this distance away, Jasmine quickly turned around with her finger to her lips and pointed for us to move backwards. Marlie took charge as we retreated and were almost back at the heat sensor room before we felt it safe to sound out our plan.

Marlie whispered, 'Okay, I go first with this one, as we planned.' She pulled out a recording device. It had been a present from her dad the Christmas before. One of those things that he had bought, she'd thought, more for himself than for her. She walked up to the air vent she must have noticed earlier, and recorded the murmur of the fan while the rest of us took off our shoes and stowed them in our bags.

'Andy, you're going to have to leave that bag of emergency blankets behind,' said Jasmine. 'I can hear them crinkling every time you move. There is no way they're getting through.'

'You sure this thing is going to work, Balooby?' Fleassy asked. Mostly out of concern that this hadn't been her idea.

'Sure as I can be. I make the most noise out of all of us when I walk, so if I get through then the rest of you will be fine.'

A few minutes later, and Marlie took the lead walking down the hall. Slowly. Really slowly. Turtle-pace slowly. Slow to the point that it was agonising to watch. She very, very, very slowly increased the playback volume of the ambient sound of the fan she'd just recorded on her little device, incrementally turning the volume up with each step she took.

The idea was that the background sound of the fan would be constant enough that the incremental volume increase would not affect the sensor. The sensor would then calibrate itself to accept the increased volume of sound from the recording device so that we could move through the space without the sensor sensing us. That was the plan, and it seemed to be working.

Fleassy, Nick, Jasmine and I watched Marlie at work from way down the corridor. She slowly put the audio device on the ground and walked past it. She crossed the room, all the way to the other side, and there were no alarms sounding.

Marlie gave us a thumbs up. Now, it was our turn. One by one, we each made the journey through the room, one slow foot followed by another. Once we were all through, we walked down the rest of the corridor without speaking, leaving the recording device on the floor by the sound sensors, playing on a loop.

We rounded another corner and there was a door at the end, just as Marlie's map had shown. Presumably, it was a soundproof door to stop any noise from beyond getting through to the sound sensor room.

Nick, who was in front of everyone, opened it a crack and peeked through. It was yet another empty corridor. We all filed through. We were getting so close to our goal. Our spirits were lifted. Our confidence was strong. Our heads were inflating.

Until an alien walked around the corner and ran straight into Nick Delancey.

THIS IS IT . . .

8:30AM

It seemed to happen in slow motion. Frankie Dwight, right-hand henchman to The Cleaner turned right-hand alien to Jenkins, now stood staring at Nick, and Nick at him. I was right behind Nick, holding my breath, waiting to see what happened.

'Hi, Frankie,' Nick said, like he was greeting a friend.

'What the hell do you think you're doing, you lot? How did you get down here?' said Frankie as he reached for the walkie-talkie at his belt.

'What are we doing?' said Nick, getting assertive with the alien, hopefully to distract him. 'What the hell are *you* doing?'

Frankie was not prepared for such aggression from Nick. We weren't, either. We really hoped he had a plan.

'I am reporting you to Jenkins. That's what I am doing.'

'I wouldn't do that if I were you.'

'Oh, and why not?'

'Because it's what you always do.'

'What?' The alien Frankie hesitated, his hand on his walkie-talkie.

'What is he doing?' whispered Fleassy from just behind me.

I had no idea.

'Well, it's what Frankie always did. Everything that Henry wanted him to. And it looks like, whoever you are now, you're just as much a suck-up as he was.'

'What are you going on about, kid?'

'Frankie. He was never good enough to be anything but Henry's slave.'

'Yes he was.'

'He was a slave. You know it. He never did anything unless Henry told him to.'

'Ridiculous. What would you know?'

'I know that you are the same. Jenkins gives you orders and you blindly follow them. You're as cowardly and pathetic as Frankie ever was.'

Frankie's face began to contort. 'You dare to insult us. We are more powerful now than ever.'

'Pfft. Some of you are powerful. But you're a mindless lackey, is what you are.'

Frankie's face was turning an off-purple colour, probably the same hue as the alien inside him.

'Pssst. Nick. What the hell are you doing?' Fleassy whispered under her breath.

But I had realised, so I whispered back, 'Shhh . . . trust him. You need to trust him, Fleassy.'

'You're just a little servant, you are. You deserve an award for being the most ignorant slave. For being played by all your masters. You're just a puppet dancing to someone else's tune.' Nick was on a roll now. The alien was starting to shake in anger. Nick had seen a weakness and pounced. And it was working.

'I am NOT!'

'Do you ever have an original thought, you parrot?'

Frankie lifted his fists toward Nick. Shaking fists. Raging fists.

'You make a robot look like it's a rebel. You are weak, you hear me? A kitten in a pillow fight.'

Frankie's fists were high and about to come flying toward Nick. Nick didn't flinch. He kept on going.

'Powerless. You are nothing. NOTHING, YOU HEAR ME? NOTHING!'

The heaving, shaking, sweating, raging alien that was about to smash Nick into a million pieces suddenly stopped. Its brain was fried. Nick had done it. He'd made it so angry it had short-circuited.

Nick turned around to the rest of us, who were standing there with open mouths. 'Easy!' He smiled and gave one of Jasmine's dorky two thumbs up with his eyebrow raised.

'Brilliant,' said Jasmine.

'Amazing work,' said Marlie.

'That was so good,' I added.

'You are a fool, Nick Delancey,' said Fleassy with a scowl. She had been furious with Nick all day. But surely even she could see that what he had just done was good work. I was about to say as such when she added, 'A bloody legend of a fool!' And then she ran at him and flung her arms around his neck in a sudden outburst of affection. I was gob-smacked.

I don't actually know which was better . . . seeing Nick Delancey talk up an alien to boiling point, or seeing Fleassy hug Nick to death. I wondered what Jasmine might be thinking, but she was just standing there with a big smile as she watched these two friends finally hug it out.

I saw Fleassy whisper something to Nick. It may have been, 'Sorry,' or it may have been, 'Dipstick.' But, in response, Nick said clearly, 'It's okay. Push me away all you want, Fleassy. I'll still be your friend.'

There wasn't a dry eye in the corridor. It was . . . you know . . . one of those moments that melts you like a cheese toastie. But, we didn't really have time for nice melty moments right now.

'All right. All right,' I said.

Fleassy let go with an embarrassed smile.

'Let's tie up and gag Frozen Frank there,' I continued, 'and throw him into one of the rooms that comes off this hall. Quick, find one that's unlocked.'

Within a few minutes, we had locked Frankie away, and the five us were now approaching the room that led into the main hall. I held my hand up to the door knob when . . .

KSSSHHHHH!

Static from the walkie-talkie again.

'Hey, guys,' came Denny's voice.

'What happened to our warning, Denny?' Fleassy said as she grabbed the walkie-talkie off me and spoke into it. 'We just ran straight into an alien.'

'Ah, I may have been, um . . . slightly sleeping.'

'We would have hired my grandma if we wanted a guard who takes naps, you –'

'Shut up, Fleassy. I'm trying to tell you something.'

Fleassy's eyes widened and she gritted her teeth at being told off by Denny. But he continued.

'About fifty more aliens have just turned up. They are coming into the school now. I gotta . . . I gotta get outta here. You guys are on your own. Over.'

'Don't you dare leave, you jerk,' Fleassy spoke harshly back to him through the walkie-talkie.

'I'm not getting taken over by an alien, Fleassy. NO WAY! I'm gonna short-circuit these computers and then I'm gone. I reckon you have about fifteen minutes to do what you've got to do down there. Oh, and by the way, there's a camera in the room beyond that door. It looks like a meal area. But there are no aliens in there at the moment. So I'd go now if I were you. I'm out. I mean, over. I mean, over and out.'

'You get back here, Denny!' Fleassy demanded.

There was no answer.

'That chicken deserves to be plucked and cooked, abandoning his post like that,' said Fleassy angrily.

Denny was going. The aliens were coming. We had fifteen minutes. Time was short. Shorter than we'd planned for. This was not looking good.

'Come on. Don't worry about him,' I urged. 'This is it. We gotta get in there and do this.'

Without another thought, I pushed open the door and we all entered. Denny had been right; the room was empty. We were in a meal area. There was a kitchen, a few tables, not much else. We quickly made our way through to an opening, which put us above one of the main large rooms from the floorplan. We were on a platform with steps leading down to a warehouse space that was filled with chocolate. The heart of Willy Wonka's. We had reached our goal.

Crouching down, we all peeked over the edge of the platform. There were big vats of liquid chocolate down one wall, scientific equipment along another. Machinery was scattered all over the place, and boxes and boxes of chocolate were stacked everywhere. Most of the space, though, was taken up with a huge semi-trailer, the same truck we had seen reversing into the mechanics' the other day. It was facing the large blast doors, and pallets of chocolate were being loaded onto it by human/alien hosts.

'I count twenty alien people,' Marlie said. The activity of the room below was so loud, she didn't need to whisper. 'But I can't see Henry.'

'And one . . . gulp . . . actual alien-thing,' Nick said, pointing over to the right as the same large, purple, jelly-like alien creature we had seen the other day entered the room. All of us gasped. It was not easier seeing this thing for a second time.

'We need to get down there unseen,' urged Fleassy, the first of us to recover from the shock. 'Do we go with a little distraction?'

'Or, perhaps, it's time for the BIG distraction?' I put to her.

She raised one eyebrow.

I motioned to the others, and we all fell back into the meal room behind us. We crouched in a circle together. 'I say this is it,' I told the others. 'We gotta do this now, or never. It's time for phase TimTam and then Cherry Ripe.'

'But –' Fleassy started.

'Yes, it is still called Cherry Ripe, Fleassy.'

Fleassy closed her mouth. A miracle in and of itself.

'So, here is what I am thinking,' I continued. 'We are at stage seven. So let's go with plan C.'

Nick put up his hand.

'The massive explosion and distraction option, Nick.'

Nick put down his hand.

I pointed out to the roof of the warehouse room beyond. 'Look, Fleassy, there are ventilation shafts with fans on the roof, so once you've poured the stuff from the drone, fly it straight up into that exhaust fan above the vats. Distraction enough?'

'Should be,' she agreed as she pulled the drone out of her bag and used our instant-drying superglue to stick a test tube onto its front. 'Plus, I get to destroy something of Denny's to save the world. I am ALL IN!'

'Of course you are,' I laughed, and pulled out of my bag a big bottle of a certain volatile mixture called Boom-shaka-laka. Nick and Jasmine took out two super-soaker water guns from Nick's bag, and we carefully filled both of them as well as the test tube that was now stuck tightly to the drone.

'So, as soon as the drone hits the fan,' I continued, 'we all go down the stairs throwing the bombs. And remember your roles. Nick is on truck duty. Fleassy, you are on all the extra boxes in this room. We must destroy *all* the chocolate. Jasmine, you are on the vats and the boxes in the other main room we saw the other day. It is through the door on the left. Marlie and I will go through the door on the right into the centre chamber room, where Henry said the Nexus thing is. There, we'll destroy the chocolate DNA-splicing recipe formula. And, if there's tech stuff, it's going to be up to you to figure it out, Marlie.'

Marlie breathed out. She looked like she was trying to summon her strength in the face of her own self-doubt.

'You got this, Marlie,' Fleassy said, looking Marlie straight in the eyes.

'I do,' Marlie nodded.

Regretfully, I had to cut into the moment between them. Time was ticking. 'Right then. We'll meet back at the truck in ten minutes. That's all the time we have. Got it? Everyone got it?'

They all nodded with mixed looks of fear and determination. I was thankful for the looks of resilience, 'cause inside I was freaking. I had no idea what was inside that chamber room, or how we would figure out what to do, or how long that would take. But I needed to trust in Marlie's brains and ingenuity, and in my . . . whatever I had.

'And, Nick. If anyone is not on that truck within ten minutes,' I continued, 'you know what you have to do.'

'I . . . It's just –' Nick looked at Jasmine.

'Even if it's Jasmine, Nick,' Fleassy added. 'You gotta leave 'em behind. You get that chocolate out and destroy it as we planned,' she told him. 'This is more important than any of us.'

'Yep. Okay,' he responded, as solemn as I'd ever seen him.

We all looked at each other. The team. The greatest heist squad in the history of the entire world. We each nodded, knowing it was time to split up. Knowing there was a good chance we would never see each other again if it all went wrong. Which, let's be honest, was HIGHLY likely. I looked at Nick. I looked at Jasmine. At Fleassy. And Marlie. Marlie, she was looking at me. Her eyes were full of fear and love. I would not forget those eyes.

Of all people, it was Fleassy then who put her hand in the centre.

'You tell anyone I started this group hurrah and I'll kill you all. Come on. Don't leave me hanging.'

We all grinned. Nick put out his hand first onto Fleassy's. Then it was Jasmine. Marlie. Me.

'All right, slackers,' Fleassy said. 'Lets go kick some alien BUTT! If the aliens actually have butts to kick, that is.'

'Yeah, I don't know if they do,' said Nick.

'Well, they might,' replied Fleassy. 'That big purple thing . . . he looks like a turd, after all.'

'But then –'

'Are you two finished?' I rolled my eyes.

'Yep.'

'Yes, sir, Captain McGee.'

'Good,' I said, shaking my head. 'Let's go save the world. Really quietly, on three. One. Two. Three.'

'Let's go save the world,' we all whispered, and moved our joint hands as one into the air.

It was so very, very naff.

And I loved it.

BOOM-SHAKA-LAKA

8:45AM

'Don't breathe in my ear, Nick,' Fleassy growled. The drone had just risen off the ground and we were all crouched around at the meal room door, looking over her shoulder at it hovering.

'Sorry,' Nick said, but he didn't move. I think he just stopped breathing instead. I don't think any of us were breathing as the drone rose higher and higher. A little wobble.

'Watch it!' I warned. 'Don't lose any of the Boom-shaka-laka.'

'McGee, I will boom-shaka-laka your butt if you don't stop it.'

'Okay. Okay.' I backed away a little. The drone started moving forward, flying over the aliens below. I dearly hoped they wouldn't randomly look up at that exact moment.

A few seconds later and the drone was high above the vats of chocolate. Thankfully, they were very large vats.

Fleassy had to get the drop-point just right. She turned the drone at what was hopefully the correct angle, one straight line over the vats.

'You sure it's right?' I gasped, my mouth now dry.

'I'm sure,' she said, with only a hint of doubt. 'Easy as . . .'

Marlie grabbed my hand.

I grabbed Nick's hand.

Nick grabbed Jasmine's hand.

'. . . THIS!' Fleassy breathed out and, in one swift movement, tilted the front of the drone down and started moving it directly forward. Out tipped the mixture and . . .

KA-BOOM-SHAKA-LAKA!

The room exploded. Well, close enough to it. It was a chocolate explosion of atomic proportions. A sticky tsunami. If you think about the volcano experiment you do at school with baking soda and vinegar then amplify that about a thousand times – I am not exaggerating when I say that, literally, every surface and every person and every alien in that warehouse was now a chocolatey, gooey mess. Including us. It was actually the best disguise we could have hoped for. Chocolate was dripping from my face and hair and hands and everywhere. You couldn't tell who was who.

All this coincided with the exact moment that Fleassy flew the drone vertically straight up into the exhuast fan above. The combined explosion of the drone, and the lava monster of chocolate erupting from the vats was . . . well . . . more than enough of a distraction. It was utter chaos. So we sprang into action.

First, we launched over the edge a number of smoke bombs we had made on the weekend out of Marlie's table-tennis balls. Fleassy's idea, of course. Then we half-ran, half-slid down the chocolate-covered stairs into the chaos. The aliens in the room were all either running scared or staring at the place where the explosion of chocolate and drone had just come from. They didn't see us coming down the stairs at all. And now the whole place was filling with smoke.

'Fire!' I called out. 'Fire!'

We hit the floor as utter pandemonium ensued. Smoke everywhere. Chocolate-dripping human-aliens were slipping and sliding in every direction.

Taking full advantage of the disorder, we bolted our separate ways, all trying to clear the chocolate and smoke out of our eyes. Nick went toward the truck and the big doors that led to the tunnel out of there, hopefully to find keys and a way to open the blast door.

Fleassy moved toward the boxes and crates and pallets of chocolates that had not been put on the truck as yet. Super-soaker in her hands, she looked like Rambo. Dripping chocolate from her face, pumping the gun in her hand, determination in her eyes. The water shooter sprayed Boom-shaka-laka over all the boxes of chocolate, causing them to erupt as the mixture seeped through and reacted with the chocolate inside. Our plan was working. Somehow, it was working. All the chocolate was being destroyed.

Jasmine, with the other super-soaker in hand, sprinted through the door toward the second warehouse room, which I hoped would soon be looking like this one we were running through. Marlie and I needed to get to the chamber room. We ran and stumbled and slid our way through the smoke. We needed to destroy that formula.

The door into the chamber was shut. Of course it was. And there was no doorhandle or button or anything. Just a big slab of metal door. I couldn't see how to open it.

'Maybe it only opens from the inside?' Marlie posited. 'Or from a remote switch or something.'

'So, how do we get in then?'

We looked around.

'There,' Marlie said, pointing at a small panel on the wall nearby. 'That'll be the electrics for the door.'

'Can you –?'

I didn't even have to finish the sentence. Marlie had pulled a tiny screwdriver out of her pocket and was already unscrewing the panel. I looked around nervously. No one seemed to have noticed us. She had the panel off in all of one minute and was now staring at the mass of wires, blinking lights and circuit boards. She looked back at me.

'I'm . . . I'm not sure.'

'Trust yourself, Marlie. Trust your gut. You've always been good at this stuff. We didn't need Denny for our tech person. You're way better. You just have to trust that you are.'

She nodded and looked back at the wires, taking a little pair of wire-cutters from her pocket and fiddling with the circuits in front of her. I don't know if she had the screwdriver and cutters for the heist, or if she just kept them in her pockets at all times. I wouldn't be surprised if it was the latter.

Before I'd even had the chance to start feeling like it was taking too long, the door slid open.

Marlie looked back at me. 'I guess I do trust myself,' she beamed.

I just shook my head in awe.

The chamber was actually more of a cave, made from natural rock and with a soft, orange light illuminating the space. It was really quite beautiful. But we didn't get far into the room before we were busted.

Marlie's hand grabbed hold of mine as we both stopped short in front of the gelatinous purple alien. A grape-flavoured jellyfish; that's kinda what it looked like. We stared at it. It stared back. Well, I guess that is what it was doing. It had a mouth, but no eyes that we could see.

Our shock did not stop there, however. Behind this alien jelly was what looked like a large clamshell, stood up impossibly vertical on its tip. It was black and about the size of a cello, with patterns of glowing blue curved lines pulsating over it. And behind this large clamshell thing was, I kid you not, a UFO.

An actual UFO.

An alien ship, as big as a bus. It kind of looked like the clamshell thing in front of it, with its sleek, curved body and glossy, black material. Etched lines were grooved in arcs and circular patterns all over its surface, almost like ripples. It made it seem, somehow, both organic and mechanical. The ship had rounded, crescent-shaped wings with a similar curving symmetry. It could have been a sculpture in a museum, except for the doorway that gaped open at its front. Out of the doorway spilled a chaotic tangle of vine-like cables that snaked along the ground where they seemed to plug into the clamshell. It was incredible.

However, at that moment, we were a little more transfixed on the very live alien creature quivering like jelly right in front of us. We could see its tentacles stretching out onto the floor. Tentacles that were maybe its arms, as they were holding a packet of chocolate.

'Umm . . . Hi.' I spoke tentatively. 'We, ah, don't want you to . . . take over the world.' I figured that maybe it hadn't realised that humans might be anti such a thing. It might not have thought about the possibility that we didn't want to be hosts to aliens. And maybe, with such knowledge, it might just apologise, pack up and fly off home in its alien ship. Maybe.

It didn't answer. It just inched slightly sideways. We inched the other way. It moved further around. We moved further around. A few seconds more of this circling and I realised the alien was now closer to the cave exit than we were. It must have realised the same, for it bolted to the door. Well, it slid for the door. Fast sliding on its tentacles – I don't know what you call that. It was obviously in a rush because it accidentally dropped the packet of chocolate as it went.

Before we could even blink, it was through the door and one of its tentacles reached absurdly out for, like, three metres and smashed the electronics panel Marlie had played with. The door before us slid shut. We looked around nervously. There was no panel on this side.

'Are we trapped?' I asked.

'It probably wouldn't lock us in here if it thought we could escape,' answered Marlie.

'Probably not.'

'Bugger.'

'I hope the others get out.'

'I hope so, too.'

We looked back toward the alien ship and the large shell.

'Well, let's do what we came here to do, Andy. Even if . . . even if it means we never get out.'

We walked over to the shell. It really was like a giant clam set up on its side. Completely black except for the pulsating curved lines that patterned it. I reached out and touched it and felt an electric charge under my fingers.

'Do you think this clam-floaty-black-thing is the Nexus that Henry told us about?' I asked.

'I guess.'

'And there was nothing when you researched Nexus the other day?'

'Nothing. It does mean "connection" in Latin, but that's all I got.'

'So the plans, the recipe or whatever . . . they are in here somewhere. And this alien vault-type thing is the likely place.'

'It looks vault-ish to me, I suppose. If an alien was to have a vault, then, yeah, this is what it could look like.'

'Right. So if that's the case, how do we open an alien vault?'

'Hmmm. Maybe from inside the alien ship?' Marlie suggested. 'As much as I never thought I would ever say that sentence.'

We walked over to the UFO. It was made from the same black material with curly lines, but these were not pulsating as the shell was.

'I wonder if they're using the power of the ship to keep that shell, you know, turned on,' I pondered out loud.

'Or maybe they're using the shell to power the ship?'

We walked to the entrance of the ship, but beyond that open first door there was another door that was very much shut. We were standing in what was like an airlock, with only one side open. The cables were all connected to the side wall in this little entrance section of the ship. I pressed my fingers around the walls, trying to find anything that might do . . . something. But there was nothing. I gave one of the cables a pull, just to see what would happen. It didn't budge. There was no way in.

'Come on,' I said. 'Let's have a closer look at the clam again. See what we can figure out.'

Stood in front of the big shell again, the pulsating blue light cast onto Marlie's face. She really was . . . pretty. A strange realisation in this moment, I know. But in that light, in the midst of thwarting an alien invasion through the greatest heist in the history of the world, her face still dripping in chocolate, I just stood there, staring.

'What?' she said, doing a double take.

'Nothing . . . I . . . Nothing.'

'Andy, what is it? Is there chocolate still all over me?'

'Well, yes . . . but . . . you . . . I just realised . . . you're . . . really . . .'

'What?'

'Pretty.'

Even in blue light, even caked in syrupy chocolate, I could see the blush. Just for a moment.

'Andy.'

'Yes?'

'Lets get on with saving the world, hey?'

Marlie traced her fingers over the pulsating light patterns on the clam's surface. I tried pressing mine into where the clamshell sides joined in the centre. Neither did anything. Marlie pushed it. I kicked it. We tried lifting it together. We even tried prying it open. Nothing worked.

I was getting angry. Marlie definitely looked like she was, too. Like desperate people do, we kept trying the same things over and over again.

'Arrgghhhh!' Marlie finally grunted in anger. She turned her back on the clam and looked around the cave again. 'We have come this far. What else can we do?'

I stopped grasping at it. It was impossible. We couldn't open it.

'I . . . I don't know . . .' My legs felt heavy. So did my arms. I slid down to the ground, my back pressed against the clam. I had no ideas. Just then, my watch started beeping.

‘That’s ten minutes,’ I said. ‘Time is up. They should be leaving now.’

‘And we’re stuck in here.’

‘Until that alien comes back to kill us,’ I said. There didn’t seem to be anything more to say or do. We were stuck. We had no way of opening this thing.

I hung my head and sighed deeply.

We had failed.

I had failed.

‘I’m . . . I’m sorry,’ I managed to squeeze out from my tight throat.

‘Sorry? What for?’ asked Marlie, sliding down next to me on the floor.

‘For failing you. For failing Henry . . . this . . . everything.’

‘This is not on you, Andy, don’t be silly.’

‘I don’t think I’m being silly.’

‘Well, you are. Look, without you, none of this would have happened. This group would have exploded before it even began.’

‘But none of it matters.’

‘None of it matters? Are you kidding me? All of it matters. We’ve done everything we could. That is what matters. You are *not* allowed to slump into small little Andy again. That little boy that let the world boss him around and tell him who he should be. The little boy who would do anything to fit in with people he thought were cooler than him. You were always like that in primary school and, up until this week, you were the same in high school. I still liked you, because I could see past it. But hasn't this week shown you that you are *way more* than that?!'

'I suppose . . . Yes it has. But . . .'

'So enough! Come on. We can figure this out. You are more than a victim to life, Andy McGee. So, GET OVER YOURSELF!'

She was angry. And she was right. I knew it. She reminded me of my mum in that moment, just with more straight-talking sass. I needed to hear it, her shutting down of my approval-seeking smallness. Her naming of my better self. Her belief in me. I still wasn't sure I deserved it, but there was no time like the present to find out. She was right, we couldn't just give up. I raised my head. She was looking at me, daring me to challenge her.

'This is what friends do,' was all I said.

She grinned.

Something caught my eye. It was the chocolate the alien had dropped onto the ground. I sat staring at it as I remembered Henry eating the chocolate all those days ago in the boys' toilets. The immediate effect it had on him, and how he progressively got worse over the next day. I thought about him at that old house on Friday, and how he'd resisted against the alien inside him. I thought, too, about when we first overheard Jenkins talking to Henry, Frankie and Lloyd in the underground hallway. Jenkins had called the Nexus a library. So that must be what I was resting against. An alien library that held the DNA formula. I wondered how the aliens would get into their own library.

And then it hit me. In that moment, just like that, it all came to me. I knew what I had to do. The way forward was obvious. No matter what, I had to save this world.

And to save this world, we had to beat the aliens.

And the only way to beat the aliens . . .

The only way . . . was to become one of them.

'I've got it!' I said, excited and terrified.

'What?' Marlie asked.

'I know what to do.' I got up and walked over to the chocolate and picked it up. I looked back at Marlie. She really was not going to like this idea.

'I, I have to eat this.'

'WHAT?!'

It was about the response I expected.

'Marlie, I have to eat this. I have to become an alien. The only way to open this alien vault thing is to *be* an alien. Or, at least, the host of an alien.'

'NO! You can't! You don't know that it works like that.'

'But I do. I've been thinking about Henry and Jenkins, and it makes sense. It must be how it works. It's alien tech, so the only way to use it is if you are an alien. I just know it, Marlie.'

'But . . . No! No! That's ridiculous.' She burst into tears. 'You are not doing it, Andy. I lost my brother. I am not going to lose you, too. I can't. I can't!'

I walked over to her and wrapped my arms around her. 'It's okay. You just told me that I had to get over myself, and that is what I am doing. Saving the world is way more important than just one little life, Marlie.

I . . . I have to. And your brother . . . he was able to fight it. It only took over him after hours of eating that chocolate.'

'Then let *me* do it!' she said, suddenly jerking away from my hug.

'No way.'

'Well, why you and not me? If it's just one little life?'

'No . . . it's not . . . you're not . . . I won't let you.'

'Well, I won't let *you*, Andy!'

I backed away from her. I had to do it. Even if it meant she hated me. Even if it meant I would lose myself. I ripped open the chocolate packet.

'Andy McGee, you will not . . .'

I cracked the chocolate bar.

'You will NOT!' Marlie lunged toward me.

She was too late. I put it in my mouth. 'It's done,' I said. 'It's done.'

She still came toward me. 'NO! I HATE YOU! I HATE YOU! WHAT HAVE YOU DONE? I WILL NEVER FORGIVE YOU FOR THIS!' She was pummelling me. Marlie Balooby used me to pull herself up, and was punching my chest as hard as she could. And she was not letting up.

I let her.

She punched and punched, screaming, 'I HATE YOU!' with every punch. It was not fun. But, only a few moments later, I realised I wasn't really feeling the punches. It felt like she was punching someone else's body.

'Marlie, stop,' I said to her, softly. 'Marlie . . . s . . . s . . . stop,' I stuttered.

She paused and looked at me.

'What is happening?' she asked, wiping away her tears. 'I feel strange.'

'Oh, Andy.'

My vision was starting to feel weird, too. Everything was taking on a greenish glow. I looked at Marlie. She was staring straight at me. And I could see . . . I know this sounds strange, but I could see Marlie's insides. Like, her heart. I could see it beating. A green outline of her beating heart. It was like I could see the blood pumping around her body.

'Andy, what can you see?'

'You. I see you. I see inside you. I . . . ARRGGHHHH!'

A jarring pain rushed through my brain. I cannot even describe the intensity of it. It was like a pounding, as though someone, something, was punching my brain from the inside. I grabbed my head. I swallowed hard. I needed to pull it together.

'Marlie . . .' I could hardly breathe. 'I'm . . . sorry.'

'You selfish, stubborn . . .'

'ARRGGGGGHHHH!'

'All right . . . All right, Andy . . . It's done. Now, make it worth it. You must do this. Come on.'

Marlie led me back to the clamshell, and I now knew exactly what it was. I just knew. Or, perhaps, the thing inside me knew. It was indeed a library. The Nexus was a cultural library of the aliens. A historical repository of the alien race. Standing there before it, I knew how to open it. In the same greenish glow by which I could see Marlie, I could now see two handprints on the device before me. I pressed my hands into them, one on the top right, one the bottom left, and the clamshell . . .

. . . opened!

Sitting inside it was an orb of the same pulsating blue light that covered the device. A curved orb that looked like a seed. Slowly, I leaned into the clamshell and placed both my hands around the orb. And then Marlie and the chamber and the whole world around me disappeared.

A PLANETARY ATROCITY

9:15AM

For a moment, the world was black. I was groping in the dark for some part of myself I had lost. Or was it something I had come here for? Something had brought me to this place, but I couldn't quite put my finger on what it was. I was here to do something, but I couldn't think of what it was.

My skin was itchy. My breath tasted dank. Something was wrong. What had happened? I didn't know. Perhaps I had died? Was that it? I pinched myself. It hurt. I still seemed to have a body. But it didn't look like my body. *It must be,* I told myself, *it must be my body. It must.*

'Welcome.' A deep voice echoed through the darkness. I was not sure from where, it seemed to be all around me. I knew it was not speaking in English, but I could still understand it. 'Welcome to the Atlaethian library. What would you like to be shown in the Nexus today?'

What would I like to be shown today? I had no idea. So I replied timidly, not sure how to address this thing.

'Hi . . . I . . . my name is Andy. Andy McGee. Who are you?'

'I am Atlas.'

'Okay. Good to know. But, um, what are you?'

'I am your guide to the Nexus. Think of me like a tour guide.'

'Great. Okay. Well, thanks, um, Atlas. Ah, the thing is, I don't really understand what's happening or where I am. Can you show me, like, where I am?'

And suddenly I was swimming through the black, moving faster than light. Or, actually, something was moving as fast as light past me. There was a blur of movement. It made me feel nauseous. But it started to slow down and then, in front of me. . . No, not in front of me, all around me, I could see . . . It was the solar system.

I knew it was the solar system from all the science textbooks I'd read. We had come into it from some place far away. Neptune on my right. Uranus on the left. I passed through the rings of Saturn. Then there was Jupiter, Mars and . . . there it was. Earth. The moon swung past me, and Earth came toward me. Closer. Closer. Closer. Blue and green. It was beautiful. Closer. Toward the little island at the bottom. Not little island, large island. It was Australia. Closer. Closer. I was staring down at the town of Bellington. Closer still, I was staring down at Bellington High School.

'You are here.' The voice echoed all around me once more. 'Bellington High School, Australia, The Earth, The Solar System, The Milky Way, Quadrant 50341A.'

'Whoa!' was all I could say. The little trip through the galaxy was enough to jog my memory. I knew where I was. I could remember why I was here. Honestly, I could even remember all those nights of staring through my telescope in primary school and reading books about space and the planets. I instantly felt sad that I'd gotten rid of all those, just to try to fit in, to be cooler. The telescope sat at the back of my cupboard with my box of magic tricks. I was going to get them out again, I decided. A weird time to decide such a thing, but it felt like something was waking up inside me.

Everything around me went dark once more. Now, I had to focus.

'Atlas, can you show me all data you have for the splicing of alien . . . sorry, I mean the splicing of *our* DNA with the humans of Earth?'

Instantly, a screen opened up before me in the dark. Like a computer screen, but much bigger. The screen showed a stack of documents, one behind the other. All I had to do was glance at a document and it would open up before me. There were diagrams, and it was in a language that was not English. But, somehow, I could understand it. I could read it. This was it! Research into human physiology alongside that of the aliens'. It looked like there were different types of this alien. As well as the jelly-looking one we had met earlier, there were others that looked a little like lizards.

Another document showed the deconstructed ingredients of chocolate, the names of things that I was sure only my dad would understand. There were diagrams of what looked like little lizards clamped onto the human brain stem. I shuddered to think that this was what was growing in me right now, what had latched itself to me. As I read, I learned it would take two days to fully develop and become one with the host. Me. The thought was horrific. But, here it all was. Everything.

I knew what I had to do.

'Atlas, please delete . . . Wait! Actually, can you tell me what a human would need to do to stop their transformation into a host?'

'A human would have to get rid of their brain stem for this to occur.'

'Wait! What?'

'A human would have to remove their brain stem for this to occur.'

'And can a human survive without their brain stem?'

'No.'

'Oh.'

'So, I'm . . . I mean . . . so a human who has already started going through the transformation . . . they can't change what is happening?'

'Not unless they would like to die. Is there something else you would like me to show you, Andy McGee?'

I blocked out my own fear as the first thought that came to me was, *Geez, Marlie's going to be SO angry with me.*

Thoughts of Marlie shook me back to why I was here. To what I was doing. I couldn't let this happen to anyone else. Let alone every inhabitant of Earth. I just couldn't. I had made the decision for the sake of the world, for everybody in existence, to destroy this research, to get rid of this program of human subjugation. This was my duty.

I spoke again, clearly, loudly, boldly. 'Can you please d–' The words got caught in my throat. 'Please d–' I could't get them out. Something was stopping me from saying the words. 'Atlas can you d–d–d . . . ARRGHHH!'

'I am not sure what you want me to do,' the voice responded.

Whatever little alien lizard thing was currently attaching itself to my brain stem, it did not want me to do this. The knowledge of which gave me even more determination. I gritted my teeth, steeled my resolve. I thought about Marlie yelling at me. I thought about Fleassy telling me to stop being a wimp. I thought about the bravery of Jasmine. I thought of Nick telling me that I was doing a great job. I thought of all that we had accomplished that morning. And this, this is what gave me the gumption to use my will to overpower the alien inside me. I forced out the words.

'Atlas . . . please . . . d . . . d . . . DELETE these files and anything else to do with this human hosting program. Permanent DELETION!'

'Are you sure? Permanent deletion of files is not reversible.'

'Y–Y–YES!!!!!' I screamed the word because it was the only way that I could get it out of myself.

'Okay. No need to yell, Andy McGee.'

'Thank you, Atlas.'

The screen in front of me disappeared.

'Is there anything else you would like me to do? Your allotted daily time is soon to run out.'

'No. Can you just let me . . . Oh, wait. Actually, could you show me how this happened?'

'How what happened, Andy McGee?'

'Ah . . . us . . . on Earth. How did this happen? Why are we here again? I just . . . um . . . forgot.'

In the dark of that space, right in front of me, appeared a huge alien. It looked like a caterpillar, but about twice the size of a human. And it was no nice caterpillar, either. It was scary, with razor-sharp teeth, six arms swinging about, an evil look in its huge beady eyes. I crouched down away from it in fear, even though I knew it wasn't really there. Then there was another. And another. And now I was looking down upon a mass of them, thousands upon thousands.

'This is how it began,' said Atlas. 'This is how the Atlaethians came to be on Earth. This is the day the Vortalix attacked.'

A massive door opened in front of the caterpillar-like creatures, the Vortalix, and down through the door they jumped, landing on the red dirt of a foreign planet. Then all around me, these caterpillar creatures were cutting down smaller alien lizard-like creatures. It looked like these smaller aliens were just going about their lives. They looked like larger versions of the little lizard beings that were attached to the brain stems of humans. But I could see, they were different sizes. What looked like adult aliens and child aliens as well as purple jellyfish aliens, like the one from outside. Both young and old.

Everyone on this planet was being slaughtered. It was a bloodbath.

'Stop!' I yelled, horrified.

The images froze in front of me.

'The Vortalix took over the planet within five days,' Atlas continued to speak. 'The Atlaethians were almost annihilated. A number of ships escaped. A fleet of them arrived over a period of many years onto the Earth.'

'You are refugees. I mean . . . we . . . we Atlaethians are refugees?'

'Yes.'

'And for how long have we been here on Earth?'

'We have been here in Bellington for eighty years. Some have been here longer. Others, less. But I do not have connection to them.'

'And what have we done for these eighty years?'

'I don't know about the others, but we who landed in Bellington, we have simply survived. The Earth is a different atmosphere to Atlaethia, so many, many Atlaethians died before we figured out how, instead of dying, we might actually survive.'

'What? How?'

'I do not know.'

'Why?'

'You have just deleted all the research pertaining to it.'

'Oh.'

With a shock that felt a lot like a slap, I realised that, in saving the human race, I had also just condemned an *entire* species of alien refugees to their demise. I swallowed. The world was swimming. No wonder the alien inside me didn't want the research destroyed. Humans becoming the aliens' hosts was their only way to survive. It made me feel sick. I didn't know what to do. Andy McGee, Species Killer.

'You are limited to ten minutes' daily usage to conserve energy,' Atlas suddenly said. 'You have reached your limit. Goodbye. Please come again to the Atlaethian Library.'

I blinked. Once. Twice. I opened my eyes and found that I was on the ground looking up at the very concerned face of Marlie Balooby.

With the stress of the entire last week of my life, of the horror and atrocity of the war I had just seen – or maybe it was the little thing inside me reliving the horror of the destruction of its home – whatever the reason, I just burst into tears. Tears and tears and tears. They would not stop. Marlie pulled my head into her lap and held me as I wept and wept and wept.

26

RESISTANCE

9:40AM

I don't know how long I was sitting there crying into Marlie for. It was a long time. And I think I would have kept on going except for one thing. The door to the cave suddenly opened.

We both scrambled to our feet, wondering who or what it might be, but there was no one and nothing. Until what looked like a ball came flying into the cave, and the door shut fast again. Thick green gas was pouring out of the ball now. Whatever it was, I was pretty sure it was lethal.

'Oh no,' Marlie said. 'Come on. Think . . . think . . . we gotta get out of here, somehow.'

'I don't know. I don't know.' I couldn't think of anything except that I was a species killer. 'Arrrgghhhh!' I grabbed my head in pain again. The alien taking up residence inside me was trying to get my attention, banging on my brain stem like it was a door knocker.

'Andy, are you okay?'

'I . . . ARRRGGHHH! GET AWAY, HUMAN!!'

Marlie stared at me, horrified. Like I was possessed. Which, in reality, I suppose I was. I pushed back against the thing that was fighting its way into my consciousness.

'Marlie. Sorry. It's . . . It's me again. But I don't, I don't know what to do.'

She still looked at me petrified, like she was unsure whether to trust me. But then she breathed out and closed her eyes in that way she does that summons all her resolve. Her eyes snapped open. 'Well, I do. If that alien got you into the clamshell, shouldn't it also let you into the ship?'

'Yes! Genius!' I exclaimed.

She smiled, but then her smile dropped and she looked at me dubiously again. 'Come on,' was all she said, and took off to the ship. The thick gas was really spewing forth now. In a few moments it would cover everything. I ran behind her to the airlock room of the ship. Everything still had that same greenish light to it. I could see two handprints now on this door, too. I placed my two hands on top of them, and the door to the ship opened. I was about to walk on when the thing inside me reefed my hands to the side and took hold of the cables. Under my touch this time, they easily came free. The power from the ship to the clamshell stopped, and the pulsating light down the clamshell turned off.

Marlie followed me into the alien ship. When we were just through the door, the alien inside me made me turn around to press another handprint, and the door closed, blocking us off from the green gas. Lights instantly lit up the inside of the ship and we walked forward.

I knew where to go. Or, at least, the Atlaethian inside me did – to the right, up some steps. The inside of the ship did not look like the outside. While the outside was black and sleek, the inside seemed to be decorated in the same substance of the planet I had just seen destroyed by the Vortalix. It was like being inside a desert house made of red rock. It felt . . . homely. Indeed, I really did feel at home. Oh, actually, that was the Atlaethian inside me again. *It* felt at home, and I understood why it would.

Up a ladder to the top of the ship we climbed. I sat in the seat that faced outside and, *really* hoping I would be able to take back control of my body, I let the alien use me to work the ship.

'What are you doing?' Marlie asked, anxious beside me.

'Turns out the alien inside me doesn't want to die, either. And, you were right, it knows how to fly this UFO.'

Through my body, the Atlaethian inside pressed a button that slid back a windscreen in front of us. Look, I guess you'd call it a windscreen, like in a car. It was my first time in an alien ship, so I really didn't know. But now we could look out and see that the green gas had indeed filled the whole room. The alien inside me knew that this ship did not have enough power for its own internal air supply and was drawing air from outside. How did I know that the alien knew this? I have no idea. I just did. I also knew that the green air would soon fill the ship and we would die if we didn't leave now.

Both my hands reached out, without my telling them to, and started touching various buttons and imprints on what must have been the control desk in front of us. Turning this. Switching on that. Pressing this. Suddenly, there was a deep rumbling hum. The ship was starting. It was actually starting. The alien pressed another button through the use of my hand and I knew that this one was to open the roof above. Although I had no idea what that meant until I looked up and saw that the ceiling of the cave had started to crack apart. One small straight crack at first, and then wider and wider and wider until the whole ceiling of the cave seemed to be open, and the ship we were in was now hovering. I stuck my hands directly into what appeared to be a very small copy of the clamshell outside. It was the steering controls.

Slowly, the ship began to edge upward.

'Are we actually flying an alien ship?' Marlie asked.

'It looks that way,' I said.

And in one swift movement I thrust the controls forward and then pulled up, and the ship did the same, hovering above the clamshell below us before moving up and up and out of the cave. The light was *so* very bright outside, it was blinding. I realised I needed to put my sunglasses on that I'd kept in my pocket from the start of our heist, or I would do the brain-freeze thing myself. I blinked a few times and opened my eyes again. I knew where we were. We were in the quadrangle between B-block and C-block. We were coming up in the school grounds.

Two things quickly happened then. The first was that the ground suddenly slid closed beneath us. The second was that the ship shuddered. A purple light was emanating from the console. It was the alien version of a red light, and it meant we were doomed. The ship had enough power to lift off, and that was it. It was out of juice. We hovered for a moment before lurching forward toward the ground, falling onto the quadrangle with a crash. But at least we were out of the death trap, I thought. At least we were free.

But then, I looked up.

Staring back at Marlie and me through the windscreen was Principal Jenkins. He looked so angry that he could call down lightning, but, I guess, he was trying to control himself so he wouldn't short-circuit his brain.

Next to Jenkins was Frankie, who had seemingly managed to escape from being tied up. Next to him was Lloyd, and around the three of them stood about 50 others. All alien host bodies. All staring at us in the ship. All wearing sunglasses. And then, from behind Jenkins, stepped Henry Balooby. It was the whole gang. We were very, very much trapped. This was not looking good.

'I DON'T KNOW HOW YOU WORKED OUT HOW TO FLY THAT SHIP, ANDY MCGEE. BUT EITHER YOU COME OUT OR WE WILL BE COMING IN!' Jenkins yelled from outside.

'What should we do?' I wondered aloud.

'Let them come in,' said Marlie, defiantly, as she rose her middle finger up at the aliens. Fleassy would be proud.

We could see Jenkins grimace and his face redden. I was racking my brain, trying to think of some way out of this. Could we stir them up to being so angry they'd all short circuit? Probably not. Was there some way to blind them all again? Nope. I had nothing.

'Did you destroy the DNA plans when you were in there?'

I looked over. Marlie was staring at me.

'Yeah. Yeah I did.'

'So it's done. We won?'

'Well, this round we did. But . . .'

'But what?'

'Marlie, they are . . . they're refugees. Their own planet was destroyed.'

'What? Really?'

'Yes. I saw it all. It was . . . horrific.'

'But now they want to take us over?'

'Well, it was their only way to survive. It was either find human hosts or let their whole species die out. So I . . . I get it.'

'That's awful.'

'Yeah. I kinda, honestly, feel bad.'

'It is you I am talking to, right? Not the alien thing inside you making all this up?'

'Yeah, it's me. I can hold it at bay . . . for now.'

'Can . . . can you get rid of it?'

But I didn't get the chance to tell her, as crashing into the room came a handful of the aliens in their human suits, all led by Henry Balooby.

'Henry!' cried Marlie as the aliens grabbed us. She was searching his face for some sign of recognition from her brother. There was nothing. Not a hint.

I hated seeing him like that. It was an image of what

I was about to become. I could feel even now the alien inside me pressing against my consciousness. It was highly disconcerting. But I was determined to not let it get a grip on me.

'Leave her alone!' I yelled at them.

'Leave *him* alone!' she yelled at Henry. 'Come on, Henry. I know you're in there.'

'Quiet. Both of you,' Henry shouted back at us. 'Jenkins wants us to take you to him. So come along. Walk, or we drag you.'

Marlie wasn't giving up that easily. She lashed out and wriggled and hit and kicked. She was not willingly walking anywhere. So, two of the aliens picked her up and carried her off as Henry grabbed a hold of me.

'Come on. Everyone out,' he ordered the others. The aliens carrying Marlie went first, followed by the other few. Last in the room was Henry and myself. As he thrust me towards the door, he yelled, 'Come on, human! Get a move on.' But then he leaned in close and whispered into my ear, 'Trust me, McGee. I got you.'

My eyes shot wide open. An alien-infested Henry Balooby was offering to help. Was this a trap? Was it legit? What did it mean? Had Henry managed to actually get rid of the alien inside him? I was so confused. But, there was a sliver of hope, and I grabbed hold of it with all my might.

Henry threw me hard to the ground in front of Jenkins. I really hoped it was all for show, but he certainly was putting on a good show. I was on my knees next to Marlie, who was on hers, too. She was whimpering. I was thinking, hoping, wishing.

'SOOOO, YOU LITTLE HUMANS HAVE DISCOVERED OUR SECRET, HAVE YOU?' Principal Jenkins yelled at us.

'YOU SILLY KIDS! YOU HAVE RUINED EVERYTHING. YOU MAY HAVE GOT AWAY WITH THE TRUCK. YOU MAY HAVE DESTROYED OUR CHOCOLATE. YOU MAY HAVE . . .'

The truck had got away! I breathed a sigh of relief. I was no longer really listening to Jenkins. Jasmine and Fleassy and Nick were safe. That was the best news ever. So good that I started to smile. But even as I did, I felt the alien presence inside me fighting for control once more, and I had to focus on shutting it down. And focus on not scratching at my skin that was getting increasingly itchy. The only thing that broke my focus and brought me back to what Jenkins was saying was hearing the word: '. . . DEAD!' And then: 'YOU WILL DIE FOR YOUR CRIMES.'

'*Our* crimes? What about *your* crimes?' Marlie looked up, shaking in her anger. 'You destroy innocent human lives and you say *we* committed crimes. You are evil, and . . .' She looked at Henry then. 'HENRY!' she yelled. 'You must be still in there. You must. Henry, come back! COME BACK!'

Henry just looked down and said, 'Quiet, human. You do not know me. I am no longer Henry, you insolent fool.' Then, he looked at Jenkins and said, 'Let me kill them. Let me show them what the Atlaethians can do to those who stand in their way.'

Principal Jenkins turned and looked at him for a moment. 'RIGHT YOU ARE. I'LL LET YOU DO THE HONOURS! TAKE THEM BELOW AND END IT. AND EVERYBODY ELSE . . .' he said, looking around at all those standing there, 'OUR PLANS HAVE FAILED TODAY, BUT WE WILL SUCCEED! FOR NOW, WE CLEAR OFF AND WE PLAN OUR NEXT MOVE. THE CHOCOLATE IS STILL THE WAY. WE WILL REPRODUCE THE EXPERIMENTS. WE MUST. WE MUST!'

They didn't know yet that I had been into the Nexus. That I'd deleted all the chocolate research in their Atlaethian library. I really did not want to be there when Jenkins found that out.

'Come on, scum!' shouted Henry as he threw us forward, walking us toward A-block. We both let ourselves be pushed forward. Marlie was sobbing as she thought she was being led to her death by her older brother. I was just trying to hold it together as the banging in my head was getting worse. We walked like prisoners of war, our hands behind our backs, through the school and to the reception. We walked past the guards, who had obviously replaced the fleeing scaredy-boy Denny, and then straight into the principal's office. The door down into the basement level was already open. Another few aliens were still standing around, looking unsure now as to what was happening, being that their chocolate takeover was thwarted. Thwarted by us. I was so proud of my crew. Whatever happened from here, we had done a good thing. A planetary saving thing. Somehow, we had pulled it off. That has got to make anyone feel good.

Down the steps into the underground Henry forced us, his hand on his sister's shoulder. I wasn't sure if he was helping her down the stairs or pushing her – either was possible right now. He led us around the corridors and through the passageways we had been in days earlier when we had first discovered this place. We passed the door on the right where we had hid and had overheard the conversation of Jenkins and Henry and the others. Around the corner, down the steps and we stepped out into the large warehouse room. I smiled when I saw it.

Jasmine had obviously done her work well in this room. The place was a disaster zone. A chocolate disaster zone. Chocolate brown goop clung to everything. The concocted mixture from my dad had done all the damage it needed to in here. A mountainous slough of now-destroyed chocolate packets was in the centre of the room. We walked through and into the warehouse where the truck had been on the other side. The room was deserted, with chocolate everywhere. The smoke had cleared. The truck was gone. The blast door to the outside was closed. There was no one around.

'Stop!' Henry commanded. Marlie and I both stopped, facing forward, away from him, our hands still tied tightly behind us.

'Now, onto the ground. Kneel on the ground.'

I knelt down. Marlie couldn't. She refused. Defiant. Tears streamed from her eyes. 'Give me back my brother!'

she screamed over her shoulder at Henry. 'I'm your sister, Henry. Don't do it!'

I started thinking that maybe I had imagined Henry's whisper to me up in the ship.

'Of course you're my sister, little squirt,' Henry then said in a cheeky, loving voice.

Marlie froze. She started to turn around.

'Don't turn around,' Henry said quickly. 'They are watching. Through the cameras. They can't hear, but they can see. Don't turn around. But it's me, Marlie. It's Henry. Not the alien. Well, it is the alien, too. Sorry, we don't have time to explain.'

'But how?' Marlie asked.

'We don't have time, sis.'

'How do I know I can trust you?' she quizzed.

Henry came over and grabbed her hands behind her back. I looked over as he did so, just in time to see the glint of a knife hidden in his hand that cut her bindings.

'That's how,' he said, up close to her now. I could just hear his words. 'I love you, Marlie. Never forget it. Now, I'm going to pull out a gun in just a second.' Henry moved back, behind us both again. 'Well, the alien version of a gun. I'm doing it now. I'm pointing it at you. This needs to be believable. In just a second I'll give you the go-ahead. I'm going to pretend to slip on the chocolate and, as I do, Marlie, you are going to turn around, grab the alien gun that will have fallen from my hands and you are going to shoot me with it.'

'What? No!' said Marlie.

'It's just on stun. It's okay. It'll just knock me out.'

Henry began pacing behind us, walking back and forth. I couldn't believe this was happening. Henry Balooby, and maybe even the alien inside him, was helping us.

'Then you run to the right of the blast doors and hit the red button to open them. There is a box-cutter knife next to the button. Cut McGee's wrist cords and then get out of there. In the tunnel, I have left bikes for you both. It's the best I could do. Jump on them and ride. When you get to the other end, there will be only two aliens in the mechanics'. You are to say to them these exact words: *The Atlaethian Resistance rises.* They will let you through. Ride as fast as you can. Your friends dumped the chocolates in the sewage refuse, exactly as you had planned. The chocolates are destroyed. Your friends will be waiting for you back at our house. But I need to go with Jenkins. We won't be able to stay after this. I'll contact you. It's almost time. But first, I need you to meet someone.'

Henry coughed a little. And when he started to speak again, his voice was slightly deeper, elongated . . . 'Don't be upset. This is the Atlaethian inside Henry speaking now.'

I could see Marlie shaking beside me, but I couldn't do anything.

'You two must know this about us: There are many Atlaethians throughout the world. We've been here for a long time. Those in power want to take over your world, they want to force humans to be our hosts. We Atlaethians will die if not, or so they believe. There are many of us who believe differently. There is another way. A world where Atlaethians and humans may live in harmony. But those in power will not listen. So, we have to take the power back. For the sake of all Earthlings, for the sake of all Atlaethians, I am asking you to join us. Please, join us. What you pulled off today was huge. But, this was only the beginning. There is much, much work to be done. Will you join in the Atlaethian Resistance?'

'How do we know we can trust you?' Marlie asked again. This time asking the alien, not her brother.

'Because I have already proven it to you today, you just didn't realise. When I saw two of you hiding under some of the seats along the wall in the quadrangle, I turned the attention of the alien I was with away from the seats so that he wouldn't see you, too.

'A bit later, a patrol of us saw three of you walking through the school. They pointed at you and wanted to come over to double check. I convinced them to keep moving. When everyone was called to the gymnasium a few minutes later, I knew it was your group up to something. So I held back. I went into the gymnasium later and saw all the others frozen. But I didn't report it. I have been on your side this whole day, Marlie Balooby. Your brother has told me how much he loves you. I want you to work with us. You can trust me.'

The alien was telling the truth. I knew it was. Its account matched up perfectly with what had happened during our heist earlier that day. It was a bit of a blow to the ego that maybe we hadn't pulled it all off as perfectly as we thought we had. Well, until we got captured, that is.

But this alien inside Henry really had been helping us all day. We would not have got away with it if it wasn't for him. Or it. I wasn't sure how to talk about them yet. And I wasn't sure whether now might be a good time to tell Henry that I, too, was a host of an Atlaethian. But I didn't get the chance as Henry's walkie-talkie buzzed.

'HAVE YOU SUCCEEDED IN GETTING RID OF THEM YET? OVER.' It was Jenkins.

'Just finishing off the humans now. Over,' Henry (or the alien inside him) spoke back into the walkie-talkie.

'It's Henry again, Marlie. I don't have time to tell you more. But, we need to help them. The rebel Atlaethians. We must. For the sake of everyone on Earth. What do you say?'

'You've changed. A lot,' said Marlie over her shoulder to her older brother. 'And I like it. I'm proud of you. And yes. Yes, of course we will.'

'Great. That's a relief. And yeah, I have changed. This alien inside me has taught me a lot. Maybe I just needed something bigger than myself to care about. Okay. That's it. You gotta go. Marlie, I love you. McGee . . . don't do anything stupid, you little dweeb, or I will flush you in whatever toilet I can find.'

'Yes, sir,' I said, amazed at how a toilet threat from The Cleaner could make me feel so good. We were about to be free, Marlie and me. Oh, and whoever it was that now lived inside me.

'All right, I am pacing, I am pacing, I am pacing . . . I am . . . WHOA!'

We heard the sound of Henry slipping on the chocolate mess of the floor. Marlie whipped herself around and lunged forward for the gun that had fallen on the ground. She lifted it up, hesitating for only the briefest moment, and then fired at her brother. He was out cold.

'Let's go!' Marlie held out her hand to me, and we moved to the great doors. Marlie hit the button, picked up the promised knife and cut me out of my bonds. The bikes were just beyond the door. We jumped on them and pedalled as hard as we could down that tunnel, although we were both shaky now the adrenaline was starting to leave our bodies. I felt weak as we neared the end of the tunnel. I looked over at Marlie. Her leg was shaking uncontrollably, and I could tell she was doing all she could to keep going. At the end, it was just as Henry had said: Two aliens who opened the back secret wall to the mechanics' for us as soon as we spoke the words, 'the Atlaethian Resistance is rising'.

We were out of there, through the mechanics' exit, and out onto the street. We pedalled and we pedalled and we pedalled, all the way to safety.

TWO HOURS AFTER THE HEIST

EPILOGUE

All of us heisters were sitting around the table at the back of the Balooby residence, arguing about where to go and what to do from here. The heist had succeeded, but now what? Were we just to wait for Henry to contact us? Shouldn't we be doing something? We argued back and forth about what that might be.

Of course, when Marlie and I had arrived on the bikes, the others had come running out, cheering and hooting and hollering. Hugs all round. Even Fleassy and Marlie embraced each other, although only for a moment. But I did notice a little exchange between them . . .

Fleassy whispered into Marlie's ear, 'You did good, Balooby!'

And Marlie whispered back, 'You were quite amazing yourself, Davies.'

They grinned at each other. But then I saw the look on Fleassy's face change.

'Balooby, I . . . I want you to know . . . I am sorry.

Like, really sorry about what I said. You know, about your limp. That was wrong. I was wrong. You proved me wrong. I was such a jerk. I . . . just . . . sorry.'

'You *were* such a jerk,' Marlie started saying. 'But I forgive you, Fleassy. I know you're better than that, but thank you for apologising.'

And with that, Nick grabbed us all together into a group hug.

'WE DID IT!' we cheered together.

It was a nice moment. Until Nick sang out, 'We smashed the aliens, we blew up their choccies. Old Jenkins is gone and we hope that he rotties.'

'Oh dear,' we all groaned. 'What has happened to you?'

'I don't know. I just . . . it just came out. Andy has had too much of an effect on me. Don't tell anyone, okay?'

'I think I preferred "McGee, McGee, you're not the boss of me",' I said.

But that got them all going. I even joined in, too. All of us jumping around in a circle and singing at the top of our lungs, 'McGee, McGee, you're not the boss of me. McGee, McGee, you're not the boss of me.'

It was a lovely moment. A worthy celebration.

Didn't I tell you this was a heist of planetary proportions? The greatest chocolate caper this world has ever seen? (Though not, of course, the Mediterranean edible variety.) Indeed, this was an Earth-saving escapade. After which, I just had to figure out what the heck to do about the alien living inside me.

Oh, and the easy task of joining an alien resistance to try to save not only the entire human race, but also the entire Atlaethian race. Ha! Easy-peasy-alien-squeezy. But, I'll save that story for next time.

I looked around, beaming at my fellow heisters, the best heist team this side of Atlaethia, as we shared our stories. They told us about their escapes, and Marlie and I filled them in on everything that happened once the chocolate had exploded. Well, except for one thing. My . . . ah . . . inside attachment. The little green freeloader. My Atlaethian compatriot. Marlie and I had decided on our ride back to hers that the rest of the team may not quite be ready to hear about that. And I certainly wasn't ready to tell them about it, either.

Besides, I didn't even know if I'd be in my right mind by the next morning. I needed to figure this all out for myself first.

Once the stories were told, the team was back at each other's throats. Though, through all the arguing and yelling, the next steps were being sorted amongst the team. Okay, maybe not sorted, more like hashed out. Or, to be more precise, violently thrashed out. A pride of highly disagreeable sharp-toothed lions trying to bite each other's heads off.

Not that I could really even hear what they were saying. My ears were blocked, like I was underwater. My skin was burning, and I couldn't stop scratching where it itched. There was a beehive alive inside me. I was shaking my head and, I realised, I had started to mutter to myself.

It was happening.

I forced myself to stop and looked around. Thankfully, no one except Marlie had noticed. Marlie was staring at me with a look of deep concern.

I got up from the table, itching and agitated. The world was a confusing mash of green lines that overlayed everything I could see. Swirling lines. Pounding head. The world was spinning. I was spinning. I was losing it, I knew I was. I stumbled my way inside, only just hearing Fleassy say, 'What's wrong with him?' as I slammed the door behind me.

I stumbled my way through the Baloobys' house. I was in the lounge room. Then suddenly in the kitchen. Not where I wanted to be. I turned . . . I was losing moments. Everything was fragmented, like my mind was dropping frames. Now, I was half-falling, but somebody stopped my fall. It was Marlie, I knew it. She smelled nice. Ugh, no she didn't, she smelled like human. Gross.

Suddenly, I was in her room, on the bed, everything dizzy, everything spinning. The world was topsy-turvy. I couldn't breathe. A wet something was on my head. A cold cloth. Marlie was looking down at me. Someone was banging on the door. Marlie was telling them to go away. That I was sick. I was sick. Was I? Who was I? I couldn't remember. Yes, yes, I was . . . no, it was gone.

'Help me,' I heard someone say, then realised it was me.

'I am,' said Marlie.

I closed my eyes. The pounding finally stopped. Silence. I heard silence. Silence followed by a voice.

Inside me. My voice. Not mine. Its voice. The alien. An alien voice inside me, and it spoke, and I was helpless to do anything but listen to it . . .

'We need to talk,' spoke the alien living inside my head.

'We certainly do,' I said back to it. 'We certainly do.'

TO BE CONTINUED IN BOOK 2:

HEIST

THE REMARKABLE ROBOT ROBBERY

ACKNOWLEDGEMENTS

Talk about finding your squad. There is a whole army of people who need to be thanked for the bringing together of this book.

The team at Penguin Random House Australia have been extraordinary to work with, but a special HUGE thanks goes to Zoe Walton, who saw the promise in this book and the entire series from the beginning. She championed it into existence and I am forever grateful for you.

A mammoth THANK YOU also goes to editor extraordinaire, Niki Foreman, who has worked tirelessly in the editing process. This book is so much better because of you. I feel like you know these characters of mine as well as I do now. Your expert eye and your on-point clarity about the story and the characters and the writing have been indispensable. Thank you

Thanks to Kristy Lund-White for the brilliant cover design, and to the incredible illustrator Aaron Blecha for bringing my heist squad to visual life. It's one of my favourite things to see, when the characters in my head become an illustration on the page. And these characters are exactly as I wanted them to be. Thank you!

Thanks to Laura Pettenuzzo, who brought her passion and lived experience and expertise into helping us create Marlie into a powerhouse of a character. Your insight was brilliant.

I have a plethora of creative friends and writer friends and speaker friends here in Australia and around the world, who constantly cheer me on and provide great counsel for my words and for the worlds I create. Thank you, dear friends. You know who you are, and I hope you know what you mean to me.

To the Wurundjeri people of the Kulin Nations, this book was written on your land. On stolen land. I want to acknowledge you, your culture and the stories told here for millennia. I especially want to thank Auntie Di Kerr who presented me with a eucalyptus leaf and asked me to keep telling my stories on this land.

The first read aloud of any of my books, including this one, is always to my children. They see what I cannot see with my adult eyes. Thank you to both of you for the way you help me write better stories. Your laugher at the right moments and your, 'Dad, that's just not funny' when I think you should be laughing is SUCH a massive help. I love you both.

To my wife, who brings me up when I'm down, and brings me down a few notches when my head is in the clouds. Thank you for your constant support of my work. It means the world to me.

To my mum, who constantly shows me how to love well. And to my dad, the one who first read me the stories of heroes and hobbits and shepherds with slings and Narnian kings. Thank you for your support of all my creative endeavours.

And lastly to you, my readers, both new and old. I've been bringing creative words out into the world for over fifteen years, and I am still just as much in love with it as when I began. So I promise you I'm going to keep writing and performing and speaking. And I hope you'll keep reading and listening. May the stories brought into our world bring about a better place for every single person.

Thanks, squad.

"Dark, lush, and intense . . . draws you into a world filled with mystery and intrigue . . . A stunning debut!"
—**CINDY PON**, author of *Want* and *Serpentine*

"An enchanting debut with a powerful and ambitious lead. Vivid and seductive . . . one of the best debuts of the year."
—**ZORAIDA CÓRDOVA**, award-winning author of *Labyrinth Lost*

"A stunning reimagining of the Evil Queen. Filled with treacherous courtesans, dark magic, terrible choices, and bloody hearts, Julie Dao's exquisite take on this classic villain rises far above the average retelling."
—**STEPHANIE GARBER**, *New York Times* betselling author of *Caraval*

"A richly developed fantasy world . . . Julie C. Dao is a talent to watch."
—**MARIE LU**, #1 *New York Times* bestselling author of *The Young Elites*

"Magnetic, seductive, and alluring . . . a lush, captivating read about desire and the lengths to which we will go to find our true destiny."
—**S. JAE-JONES**, *New York Times* bestselling author of *Wintersong*

★ "A masterful reimagining of the early life of Snow White's Evil Queen. Subverting the all-too-white world of fairy tales, this novel will trap readers in a lush, dangerously dark, and often beautiful world from which they will want no escape."
—*Booklist*, starred review

★ "Lushly written . . . tantalizing reading. A fascinating examination of destiny, responsibility, and how choices shape a person."
—*Publishers Weekly*, starred review

"Readers will appreciate the sweeping fantasy saga lifted from East Asian dynasties and endearing characters that are beautifully rendered."
—*Kirkus Reviews*

"Readers will be drawn into the lush, fully realized world of Feng Lu and be intrigued by the sinister forces that awaken within and around Xifeng."
—*BCCB*